DOWELL'S DISAPPEARANCE

BY

BERNARD BANNERMAN

ISBN (Print): 978-1-911124-94-8
ISBN (Ebook): 978-1-911124-95-5

This one can only be for
Sheila, Jo and Emma...and Joe!

CHAPTER ONE

Fridays I went to the Dowells. I usually got there sometime between midday and midnight. That's the kind of man I am: precise, accurate, reliable.

Fridays I went to the Dowells to pick up Alton, my two year old son. He stayed with them during the weeks; I took care of him at the weekends; the next week they spent making good the damage.

The arrangement with the Dowells had never been planned. It just happened and kept on happening. The day Sandy died, the day my last investigation ended, Tim Dowell took me home from the hospital, and the next day Carson and Natalie brought Alton over to his house in Ealing in West London. Sheila, Tim's wife, fell in love with Alton: who doesn't? For a few days, we stayed there together.

I thought and thought it around and around. There were plenty of combinations. I had a big empty house in Barnsbury - in Islington, North London - into which Sandy, Alton and

I were just moving when it all came tumbling down. Jada Jarrynge and Frankie Mellor - the other two casualties of that period - were down the road. There was room for Carson to stay with me, even Natalie if I'd asked nicely, or maybe a live-in nanny, to help with Alton; there just wasn't the room both for them and my grief. I'd known Sandy most of my adult life; we'd been on-off lovers for less than a quarter of it; we'd made it work properly - if there is such a thing - for little more than a year before she died; I was still trying to make it work nearly a year afterwards.

So Alton stayed in Ealing, over Tim's calculatedly callous comment that he was damned if he wanted to live with that little bastard Woolf's little bastard but he'd put up with it if Sheila insisted while I went back to Barnsbury to sort my head out. There was a lot else to sort out: Natalie could manage the club on the Old Brompton Road that I had accidentally inherited from Lewis but there was also the law-firm that Sandy and I had set up together when we left college, to which I'd grudgingly returned as some sort of acknowledgment that I was - at the time - about to become a father and therefore by default a grown-up, and of which I was now the sole surviving full equity partner. There were salaried partners and assistant solicitors but to my chagrin the firm was now all mine.

I could add to the list of what needed sorting out an ill-defined, residual responsibility for Jada and Frankie, derived from a last minute promise I'd made Russel Orbach that I'd help the former look after - bring up - the latter, a promise which I had at the time presumed Sandy would be around to discharge on my behalf.

I'd like to record that I got a grip on myself, distracted myself with work and pulled all my affairs - on which a number of other people's daily lives and incomes depended - into order. I'd like to record how I foreswore alcohol, cigarettes and McDonald's, took up jogging and Nautilus work-outs, ate brown rice and fulfilled my parental obligations to Alton with tender, loving skill. I'd like to record these things, but I don't like to lie unless someone is paying me to do so. The truth is I single-handedly increased the sales figures for both Southern Comfort and Camel cigarettes so much their directors are all driving Porsches I personally paid for. I left Carson to sort out the firm, by which she was in any event technically employed. She's not a qualified lawyer but she's a qualified human being and I figured that was enough. I sat and brooded and drank, looking back on it for what seemed like months on end until it began to drain out of me and, gradually, I started to try to put my and Alton's lives back together.

We didn't try and do it all at once. Like he would've said if he could talk: kid, you've gotta lotta problems, I can't take too much of it at a time. So, Sheila and their kids kept him during the week, and he looked after me at the weekends. Which is why Fridays I usually went to the Dowells.

* * *

That Friday, I got there from the office about seven. Every week I swear I'm not going to take Alton back on Sunday; driving west through London any time after midday on a Friday is like taking part in a funeral cortège with a million mourners. On the way, I listened to the radio. They were talking about the results of the recent by-election, the second suffered in the short life of the present Parliament, cutting an already thin majority to one that was - I was informed - approaching the barely tenable.

What was more, there had been another parliamentary death, which meant another by-election yet to come. Given the magnolia colouring of the government (the faintest hint of pink), revivalist hymns could be heard on the floor of the stock exchange and the pound was strong against the dollar. Ordinarily, I would have brushed this sort of information aside as trivia irrelevant to my - and probably anyone's - life. For once, it attracted my attention. The reason was rooted in a strange re-encounter just the night before.

* * *

'I don't do investigations anymore,' I replied, and replaced the receiver.

The caller had been Margot McAllister, the MP, now a junior minister of state. I didn't want to talk with her. There were too many bad associations: in particular, she had at one time been the person in the world closest to Russel Orbach and, however many fine qualities she might have in her own right, that was enough in my book to damn her forever. At the time of his death, Russel and Margot had not lived together for many years, since she went into Parliament. Even beforehand, they had lived together as 'just friends' for a long time. Subsequently, they had stayed friends, still meeting regularly, until Russel was appointed to the High Court bench and Margot married Horace Black, another MP. Russel, with cause ever cautious about the faintest scent of impropriety, deemed it injudicious to remain in open contact. After the general election, both Margot and her husband had become ministers in the new administration. She and I had never been close. Which is why I was surprised to hear from her:

'Is that Dave Woolf?'

'Mm,' I mumbled, annoyed I had not switched on the answering machine before boozing into my standard evening gloom.

'It's Margot McAllister.'

'Uh, Margot,' was my witty repartee.

'Yes, Margot McAllister. I'm...'

Her standing as a politician notwithstanding, she was so innately modest she had misinterpreted my reply as meaning I might have forgotten her.

'I was sorry about Russel, Margot,' I made clear I had not.

'Were you, Dave?' I had seen her during the case; she knew the direction in which I was driving it; if she did not at the time know the details of its destination, it was only because she did not want them spelled out. She added: 'I was sorry about Sandy.'

The difference was, she was probably not lying.

'What do you want, Margot? What do you want of me?'

She said:

'We - I - we need your help, Dave.'

'This the royal we or do you mean you and Horace?'

She laughed nervously.

'Closer to the first - in the sense of HMG.'

'HMG?' I never was strong on acronyms.

'Her Majesty's Government.'

I shrieked with acid laughter.

'That's a first. That's rich. The government wants my help? I don't even vote, Margot. I left all that political stuff way behind.' The way I knew Russel and thence Margot was from when we were all young, left-wing and full of the cause and ourselves. A different lifetime.

'Not politically, Dave; professionally.'

'Listen, Margot, I don't know what this is about, but whatever it is I'm not interested. You've got enough lawyers at your disposal to... Oh, hell, I can't even think of to what and they probably can't either. I'm not practising, Margot, not really anyway.' I went in to the office a couple of times a week, theoretically to check things out, more to have somewhere to go. I was supposed to be negotiating full partnerships with the two salaried partners, Ruth Binder and James Coatman. Another, Neil O'Rourke, had quit over how long it was taking.

Patiently, she reminded me she had known me too well and too long to be so stupid as to seek my services as a solicitor:

'That was never your greatest strength, Dave.' She wasn't being sarcastic or insulting, merely accurate. I didn't disagree. 'I meant I wanted you to carry out an investigation for us.'

I didn't bother reminding her that she had at her disposal the entire police force plus the security services, the army, navy and air force and a bunch of other available people who don't even technically exist. I just said:

'Sorry. I don't do investigations anymore.'

* * *

She had rung at about nine o'clock of a Thursday evening.

I returned to my booze mildly disturbed by the call; despite myself, I was more curious than I had been ready to admit.

When Margot had been a lobbyist, before she went into Parliament, she had an unequalled reputation. Governments of every ilk quaked before her well-researched wrath. She hadn't changed much since she was elected that I had noticed when I met her before Orbach's death or from what I had occasionally seen of her on the news. She sounded the same on the phone: a deep voice that could pass for a man.

She was a slight woman in her early forties, with reddish hair that used to fall as it grew almost to her waist but that in recent years had been cut and styled to shoulder-length. She had a pronounced nose that when I'd last seen her had been partially offset by blue-rimmed glasses; she had the sweetest smile of anyone I knew and spoke with a sincerity and an integrity few achieve on this side of the silver screen.

I was still thinking about her when the doorbell rang. I toyed with not going to see who it was. The people close to me have keys and could let themselves in if they wanted: Carson; Jada and Frankie; Tim Dowell too had finagled a copy, allegedly in Alton's interests so he or Sheila could check for child abuse at the weekends.

The doorbell continued to ring. As with the telephone, I could only take so much. Reluctantly, I opened it half an inch. On the stoop stood Margot, together with her red-faced, beefy husband Horace and, hovering behind them, another man I couldn't quite make out. On the street itself there were four more besuited men, facing away from me. Recognising the stance and intuiting they were probably not wise guys, I said dryly:

'I didn't know junior ministers rated so much security these days.'

'They don't.' The man behind Margot and Horace thrust himself and his hand forward. 'I do.'

'Yes, I suppose you do,' I managed to muster as, impressed despite myself, I took the Prime Minister's hand.

'Can we come in, Dave?' Margot asked.

'You really meant you needed my help, didn't you, Margot?'

'Can we come in?' she repeated, flashing her eyes behind her glasses at the watch-dogs.

I shrugged; it was all the same to me. I could tell them to piss off inside just as easily as on the stoop.

* * *

What I knew about Boller, the Prime Minister, was everything I wanted to know. I knew he was tall and thin, in his late fifties, with a lean, weathered, outdoor face, widely considered to be wholly lacking in personality or charm, let alone charisma: he had risen to the top by default, in the absence of anyone else about whom any three members of his party could agree.

I also knew he was from the West Country, and in public - though, as I was now to learn, not so much in private - stressed the broad burr to the maximum of its voter potential. I knew the satirical magazine Private Eye always printed his name with an added 'x'. I knew he was supposed to be a man of the people and insisted on being known as Alf rather than Alfred. I didn't know what his policies were but couldn't have cared less.

Once we were settled in the living-room, all three of us men drinking, Margot - who only occasionally drank - sipping neat mineral water, the policemen left outside drinking the cold night air, I asked, addressing Margot:

'So? You were worried about me and decided to come over to make sure I was alright? You had nothing better to do? This is what they mean about caring government?'

The Prime Minister replied.

'I, uh, understand from Margot that you had a personal loss last year. I would not seek to intrude if it was not important.'

'Trouble is,' I said: 'Politicians think everything they do is important.'

I could see Horace bristle. His thick Scots accent napalmed the twilight atmosphere in which I liked to linger as if a sudden explosion had taken place:

'Mr Woolf, Dave, the Prime Minister doesn't get into a car in the middle of the night and go to visit a complete stranger to ask for his help if it isn't important.'

Margot smoothed the ruffles.

'Dave, I know this is all a bit of a surprise; we just want you to hear us out.'

I shrugged.

'I've got nothing better to do.' I rose to pour myself another cannon-blast of Southern Comfort, proffering the bottle of scotch to Horace to help himself and the big man. Neither refused my hospitality.

She explained apologetically:

'When I rang, it was from Downing Street. We - and some others - had been talking for a while about our, er, problem; that's when I thought of you. After you hung up, Alf took the initiative in this visit when I, er, suggested that there was not a lot of point inviting you to come and see him.' She obviously found it difficult to repeat in front of him that there were some people who would not beck to his call.

Alf took over.

'Can I feel sure that anything I say here will be treated in the strictest confidence?'

'Are you paying me for this interview? As a solicitor or as an investigator?'

'If that's what you want, Mr Woolf,' the Prime Minister was unconcerned.

As it was the only way to disappoint him, I waved it aside.

'Just asking. Go ahead.'

For some bizarre reason, he took my remark as confirmation of confidentiality. And he was running the country? I shuddered; we'd be lucky to make it through the night without an invasion.

He said:

'We have been in power for ten months. We had the smallest majority since 1974. Many of our seats are wafer-thin marginals.

Any mid-term by-election is stacked against the government; it's natural; the protest vote, rebelling against the authority of the time being, whatever it may be; in addition, the City has not responded as well as we hoped.'

By golly gosh, it was riveting material. I made a mental note to enrol in a political studies seminar and join the next several parties to canvass my support.

He sighed, realising I still didn't know - or care - what he was talking about. Margot took over.

'Dave, there have been three deaths on our side in the last ten months, all of them marginal seats. There have been two by-elections, both lost, and one more in a few weeks' time which we have no chance to hold.'

'All of them had heart attacks; none of them had any serious health problems,' Horace added.

I didn't contradict him, though it occurred to me that a fairly serious health problem was the one thing they most certainly did have in common.

'The oldest was fifty-seven; the youngest, forty-two. All three of them were within the ten closest marginals. Doesn't that strike you as a bit much of a coincidence?'

'Maybe God doesn't like your policies either?'

The 'either' was gratuitous.

'You don't believe in God,' Margot reminded me.

'It's not coincidence,' I said, so flatly they thought I was telling them I already knew something about it. I shook my head:

'No, of course not. But the odds against it are astronomical. What are we talking about here? Six hundred odd MPs.' I meant I didn't know exactly how many, only subordinately that all MPs are odd. 'Allowing for independents and all those exciting little ethnic parties - the Irish, the Scots, the Welsh, the Jews - we're talking about approximately three hundred of your own. You're telling me one percent of them died within the last ten months, and they were within the ten slimmest majorities, at no great age, in perfect health - well, acceptable health, anyway. I'm telling you, there's no way you can regard that as coincidental. It might be God's will, it might in the end turn out to be coincidence, but since for some obscure reason that you haven't yet confided you've chosen to consult me as an investigator, I'm saying - as an investigator - that there's no way you can avoid being suspicious. That's all I'm saying.'

Their relief that I shared their reaction was evident, even if I proposed it to be short-lived:

'Which brings us to the crunch question. What are you doing here, telling me about it? There's a place called Scotland Yard; even if you wanted to talk to them in the middle of the night, like now, you could probably find a bobby on guard duty or sweeping the hall. Besides, surely they've realised it for themselves. Were they autopsied?'

Horace answered.

'Yes. Nothing; coronary occlusions, that's all.'

'As for the police,' the Prime Minister said: 'This is where it starts to get complicated. There has been no formal suggestion by them that there should be an investigation. Informally, the Home Secretary has had a word with the Commissioner.'

In the rest of the country, locally elected Police Commissioners supervise their forces; in London, uniquely, the Metropolitan Police is supervised jointly by central government and the Greater London Authority.

'Sir Randolph agreed it was unfortunate, promised to have someone take a look at it, but said that unless we, the government, made a formal request for an investigation there was no material on which to do more.'

'And did he? Have someone take a look at it, I mean.'

'If he did so, he hasn't brought anything back to us,' Horace said hotly. 'The man's a bloody buffoon.'

I held my peace: I knew Dunlop's public image; I also knew there was a lot more tread in him than the public realised.

'So make a formal request, for Christ's sake.' I was getting bored. This time, I brought the bottle back to the sofa where I was sprawled. Fetching it was too much like exercise; my junk-food jelly-belly was at risk. Horace, sensibly, had clung onto the other bottle since I last handed it to him. I was pleased to see Margot weaken and accept from her husband a slug of scotch to go into the remains of her mineral water. I hate people with complete self-control.

The Prime Minister, his own drink refreshed, smiled thinly.

'Now you're getting to the point.'

If I was, I hadn't meant to and didn't know what it was.

'Let us suppose we ask for an investigation. Into what? The individually unsuspicious deaths of three of our members, which - when the by-elections are in - will have more than halved our majority. Unless we come up with evidence of some sort of plot, we will look thoroughly stupid, as if we can't accept fate or, as you put it, God's will, or the consequences of democracy - as if we can't accept losing. It will look as if we're trying to win sympathy at the polls, and it will backfire on us. Can you not see the dilemma, Mr Woolf? With no evidence, no proper investigation; with no proper investigation, no evidence.'

How powerless can the powerful be? I had encountered this before: people trapped by profile and position, unable to take a tiny step that is not the immediate subject of public scrutiny.

Just look at Henry Eight; all he wanted was a new wife. Half-heartedly, I suggested:

'Insist it be a confidential inquiry, then.'

Horace spat scorn.

'I doubt such a thing exists. Especially not when the police would hardly be likely to want to keep it quiet.'

I pondered this for a moment before I realised he was hinting that most members of the police force are somewhere to the right of Sarah Palin, would be only too happy to embarrass the government and have the Daily Mail on their speed-dials.

'What about the security services?'

'MI5?'

'Yeah, though I thought you weren't supposed to admit it exists.'

'That's MI6,' Boller corrected me and contradicted himself. 'Consider what I'm suggesting for a moment.' He paused to see if I got his point without prompting. Once it was clear that I didn't, he continued. 'If there is some sort of plot behind these deaths, where will it be coming from?' He paused again.

I said:

'Yes?'

Sighing in frustration, he said:

'The right, Mr Woolf, it will be coming from the right.'

I shrugged.

'Maybe. What about the Irish? They're always good for a laugh. I would have described killing off British MPs by the IRA not so much as a plot as the pursuit of a long-standing policy.' I was following their lead to this extent: I was treating it as an internal, domestic issue rather than international - this sort of warfare did not fit the more modern terrorism that Islamic State, Al-Qaeda and their ilk have popularised.

'The Real IRA don't have the ability to wage this kind of war,' Boller dismissed out of hand. 'Maybe the Provisionals might have...' His voice trailed away almost wistfully. The Provisionals had abandoned armed struggle and their leading figures had joined government in Ulster. 'No, if it comes from anywhere it must come from the right.'

'And if it's from the right, Dave,' Margot pre-empted my next wilfully stupid statement, 'then there is no way we can entrust any part of it to the security services.'

I knew what she meant. I had read the book, however appallingly it was written. If there was a right-wing plot to bring down the government, the question would not so much be whether members of MI5 were involved in it, but how many of them, how senior and how much of the government's own money was being spent on it.

There was a long silence after she spoke. I still wanted to know:

'Why me?'

'You're, uh, not unknown,' the Prime Minister said. 'In the field.'

Nor was I. My cases had all been close to the centre of power. The Disraeli Chambers deaths: they might have been left-wingers but they were still members of the English Bar, from which elite emerges a disproportionate number of our legislators and almost the whole of our higher judiciary. The Mather's madness involved one of the main firms of solicitors to service the freemasons, than whom there is no one more powerful or influential within the establishment. The Pulleyne problem and the Orbach exorcism both involved backsides on the High Court bench. On the other hand:

'My cases do have a tendency to resolve themselves without getting to court.' This was the principal part Tim Dowell played in my life and career: keeping my cases out of the public eye; not, I hasten to add, in my interests, but in those of his paymasters.

'Mr Woolf, I do not give a damn,' said the PM, 'if the people involved never see the inside of a police station. Even if the truth could be proven - a year or more from now by the time of trial - it might not even affect the outcome of any by-elections. No, Mr Woolf, I only have one interest, and that's to see these killings stopped. Do I make myself clear?'

As a bell. I'd half-bought the story about keeping it out of the hands of the police because of the publicity, and out of the hands of the security service because of their prejudice. Each might be true but neither was a full account of Boller's reasons. What he wanted from me was that which explained why my cases never got to the court door: there was rarely anyone left alive to put on trial. I studied the trio with genuine curiosity. My much-respected Margot; Horace the orator; Boller, the master of dignity. They were sitting in my living-room, in the middle of the night, not an independent witness, civil servant or even a political assistant to hand, asking me if I'd awfully much mind, in the interests of the administration, getting off my butt and making sure their enemies died, whether by my hand or by any other available means.

* * *

It was after midnight when Boller & co left. I agreed I would look into their problem, but not until after the weekend, insisting there was nothing that could distract me from my parental duties. What I meant was that I needed the time to adjust to the notion of working again. I asked if they knew who Dunlop had put onto the case - to which they replied that they did not - and whether they intended to inform him of my involvement.

I could have worked the answer out for myself.

'That would not be appropriate,' said the Prime Minister.

'No way,' expostulated Horace. 'That would be even worse: imagine what the papers would make of it? So little to investigate the police won't touch it and we hire a private detective. We'd be a laughing stock. I can see the headlines now: Boller's Marlowe. We've got to keep the police out of it formally - in any way that might get known - until we've got more evidence. That's imperative.'

Nevertheless, I proposed to find a formula to run it by Tim Dowell. For all I knew, he already had the Dunlop brief. It was his sort of gig.

At the door, Margot hung back.

'Do you see anything of Frankie, Dave?'

Frankie Mellor was Orbach's goddaughter and, after the death of her parents, his ward. Because once upon a time Margot and Orbach had been a couple, Margot used to have a quasi-formal relationship with Frankie.

'They live down the street. In Russel's old house.'

She looked surprised. I explained:

'It was home to Frankie. She had lost enough.' Her real parents - Mick and Eartha Mellor - and then Russel.

'I've wanted to go and see her, but...' She shrugged apologetically. She hadn't known how she would be received; she didn't know what Frankie might have been told.

'Uh, Frankie, well, she's just an unlucky kid.' I was telling her that Frankie still knew nothing about the true circumstances of her own parents' deaths or that of Russel Orbach, her guardian, although she was bound to read about it one of these days and maybe soon. 'And Jada's too wise to make any unfair or unnecessary associations.' I meant that she would not blame Margot for Orbach's behaviour.

Jada was Frankie's half-sister. When I first met her, she was already a successful singer and at the beginning of a supplementary career as an actress, which was also expected to be successful, if her first part in a TV mini-series was anything to go by. A later-released movie suggested it had been everything to go by. Though not long out of art college, she had also put together an autobiographical collage entitled Where I'm Coming From, which on publication was to earn her yet another critical notch on the totem pole of public esteem as well as a healthy chunk of cash - half a mill, if I remembered rightly. My investigation of the manuscript of her book on behalf of her libel-fearing publisher was the spark that led to Orbach's death: it did not explicitly accuse Orbach of murder but used fiction to claim that he had wanted Frankie's parents to die and imply that he had some, more than oblique, responsibility for the accident which had cost them their lives.

Jada had not shirked the resulting responsibility for Frankie. Her career was on temporary hold and, at the age of twenty-two or three, she was mother to a child approaching adolescence.

'Why don't you come to lunch one Sunday? See her, them?'

She smiled wanly.

'I'll think about it. It's still painful. It's hard to think... I loved him once...'

'No one's all good or all bad,' I said. It was something Orbach had commonly remarked. 'I used to like him too.'

'Right.'

Our eyes met and held; sad memories and guilt by association.

The Prime Minister's impatience darted from the car like a stingray.

'I'll think about it,' she repeated, clambering into the back seat.

* * *

By the time I got up the next morning, there wasn't much left of Friday. I pottered, shopped, made a half-hearted effort to tidy Alton's room, popped into the rental for some DVD cartoons to keep him quiet and drove off to fetch him. When I drew up at the Dowells' house, I thought at first they must be having some kind of a party or maybe a police convention: there were marked cars on the street, some of them still occupied by stuffed uniforms, and one smart Rover in the driveway that certainly didn't belong unless Tim had finally come out as a pig on the pad.

I double-parked Sandy's Renault beside one of the marked but empty cars, to make sure the copper couldn't get away. I wasn't planning on stopping: Tim's the only policeman I've ever exchanged a half dozen pleasant words with; and a half dozen is about as many in the years we've known one another. There was another uniform on the door:

'Can I help you?'

I thought of several smart answers but it was beginning to dawn on me there might, just might, be something wrong. I said:

'I'm Dave Woolf; my son lives here during the week.'

It worked; he stood aside. I had established myself as 'family'. Tim would be mortified.

In the kitchen, I saw a policewoman bustling about as if she owned it. In the living-room, Sheila was seated at the dining-table, motionless, expressionless. There were three others in the room with her: a uniformed senior officer - Commander, probably - another uniformed woman police constable, and Walter - Wally - Wadd, the last and longest-surviving of Dowell's Detective Sergeant personal assistants. I could hear the children upstairs watching TV. I took in the tableau in silence. I knew what it meant. I spoke hollowly, my breath too shallow to paddle in:

'Oh God, no. Sheila.'

I tried to put my arms around her shoulders but she pushed me away savagely. Then the torrent - the torrent for which I sensed the others had been waiting - broke, and she put her arms around my waist and sobbed against my ample stomach:

'He's gone, Dave, he's gone.'

'I know, I do know how you're feeling.'

Oh, Christ, did I know.

The Commander coughed discreetly.

'It's not what you're thinking, sir. He's not dead. He's, well, disappeared.'

'What do you mean?' I howled in anger. I felt let down; I'd shown I cared about Tim, which was the most prohibited of all the feelings between us. I'd been cheated.

I continued to stand beside Sheila, my arm around her shoulder, her arm around my waist, as Wally Wadd explained.

'He hasn't been seen since Tuesday, Dave.'

The Commander's eyebrows shot up. The second time around, he realised who I was. Oh, that Dave, his eyes read. Now he knew, he could stop pretending to be polite.

'So? Three days? Couldn't he - well, you'd know - isn't he working a case?' Clearly they thought about it in domestic terms no more than did I. My sneaking suspicion was that he'd never even been with another woman; I was absolutely certain he had never been unfaithful to Sheila. She was the guardian angel of his good nature. Some sort of nervous breakdown was, for pretty much the same reason, unthinkable.

Wally didn't answer. He looked towards the Commander for guidance. The Commander said:

'Obviously we're aware what Mr Dowell was working on.' This was probably a lie, but he had to save face. 'None of it would have called for his absence. Besides which - you know him quite well - he would hardly disappear without a word to his wife.' He spoke as if on familiar terms with the family; until today, he probably hadn't known or cared if Tim was married.

'What are you doing about it?' I was expressing Sheila's hysteria for her. 'Why are you here? Why aren't you out looking for him? What was he working on?'

'I can't tell you that, Mr Woolf,' the Commander said with - I detected - a measure of satisfaction. 'We're taking all the steps we can. We came over to offer Mrs Dowell some support.'

I snorted.

'All of you? You're keeping something back. You think he's dead, don't you?' It might have seemed cruel to say it in front of Sheila, but she squeezed my hand gratefully; if it was going to be bad, she wanted it all at once.

'I can't say any more than I already have done, sir.'

'Which is sweet...' I remembered Sheila's views on language and swallowed 'fuck all': 'Nothing.'

'Because there is nothing to say, sir. I'm not keeping anything back. As soon as there is any news, we'll let Mrs Dowell know.' He addressed her directly: 'I'm leaving WPC Rankin here to help you, Mrs Dowell.'

'I don't want her. I'm sorry.' She realised how rude it was to talk about her as if she was not there: 'I'm sorry,' she repeated.

'It's very kind of you, Miss Rankin, but I don't need any help. I just want... Find him. Please.' She got up and left the room. I could hear her mounting the stairs heavily; she would find her strength in her children - and in mine.

The Commander looked confused; he wasn't used to being walked out on. I couldn't imagine why not; he wasn't good company. He said:

'What do you think, Wadd?'

'Are you going to stay around, Dave?'

'Sure. For a while, anyway. She's got a sister a couple of streets away; I'll call her. And Carson can probably come out - if I can find her.' Wally knew Carson. He, too, raised his eyebrows. I said: 'I know, but they get on pretty well; Sheila's sort of adopted her too; they meet in town.' Not at home, where Tim and Carson would feel compelled to compete and clash. 'You know, shopping, girl-stuff,' I added, and batted my eyelashes at the Commander, who was the only one who didn't understand I was telling him to piss off and leave us to sort out the boy stuff on our own. WPC Rankin rose and politely suggested they all leave.

Wadd said:

'I'd like to stay around myself for a bit, if it's alright with you, sir, of course?'

After the Commander left, I asked:

'Does he always take half the force with him everywhere?'

Wally hadn't answered by the time Rankin came back in and asked whether by some chance the Renault blocking her car happened to belong to me.

When I returned, Sheila had come back down, carrying Alton but leaving her own pair of brats upstairs. I picked up my boy and cuddled and kissed and cooed at him as she said:

'Do you want to take Alton, Dave?'

'Don't be daft, Sheila; I'm not going anywhere; not unless you want me to.'

'I'll keep him this weekend, then.'

'I said: I'm staying, Sheila.'

'No you're not, Dave. You're going.'

I knew exactly what she meant. She looked pointedly at Wally until he too understood. He groaned.

'You'll get me crucified, Sheila.'

She said flatly:

'It's what I want, Wally; it's what Tim would want.'

Just like buses, two cases had come along at once. Or had they?

CHAPTER TWO

With Sheila's consent, we tossed the Dowell dwelling to see if there were any papers around that might give us a clue, and to give us something to do until Mary, Sheila's sister, arrived. She was a librarian, and her husband something in computers: I've never really understood computers, so I can't say what. Mary was younger than Sheila by about five years but, although she'd had only the one child to the Dowells' two, looked a lot older. It's worry that does it; Mary was a worrier, someone who struggled with life where Sheila took it all in her stride.

Wadd appeared to have little idea what Dowell had been working on, so I wasn't much use at looking, but I found the secret place in the unfinished attic room Tim used as a study where he hid his own supply of Southern Comfort - our shared hobby - which Sheila had banned from the house after he'd once drunk his way from top to bottom of a bottle and threw up all over the bathroom. It was reassuring to discover that he could deceive her a little; their relationship would otherwise have been that bit too perfect. Was it significant, I wondered, in terms of the assumptions we had all made that he would not disappear because of her, or could not have had some sort of breakdown? Had he gone on a Southern Comfort jag? I was still wondering about it as I wandered back downstairs and Sheila said:

'You can't have looked very hard if you didn't find his stash.'

'What makes you think I didn't?'

'I can't smell it on your breath.' Sheepishly, I returned to recover it and brought it down to pour myself a shot.

Sheila, who hardly drank, said:

'Pour me one, too.'

* * *

Wadd had arrived with the Commander, so we drove back to town together. On the way, probably more to distract himself from my driving than usefully to apply the time, he filled me in on what little he knew.

'There's a couple of things he's been interested in,' he began grimly, 'but I couldn't tell you whether they're separate, or aspects of the same case.'

'Yuk.'

There's something I should explain about Tim's work. Tim - and whoever is working for him for the time being, which as I say had for a while been the unfortunately named Wally Wadd - didn't really fit into any acknowledged category of police department or work. He worked out of Scotland Yard, but he worked only the most elusive kinds of case. He was called in when the matter was sensitive - for this reason or that - and couldn't be handled in any conventional or even a structured way.

If it was directly political, Special Branch caught it. If it was merely murder, the usual semi-comatose bodies crawled over the wholly moribund. Tim fit in when a case was perceived as in some way or another likely to have undesirable implications, which implications might be avoided depending on how the matter was handled. The cases I'd worked when he'd 'happened' to show up all fit this definition. The common denominator was the establishment, whenever it had an interest in the outcome.

The reason I said 'yuk' was because one Tim-class case would be problem enough. Their nature invariably limited the involvement of other officers. Written records would likewise be kept to a bare minimum. Even Wadd, as his full-time assistant, could be partially in the dark - perhaps without knowing it. Tim was a loner not by nature but by trade.

'I've got to tell you, he's been even more secretive than usual this time; a lot more,' Wally said: 'He's reporting direct to the Commissioner, so he says; what I mean is, if he's reporting at all'.

'Great. Go on. Break my day.' I had already clicked to the connection but wasn't yet ready to tell Wadd: Dunlop had promised to have someone take a look, even if he wouldn't do more without a formal request. If someone was taking a look on Dunlop's behalf, it would be Tim.

'Okay. Number one: Doctor Kildare.'

'Doctor Kildare? This is a person? They're showing repeats? He's watching them? How come you ruled out nervous breakdown?'

'Shuddup, Dave.' Since Dowell wasn't around, Wadd had to assume his role: how else would I be able to work with him? 'Doctor Kildare. This is what we called it since he wouldn't tell me what he was interested in. All of a sudden here, he's studying drugs, development, research.'

'This is drugs? Drugs stolen from hospitals? Drugs stolen by doctors?'

'If it was anyone else's working name, yeah, sure. Not his line, though; no reason not to leave it to Drug Squad.'

'Unless you happened to want to catch anyone at it.'

He grinned amiably; he shared my view of the National Drugs Intelligence Unit on the ninth floor of New Scotland Yard. Even with the benefit of their team of external - expatriate and indigenous - undercover agents, there was one word in their title that was entirely misplaced and another that probably explained why. Like most else, all that was important politically was the fact that a National Unit had been established, the hell with what it achieved.

'No, I don't think so. The sort of thing he was interested in was drug development - how new drugs came into being, specifically toxics, but search me...'

'Double yuk, no thanks.'

'You can't help it, can you, Dave? I mean, it's like a compulsion with you. It's gotta be a wisecrack a minute or you think you don't exist.'

I slammed on the brakes in shock: this was Wally Wadd; he wasn't supposed to enjoy intelligent insight. I sighed: no one could be relied on.

'Go on.'

'That's all I can tell you about Doctor Kildare.'

'Gimme number two. What's this called? Lou Grant?'

'Not fair; better programme.'

'Granted.'

'Rhode Island Reds.'

'Rhode Island Reds? This is a new drug, a pill? Uppers, downers, hallucinogenic? Where can I get some?'

'You mean you aren't selling them out of that club of yours?'

'What's a Rhode Island Red?'

'It's a cock, actually.'

I suppressed the more obvious riposte, settling instead for:

'Voodoo, maybe?'

'Maybe, for all I know.' Suddenly, unexpectedly, he slapped his hand on the dashboard, furious. 'Damn the man. Damn him and his secretiveness. Damn him and his inability to trust anyone, me. Just damn him, that's all.'

He cared too.

After he calmed down, he went on.

'Newport, Rhode Island. It's where they used to hold the America's Cup for years, until Australia won it and it got transferred to Perth. Then there was that stuff about New Zealand. It's been in Valencia recently; now it's heading for San Francisco.'

'Right. Of course. Should've realised it straight off.'

'It's a very big deal; huge money involved; people pay millions to design a yacht to win; there's a billion dollar tourist industry around it.'

'That dollars US or Australian?'

'You know the exchange rate?'

'Nope.'

'Then why ask?' Wadd snarled.

'What's the America's Cup got to do with this?'

'Nothing I know of. It's just the only other thing I happen to know about Rhode Island,' he admitted, returning to form. 'But Tim went to Newport end of last month.'

'I didn't know that. He went to Newport? He came back?' The latter was the more surprising: I've been to Newport; it's beautiful. The old part of the town is full of wooden houses, a redwood library, a clock that I think plays the opening bars of God Save The Queen but they think plays My Country 'Tis Of Thee (which in turns makes me think of Buffy Saint-Marie's magnificent protest song: My Country 'Tis Of Thy People You're Dying), a plaque commemorating someone called Michel Felice Corne, who brought the tomato to America, a sign in the empty lot behind a church which says Park And Thou Shalt Be Towed, and a whole bunch else that looks pretty, including - especially - the women.

'He was only there a couple of days. When he came back, he started reading up all about oceanography.'

'That's okay, makes sense. They've got one of the most highly developed oceanography centres just outside Newport; comes out of the naval research establishment originally, I think. Gant's Gully, it's called. Some people rate it more highly than Wood's Hole,' its better known Massachusetts kissing cousin. 'The U.S. Naval War College is in Newport, too.'

His turn to be surprised that I could make an intelligent contribution.

'So?'

'So, whatever he went to Newport for had something to do with Gant's Gully and oceanography.'

I pulled up on the Old Brompton Road outside the club and parked on the yellow lines they never bothered to enforce in the evenings. I couldn't come to the club without thinking of Lewis. In his will, he'd left the club to me; in a separate letter, he told me it was to hold on trust for Malcolm, his manager and one-time lover, until Malcolm's criminal convictions had been spent and he could hold a liquor licence in his own name. Malcolm never made it, there was no one else around to inherit, Tim tore up the only other copy of the letter, and so it became mine. Carson's friend Natalie took over running it for me, and turned it from a seedy, out-of-hours drinking den serving food bought second-hand from the Salvation Army into a quite pleasant place to go for an evening with a chef who knew more than how to microwave a frozen burger. I liked it, and it even made me money, but I still missed the way it was in Lewis' day and night: tacky.

* * *

I'd rung from the Dowells' to forewarn Carson to be at the club when I arrived. For once, she'd done what I told her.

Carson and I as a team was Sandy's suggestion. When she introduced us, after I went back to work at Nichol & Co., we came very close to immediate blows. She's Australian, five eight or nine, and gives the impression of being built like a brick-shithouse, though that stems not nearly so much from size as it does from the wall of anger and pain built up during and after a childhood which came to an abrupt end when she saved her crippled father from savage assault by killing her drunken uncle with a meat cleaver. She was fifteen at the time. She was acquitted on all counts - congratulated by the court for her courage - but fled the memory in favour of a variegated life in England that led her by a tortuous route to Sandy, by whom she was despatched to college to train as a paralegal.

At the time we met, she was living in an illegal squat in Finsbury Park, along with - among others - Natalie. I'd stayed there for a short while when some unpleasant people wanted to ventilate me. Carson and I had slept together twice. Once without sex, and once with, both during the same case. I always suspected Sandy knew about it and I liked to think that -

notwithstanding her innate and immoderate jealousy - she had understood and tacitly condoned it as a necessary result of the tension we were under; better each other than someone else.

Soon after, Alton was born and Carson went back to Australia to sort herself out and maybe to leave us to sort ourselves out on our own. When the time came that I needed her again, Natalie - by then running the club and living in Lewis' old flat above it - coughed up a contact number, and a few days later she returned.

I don't know how she manages it - perhaps because she owns a minimum of clothing and other personal possessions - but Carson remains of no fixed abode. She leaves some of her stuff in Natalie's flat, and stays there much of the time. She has also co-opted one of the empty rooms in Sandy and my house in Cloudesley Road for her own use, keeping a few books and a change of clothing in it, staying whenever she feels like it or thinks that - even if I won't admit it - I need the company. She's often there for Alton at the weekend. I don't know why, because I am still very attracted to her and I sometimes sense she wants more with me, but we've never gone back to bed together. Maybe it's too early; I think if we did so, it would be the start of something so serious we'd know we'd be in it together forever, an idea each of us has our own reasons to fear.

As for Natalie, well, she's altogether different, which is possibly why they are as close as two women can be. Natalie is of Russian Jewish extraction, a sometime dancer, small and dark - to that extent, like Sandy - but with the biggest boobs and the most electric body I've ever encountered. I wanted her in the most blatant, physical sense from the first time I saw her. Before Sandy died, there was one night when I thought Nat and I were going to make it, though we didn't; it was the night I read, with deepening gloom, Jada's manuscript.

While Sandy was alive - and except for the duration of that last case - I was only allowed to go to the club - my own club! - once a week, to go over the books but nothing else with Natalie. Sandy would wait up for me to return to check I'd behaved. Like those machines you have to walk through at the airport, which screech if you've any metal about your person, Sandy would have known even if I'd taken ten baths and changed clothes fifty times since. After Sandy died, when I wasn't sitting alone at home getting drunk, I used to go down to the club a lot more often.

Natalie's grown older and wiser - and sadder - since she took over the club. She's watched all the lonely people, and recognised as myth that what a loving couple do with and to each other is stretch out naked in front of the fire and make languorous love accompanied by a bottle of Veuve Cliquot and - say - the Sweet Baby James CD. One night - maybe three, four months after Sandy died - too drunk to drive home, she took me up into her bed and we made love gently and with genuine warmth. A few days later, I went back for more. With hindsight, I'm pretty sure she knew it wasn't going to work again before we began, but also knew I had to find it out for myself. And that's what happened. I don't mean nothing; I functioned; she functioned; it was much worse than if neither of us had been able to do so.

I still yearn a bit for Natalie, and wonder whether in the right combination of circumstances we might not yet be able to come together in a relationship. I haven't tried to find out, neither has she and it is the one subject Carson will never discuss with me. That means quite a lot, since there's nothing else she won't talk to me about or say to my face, like, as Wadd and I entered the club:

'What the hell have you done, Dave? How could you?' As if it was my fault Tim had disappeared.

I held my arms out wide: search me; I have nothing to conceal; nothing to feel guilty about. It wasn't good enough. She said:

'You and your bloody games with Tim. You're his best friend, damnit, and he's your only one. If you both didn't pretend you couldn't give a toss about each other, you'd know what he was up to, you'd know where to find him.'

She was close to tears and, as usual, coping with it by getting angry at me. She had spoken to Sheila; it was Sheila's pain, so it was hers.

Natalie joined us at my usual corner table, from which we could watch the club while we talked. Tom, Malcolm's tantalising toy-boy to whom I gave a job at the club after Malcolm's death, had recently quit to go back to Scotland. Like Carson when she went to Australia, part of his growing up was to confront where he'd come from. He, too, would probably return one day. Apart from the chef and his assistant, there were three other staff, but we trusted them only so far as we could see them. Every time the barman approached the cash register, Natalie twitched.

'What do you know?' Carson demanded. Unusually for her, she was quite pissed. 'What's he told you?' She tossed her head at Wadd as if there was no prospect of direct communication between them. He grinned: she was only dealing with him the way she dealt with Dowell, the way earlier he'd started to deal with me. And she put our ignorance and his disappearance down to the games I played with Tim?

I glanced at Wadd. He shrugged. There was no way he could stop me telling her, nor did he want to, though he still looked uncomfortable at the extent to which - following Sheila's diktat - he was throwing the Commander's orders, police regulations and maybe his career out of the window by sitting there while I did so. He was so uncomfortable, he made like he wasn't really listening, especially while I was simply repeating the information he had given me. Accordingly, he did a double take when he heard me conclude:

'And now I'll tell you what he's really working on.'

* * *

Wadd said:

'But how can I not tell him?' Meaning Millward.

I said:

'Tim hadn't.'

Wadd said:

'Is this because Boller told you not to?'

I said:

'I think it was Horace Black, actually.'

It was an evasion. There was a conflict of interest. I was certain the cases were connected; Tim's life had to be considered more important than votes. On the other hand, if the police were brought in, I'd be out - and so would Boller in another death or three - and that was probably the same as a death sentence for Tim.

* * *

We could have divided up the areas of interest and separated for the night to ensure a bright and early start in the morning. Alternatively, Wadd could have snuck into the Yard to extract copies of what little Dowell had recorded.

'I'll have to print it out, though; it's all on disk, you know.'

I knew that Tim was something of a fanatic about his computer, and kept programmes and files all of his own, in flagrant breach of the Data Protection Act, containing bits of information no human being ever ought to know about another. His brother-in-law, Mary's husband, had devised a programme for him that only Wadd and the two of them knew how to run.

Then again, we could have continued to concentrate on the information to hand, trying our damnedest to think it through the way Tim would have meant it. I guess we must all have been overwhelmed by shock, grief and fear, though, because all I can remember of the rest of the session is being driven wearily home by an equally weary Carson, the way she was driving mostly wondering - if Tim was still absent without my leave - who would be left to attend our funerals. Nor did we get an early start next day. I didn't even wake up until Carson shook me to tell me Wadd was coming over.

'Time is it?'

'Three.'

'Day or night?'

'Cucumber sandwiches.'

There was more in written form than I had expected. Wadd had borrowed the books Tim had been ploughing through, though he had to return them during Sunday. Important though Tim's disappearance was, sufficient to justify a personal visit to Sheila by his Commander, it was not important enough to qualify as the sort of emergency for which additional overtime could be authorised: Tim was neither a politician nor a millionaire and nothing was different since Friday.

I've spent some dull Saturday evenings since Sandy died, but none came close to the boredom of the books on oceanography and medicine Wally insisted Tim had been interested in. They united to impose the most obscure ones on me, reminding me that - as a lawyer - I was supposed to be trained to grasp the essentials of numerous alien disciplines. They wouldn't let me off even when I reminded them that, if nothing else, I was one of the world's worst lawyers, not even when I told them Margot McAllister thought so too.

'New theory, people,' I cried. 'It drove him crazy.'

'Already was,' Carson commented. 'Shuddup.'

Tim had marked several passages, and though I skimmed the rest, these were the ones I read closely and struggled to master. At about five in the morning, Wally snoring on the sofa with a handful of print-outs clutched to his face like a teddy bear, Carson determinedly doodling the way she always does when she wants me to think she's concentrating but which means she's asleep on her feet, I brought the troops to attention.

'This is what I got. Tim didn't buy coincidental death any more than I did. Tim's looking at how in the hope it'll tell him who. Gant's Gully is what takes him to Newport, and my guess is, from this, that it gave him a fair idea of what he was looking for. Now all we gotta do is find out where it took him next. Wally?'

'If it's a drug, how come it didn't show up on any autopsy?'

I shrugged.

'That's another good question.'

'What was the first?'

'Tell us about the drug, Dave,' Carson forestalled the descent into mutual abuse.

'Not sure I can. I don't know if it's the sort of drug intended to get high on, which may have turned lethal, or designed to kill. All I know is, obviously, it's something that grows in the ocean, but I haven't got a clue what.'

'How're you going to get one?'

I batted my eyelids flirtatiously.

She groaned.

'Oh no.'

'Oh yes.'

* * *

Which is how come Monday afternoon - evening in England - I touched down at Boston's Logan International Airport and picked up my Alamo compact rental, thankful the lethal lifestyle of MPs had improved the exchange rate. Don't ask me the model; I have a hard time distinguishing English cars, let alone foreign makes. I also have a hard time driving on the right-hand side of the road; I nearly gave up the investigation once I hit the Callahan Tunnel that was the only way to get anywhere from the airport.

Over the weekend, I had rung Margot McAllister to tell her what I believed and where I was going. At her suggestion, I also rang Ted Farlowe, Boller's political assistant and principal independent adviser, external to the civil service, who had been identified as my main route to the main man. I asked him to ask Boller how much he trusted the Americans, and how much good he could do me in terms of contacts and aid. Farlowe rang me back Sunday afternoon and quoted Boller.

'He said to tell you he trusts them about as far as Osama bin Laden did.'

'That means no one?'

'He also said to tell you, if you get into trouble he's never heard of you and he'll revoke your passport if you go anywhere near the Consulate.'

'Tell him...' I paused, my head hurting from the war between the epithets. So I just said: 'Thanks. I'll do the same for him some time.' I hung up, leaving Farlowe to work out what - if anything - I could have meant.

I did not drive directly to Newport, Rhode Island. As I said, I'd been there before, and had friends in the town, though it had been so long since I'd been in touch with them I had no idea if they would be around. They were, in any event, the wrong type of friends for what I needed, unlikely to have appropriate contacts.

I planned instead to drive to a small town called Pelham, still in Massachusetts, which merges with another town called Amherst, like you don't know if you're in Brighton or Hove, or Southend or Raleigh. I tried to call ahead, but all I got was a busy signal. I took the chance. It'd be harder for them to tell me to piss off in person.

After a few wrong exits off Route 90 - the Mass Pike - that added a couple hundred miles to the meter and would correspondingly add more than a couple of bucks, I found my way to the familiar, rambling, wooden corner house at the beginning of Harkness Road. The garage doors were down and there were no cars in the drive. Another of my hunches gone wrong. I wondered if the spare key for when someone got locked out was still in the same place. It was; I let myself in. In the untidy kitchen, I found the makings for a cup of coffee; I was beginning to flag; it had been a long day and it was late back home.

I heard a car drive up. I watched from the window. Karen had emerged - stiffly, hesitantly - from one side, and was examining my car curiously. A small boy jumped out from the other side - Abe? Noah? How old would each of them now be, and which was which? I'd only ever seen a photo of the younger, and when

I met the older one he'd pissed on my red flared jeans. Karen glanced towards the house without seeing me, and then back to the car. I was about to go out and announce myself when I heard her peal of merry laughter. Then, as if she had just remembered something, she frowned and stormed into the house.

We collided at the door:

'You bastard,' she slapped my face. She was heavier than my memory of her: it hurt.

Then she remembered something else.

'Oh, God, Dave, I'm so sorry about Sandy. I'm so sorry we never knew her.' I had nonetheless sent her a copy of the printed announcement card.

She put her arms around me and we hugged and hugged, both of us in tears.

'How'd you guess?'

'When I saw the rental sticker. Who else is going to turn up, let himself in, after - how long has it been, Dave?'

'I don't know; ten years, twelve, maybe?'

The boy had followed her into the kitchen, presumably disregarding instructions to remain outside until Karen had dealt me her opening hand. He was wearing a martial arts tunic. All the same, he was about as scared of me as I was of him.

'Come here, Abe. This is Dave Woolf. Remember? I told you about him?'

'Oh, yeah, sure.' Obviously it had not been a memorable account. He stuck out a hand:

'Hi. I'm Abe.'

'Dave,' we shook solemnly on the occasion.

'Do you know Noah?'

'Uh, yes, I do. But, well, I don't think he'll remember me. He was just a baby at the time.'

'He still is, sometimes,' Abe replied tartly.

'Cute, Abe, cute,' Karen scolded while she busied herself making a fresh pot of coffee: 'How long are you staying, Dave? You are staying, aren't you?'

'Overnight, anyway. If that's okay, that is?' I remembered my manners.

'Sure. No problem. Noah's sleeping over at a friend's house tonight.'

'I remember about you,' Abe announced. 'You're the one that got them into trouble. Right?'

'Uh, right. I think your Mom remembers it too.' It was what had earned me the reception. 'You still got the tape, Karen?'

'Uh-huh. They impounded it.'

A while back, in the middle of a case, I needed somewhere safe and preferably out of the country to stash what was, to the naked eye, about as openly pornographic a video as one would want to imagine. One of the participants - Malcolm's then lover and my future employee, Tom - knew he was being filmed; the other - a most distinguished member of the English Bar - didn't. You can work out for yourself what was up whom at the time, and why this particular posterior was being preserved for posterity.

Anyway, I thought it'd be alright to send it to Karen for safekeeping, because I knew that English and American videos were not compatible. What I had not known about was the conversion equipment used by the American postal service. Only Tim's long-distance intervention prevented a prosecution. If memory served, Sandy fielded an angry call just about the time Alton was born; possibly it brought him on. I had forgotten that during a later call, when Karen rang to proffer condolences, she had also promised me a slap in the chops for their trouble.

Abe's curiosity reasserted itself.

'Did you know my Mom when she was a hippie?'

Karen laughed and tousled his hair.

'Sure,' I said, and glanced at Karen.

The look was enough. We broke into an old mantra:

'Omni-ma-shevaya, omini-ma-shevaya, omni-va-shevaya, omni-ma-shevaya. Omni-manal-rayal-nayal, omni-manal-rayal-nayal, omni-manal-rayal-nayal, omni-manal-rayal-nayal...' (Though don't ask me if that's how it's spelled).

Abe held his hands over his ears and, as soon as he could be heard, shrieked disgustedly:

'Oh, yuk. What is that? On Top of Old Smokey in yiddish?'

Like Karen said: cute, Abe, cute.

After dinner, when Abe had finally exhausted himself only moments before he wiped me out, I told her why I'd come. Amherst has no less than five universities. It was why I used to enjoy coming to visit them; in those days, at least one or maybe two of them were women's colleges. I didn't figure her for contacts with the naval people at Newport - not, anyway, unless there was some sort of protest meeting at the gates. I did figure her for finding a contact within the universities who in turn might be able to put me in touch with the right people. It took a couple of days, but she didn't let me down.

* * *

The trip from Pelham to Newport took less than a couple of hours. I read licence plates. New Hampshire's Live Free Or Die is my favourite. I listened to the radio. How come theirs is so much better than ours? Maybe because the pop music I like is American, so it needs Americana for it to work for me.

I was deep into this debate when a cop car overtook and drew in ahead of me, slowing down and flashing a sign telling me to pull over. I was disappointed; I wanted to be hollered at through a loud hailer. I followed the car onto the hard shoulder and, remembering what I'd been taught from all those years before when I was last in the States, put my hands on the steering wheel in plain view.

They came at me from each side. The one on my side was about eight feet high and jangled as he walked: radio, gun, stick, shades.

'Sir, may I see your licence?'

I shrugged and extracted it from my wallet. He examined it with curiosity, holding it up to show his partner. They both relaxed, and he grinned.

'That explains it.'

'Explains what?'

I'd been driving slowly in the fast lane, then speeding up, moving into the slow lane at well above the limit. They'd been following me for a few miles; I hadn't noticed; that, if nothing else, worried me. They let me off with a warning, and what Tim liked to call a 'HAND.' (Have A Nice Day).

In Newport, I checked into the Treadway Inn. I'd never stayed there before, couldn't afford it. The oddest thing to come to terms with was that, for all my attempts to squander my money, I was wealthier than at any time in my life. The mortgage protection policy had paid off the house on account of Sandy's death before I'd made the first payment; the firm was still ticking over enough to generate a profit; the club brought me money, too. What's more, if I did find Tim, I could bill him time and expenses.

I took a room, paying extra for a view over the harbour. Checked a Miller Lite out of the pay-fridge. Sat on the balcony, feet on the railing, and studied the boats from a professional perspective. Some of them were sleek racing yachts; many were serious fishing boats; most of them, though, were qualified to do no more than show off how much money their owners had. It was awesome: I had to be looking at a billion bucks of dedicated vanity. I sighed: and I thought I was well-off?

Having established in the phone book that they were still in town, I didn't want to call my friends yet. As soon as I did so, I would have to see them. I'd already been in the States for three days, and all I could show for it was the beginnings of a tan. Guiltily, I picked up the phone and dialled Gant's Gully.

'I wonder if I might speak with Professor Chambers,' I used my poshest accent. 'If he's available, of course.'

'Who shall I say is calling him, please?' a man asked.

'He won't know me. My name's Dave Woolf; Professor Partington of Amherst suggested I make contact with him.'

'Hold for a moment, please.'

'Chambers,' a middle-aged, clipped voice came on the line. He had to be clenching a pipe between his teeth. I put him as male Caucasian, late forties or early fifties, silvery hair, probably expanding an inch a year, with children who grew up calling him 'sir' and now brought their own families for Sunday lunch - at a table, not a barbecue, served by a black or Filipino maid. Probably, he wore half-glasses to read, or rimless spectacles all the time. I nearly barked back at him: 'Woolf'. Instead I spoke in my most modulated English upper-class tone.

'Oh, Professor Chambers. Good of you to take my call.'

'How can I help you, Mr, uh, Woolf?'

'Just Woolf.' Wadd was right; I couldn't help myself.

'Excuse me?'

'Sorry, nothing.' I gave up on the accent. 'Professor Partington - Amherst - I was visiting some friends, said I was coming down here. Doing an article on oceanography-related research. Interesting chat with. Suggested I call you, thought you'd be willing to see me.'

The reason so many private eyes - and conmen - select journalism as a cover is because few people can resist the notion of their name in the papers, not even if they are already well famous.

Chambers chuckled.

'What you mean is - give you the tour and the talk?'

'Well, uh, yes.'

'How does Friday afternoon sound to you, Mr Woolf?'

'Dave,' I said: 'And fine.'

'Know how to get here?'

'I'll find my way.'

For some reason, he didn't seem to share my confidence and insisted on giving me detailed directions, all the way from my hotel to his office. Afterwards, I rang home; I spoke, in order, to Sheila - who had no news, Carson - who had no news she was prepared to tell me, and Wadd - who had no news he was prepared to tell me over the telephone. He did, however, have some information.

'He was in touch with the local law; he was scrupulous about that; it's a copper's convention; about the only one he ever honoured.'

'Any thoughts how I might...?'

'What? Find out who? Dear me, no; I mean, that would be something Millward would have to find out, formally.'

'You wanna know what this call's costing you, Wally?'

'Me?' His voice travelled from his feet through the top of his head and out into orbit.

'If we don't find Tim, I'll bill you instead.'

He coughed and spluttered and in the middle slipped out a name.

CHAPTER THREE

I entertained my old friends at Le Bistro, overlooking the harbour, where the best dishes are fish and the cheesecake so memorable I could still taste it from my last visit which, if Karen was correct, was at least a decade before. I had known Dannie and Lucy from the beginning of my Earl's Court days, when I was still at university. An American Jewish family, Warren - Dannie's husband, Lucy's father - was a painter not especially well-known but commercially viable before he died far too young to bear thinking about. He and Dannie had liked to spend half their time in England and the rest of it in New England, which is how come Lucy still isn't sure what kind of an education she got, except it was different. In my own eyes, Warren had half-adopted me and after his death Dannie kept up the relationship, although we could go for years without meeting or talking.

There was a lot of ground to cover. Lucy had met Sandy a couple times when she was over in England but Dannie never did. They knew a little bit about my extra-curricular activities from the occasional - usually drunken - catch-up call in the middle of the night when I couldn't sleep and there was no one awake to keep me company within a cheaper zone. They had also been amongst the select few to whom we had sent Alton's birth announcement.

I think Lucy was game for the sort of all-nighter in the waterfront bars of Newport that we had engaged in when we both young enough to remember the next day what had gone on the night before. Tonight was not to be. Lieutenant Luke de Vries - the name I had scored from an unwilling Wadd - was on the night-shift.

'I could use the company,' he had said. 'Gets slow around here when the jet-ski-set's gone to bed.'

'I didn't think they went to bed?'

'Well, okay, when they pass out on the Persian carpet.'

He hadn't sounded surprised to hear from me, though I was surprised Wally had taken the time out to call ahead. Booking a call abroad from New Scotland Yard requires so many forms I doubted Wally's capacity to complete them without Tim to guide his hand and show him how to make the loops in all those letters.

'Didn't. Remembered the name,' he explained. 'Spent an evening with your Dowell; took him pub-crawling.' I hadn't known they used the same term in the States. 'He hit the Southern Comfort pretty hard. Some point in the evening, started talking about you. Seems you turned him onto it; sort of road to Damascus, huh?'

'Could say. We get to do the same?'

'Hell, no. I'm on duty.' But he was prepared and when I met up with him he had brought in a bottle. I was impressed. Unlike any English police station I knew, they even had an ice-machine. I was even more impressed.

De Vries was a tall man, about thirty-two or thirty-three, with thinning hair, horn-rimmed glasses, a moustache and of indeterminate ethnicity until he explained that he had a Puerto Rican mother and a Dutch father.

'Without the name, no way I'd be on the Newport force,' he added grimly.

Newport is snob-town. One long road along the coast - Ocean Drive - is lined with the mansions millionaires built as summer homes - Vanderbilt, Woolworth; Jack and Jackie were married from her parents' house on the shore. Though much of the wealth is gone, the tradition lives on. It was also why night duty was a soft call; leaving aside the occasional high-society death, there weren't too many street brats allowed to stay in town.

'What about the navy?'

'Prestige posting; mostly officers. Naval research, naval hospital, war college, honour guards.'

'Gant's Gully?'

'Not navy. Is that why you came? Why did Tim send you?'

'Uh, right.' We were a quarter of the way down the bottle and I still hadn't disabused him of the notion that I was present on Tim's precise instructions. 'Tim doesn't know I'm here.'

He froze: he looked like a popsicle with spectacles.

'Now maybe you'd better tell me what this is about, Mr Woolf.' Two seconds earlier it had been 'Dave' and 'would I like another drink'. 'Or maybe I should call Chief Inspector Dowell?'

'I wish. He's missing, Luke. MIA.'

He nodded slowly, digesting the information, relating it to whatever Tim and he had discussed which, if I knew Tim, wouldn't be nearly enough for my purposes.

'How official are you? No. You're not official,' he confessed just how much Tim had told him about me. 'Maybe I'd better make that call all the same.'

'It's tempting. It's five in the morning over there. Can I listen in when you call Commander Millward?' But it was the last thing I wanted. 'Okay, so he doesn't know I'm here. There's a DS - Detective Sergeant - who knows. He's who gave me your name; you spill that and you spill him. Wally Wadd? Maybe Tim mentioned him too?'

'Nope. Talked about his wife, talked about his kids, talked about you, talked about yours. Some kind of weird name?'

'Alton,' I said dryly, appreciating that he was still testing me. 'He tell you the story of it?'

'Well,' he grinned and finally relaxed again. 'I couldn't truthfully recall. Maybe you'd better tell me what you got, okay?'

'Okay.' So I did. All of it. A lot more than Tim had told him, it was clear from the expression on his face and the frequency with which he reached for the bottle. By the time I was finished, so was it. 'What can you tell me about Professor Chambers?'

'Oswald Chambers, sure, I know him. He's one of the friendlier ones from out there. I've played in a bridge tourney with him.'

The vision of this lanky copper playing bridge amused me. He scowled.

'Good game; serious game.' Then he too grinned. 'Make a few bucks at it, too.'

It was a small permanent community. Big enough, and well-enough resourced, for the substantial summer population influx. Those left around for the winters naturally enough viewed themselves as the 'real Newporters'. They divided into two classes. The straights - which would certainly include Chambers and, apparently, de Vries - and the artists, like my own friends Dannie and Lucy. There was little overlap between them. This sub-divided the permanent community yet further. It was accordingly unsurprising that de Vries was able to tell me a bit about Chambers.

'Did Tim meet him?'

'Not that I know of. He was only here a few days. What're you saying here, Dave? What he was looking for comes out of Gant's Gully? Or, just information?'

'Ask me again when I've seen Chambers.'

A uniform put his head around the door, studiously looked in every direction other than the bottle and said:

'Word, loo?'

Which abruptly terminated the interview.

* * *

I killed a day wandering the town. In the Red Brick Market, I bought gifts for the kids; I figured Sheila wasn't in the mood and the bric-a-brac was far too classy for Wadd. For Carson and Natalie, I was daily snitching the supplies of almond soap and shampoo the staff left in my room at the Inn. In Leather Feet - still there after all those years - I bought myself a belt and a soft-leather cigarette case. When I used to come over to the States, I did a lot of shopping there: I still have a couple leather shoulder-bags from when I was a beardie-weirdie with a headband. I'm an aging hippie at heart and such as passes for style, though more recently, looking for things on which to spend my unsought and unearned loot, I've gone upmarket to Timberland. They had a store in Newport, too, but it didn't have anything I couldn't've bought in London without the added risk of being stopped at Heathrow Customs.

In the evening, I ate again with Dannie - Lucy had departed for Providence - but this time at the Black Pearl where, perversely, I chose Maine lobster. Almost idly, but because I'd trust her with my life and she has one of the better minds I know, I sketched the story in outline. Half-way through, she started taking it seriously. At the end, she said:

'I don't know if it's relevant, dear, but about six months ago there was some trouble at Gant's Gully. A woman got killed - shot. She worked there; a mugging.' So much for de Vries' claim he had no street trouble. 'It's all I know, because after the first two or three days the whole thing went quiet. That's why it's curious. Didn't de Vries mention it?'

'Nope.' Which was also curious.

One of the other things de Vries had omitted to mention was that Oswald Chambers was as black an American as ever I've seen, blacker than a West African. He was also considerably younger than I had imagined. He was also very much larger; he should've been the cop, not de Vries. Nor was he wearing glasses. As we shook hands, I said:

'They don't look like bridge-playing hands, Doctor.'

He was amused.

'Who did you get that from, Mr Woolf - Dave?'

It had been a piece of crass one-upmanship which I had to wriggle out from under.

'Policeman called...um...Vries? I have some friends here - maybe you know them?' This was safer ground: Dannie had confirmed she knew none of the Gant's Gully people. 'They know him, we got chatting. He said he played against you in a bridge tournament, right?'

His face didn't register any dismay. He asked about the article I was writing. I'd done enough reading around in Tim's books to sound convincing.

'There's a lot of work still going on about medical applications of ocean life, right?'

'That is correct.' He led me down a corridor and we emerged into what might have been called a laboratory but which was far larger. It was a huge hall, filled with vast, glass vats in each of which swam or grew the most disgusting colours, shapes, textures and growths - fungi, algae, plankton - you could dread being served up as a seafood salad. A slice of sewer seaweed would have been more savoury. I gulped. This was what last night's lobster had been eating while awaiting its - his? hers? I didn't want to think about that either - destiny as my dinner. They had the most perfect killing apparatus in the world: dunk me in one of those vats and I'd die of horror. 'That's a lot of what we do here,' he added, meaning medical research, not death by a thousand upchucks.

'What's that?' I pointed at a particularly repulsive moving mass.

'Jellyfish, Dave, plain old Portuguese Men of War.'

'Oh yuk.' I'd meant to keep it under my breath but it slipped out.

He laughed.

'You can find one at almost any beach around here. If you feel like that about it, don't go for a swim.'

'I won't,' I promised with convincing sincerity. 'What do you do with them?'

He launched into a lecture he had probably given a dozen times a week for the last five years.

After a while, my head spinning, by now in our third 'facility', as he called each new part of the complex, I asked:

'And you're the director of all this research?'

'Hell, no, Mr Woolf. No one person could direct all the research at Gant's Gully.' We stopped by a coffee pot, which he picked up and tilted with an inquisitive gesture. Then he sighed and shook his head.

'Might be good for making cultures; not for drinking. Tea?'

'Sure.'

We carried our mugs to his office. He stopped behind for a quick word with his secretary.

'You were saying,' I reminded him when he had settled behind his desk.

'I direct the medical research facility,' he confirmed. 'We were responsible for Diasamynyl, did you know?'

'I didn't,' I said dryly. 'Nor do I know what it is.'

It's better to look like a schmuck than be caught out by a trick question.

'Diasamynyl is a culture used in heart treatment, basically, in lay terms, to loosen the valves; you might think of it like a lubricant for the engine of the heart.' He followed the lay introduction with a technical description that was appropriate to someone avowedly writing an article about the establishment.

'What happens when you discover something like that? I mean legally, who owns it?'

'Most of our research is under contract. There'll usually be a deal where if something is successful, both the facility and the people involved will benefit - financially, I mean. Incentive. Performance related pay comes to academe.' The last sentence was a quote he wanted to see in print; I dutifully wrote it down in block letters, which was as near as it would get.

'Do you view yourself as an academic?' He had told me earlier that he had qualified as a medical doctor, but subsequently developed his work in toxicological research.

'Sure. Gant's Gully is a spin-off from the university. Brown. I was on the research staff at JH - Johns Hopkins in Baltimore.' Something tweaked in the back of my head. I reached around to massage my neck muscles, but it was inside my head not outside. Johns Hopkins. Baltimore. It featured in the material Tim had filed under the asinine title Doctor Kildare.

It didn't mean much. As Chambers explained, Johns Hopkins Hospital was one of the most important medical centres in the USA, and no one of any real medical worth had not at some time enjoyed a connection either with it or the University with which it was associated:

'Like Oxford or Cambridge,' he added. 'Did you go to Oxford or Cambridge, Dave?'

I pulled a face.

'Like hell.'

He chuckled.

'I didn't think so. Where did you go?'

'UCL. That's…' I was about to tell him University College London when he surprised me.

'I know what it is. I did some work at UCH.' Its affiliated hospital. 'Then spent some time in the West of Ireland. We have a lot of people come over here from Ireland; there's some surprising resources off the coast.'

I was about to pursue the subject, with its inevitable association, when Chambers' secretary poked her head around the door.

'Doctor Somers is here, doctor.'

'Here's someone who can really tell you about Diasamynyl. Do you mind, Dave?'

I shook my head.

Doctor Somers was not black, large or male. She stood maybe five two in low heels, and was as skinny as a rake, with a face freckled and pert like a fifteen year old, though she had to be at least in her late twenties, probably early thirties. Beneath her white laboratory coat, she was wearing jeans and a t-shirt. Beneath them, who knew? Chambers did the honours. She said:

'Julie,' in response to my invitation to call me Dave. 'From England, right?'

'Right. Have you been there?'

'Julie did her undergraduate degree in London,' Chambers explained proudly as she sat down.

'How come?'

'My father was in the diplomatic service. I was educated all over.' Like Lucy. 'But latterly in England. Then J.H. Then Oswald offered me a spot here. Are you from London?' She had a lovely voice: firm, but melodic. Mellifluous was the word that came to mind, reminding me of an old friend at home who had spent part of her childhood in the Isle of Skye.

'Yes,' I answered, not entirely accurately. London's like New York; hardly anyone was born there; the intervening years until arrival are written off to misadventure. 'When were you last there?'

'In England? Not for a while. But I'm going over this week for a conference.'

Chambers explained.

'Julie's presenting a paper on some of our work here. Usual thing - looking for money. Most of the drug money is in Europe now.' I'd thought it was in Colombia. 'For research,' he continued. A quick scowl crossed his face. 'Well, a lot of it, anyway.'

'Perhaps we could get together,' I suggested politely. 'Follow up some of the questions I've been asking Professor Chambers, here?'

Before she could answer, Chambers said:

'I was, uh, going to suggest Julie take you over from here in any event. She and I just need a couple of minutes first. Is that alright with you? I'm going up to Brown - Providence - on Monday, so this is our last chance to connect before Julie travels to Europe,' he explained.

'Sure.' I rose. 'I'll wait outside?'

He got up too and we shook hands.

'See you again,' he said politely.

When Julie emerged, she seemed distracted but quickly remembered her manners.

'You want to see the ocean, Dave?'

We wandered down a long path between low buildings towards the shore, where she pointed out the reservations and reservoirs where their own fish, shell-fish and some of the unmentionables I had seen in the glass vats were raised and cultivated for research. She pointed out the gully where the sea had eroded between the hills, which gave the place its name. The loudest noise was the ripple of the ocean on the rocks. Casually, I said:

'It's not all so peaceful around here, I've been told.' She looked up at me quizzically. 'I was told you had a murder around here a while ago.'

A black cloud crossed her face.

'Helen,' she said tersely. 'Helen Thornton. She was a friend of mine.'

'I'm sorry. Were you very close?'

'As close as can be; we qualified together, were room-mates for a time up here. Why do you want to know?'

'No reason. I was told about it last night. It just struck me as, well, incongruous; it's so quiet here. Mellow?'

'Yes,' she said curtly. 'Mellow.'

I had turned her off which was a pity as I'd planned to ask if she was free for dinner. We strode back towards the main buildings, but she veered away at the last moment to show me directly to the car-park. Nonetheless, when I asked about meeting in London she took down my phone number and promised to get in touch.

* * *

Instead of Julie Somers, I spent my last evening in America with the secretive Lieutenant de Vries.

Helen Thornton - like Julie Somers - had studied at Johns Hopkins under, among others, Oswald Chambers, and had subsequently been brought by him to Gant's Gully to participate in a new programme of toxics-related medical research, predominantly heart-oriented. Seemed like a lot of his staff had studied under or worked for him before. The accent on heart research was not new: because of the navy connection, Gant's Gully had for years been involved in deep-sea heart conditions. Her murder was not, in de Vries' opinion, a mugging, as it had been treated in the press, though it had been intended to look like it. He had not told me about it during our first talk because he had seen no relationship until I had finished talking, at about which time we had been interrupted; the conversation had not been resumed that night.

By this second occasion we talked, he'd had more time to think about it. Though clear in his own mind that the death was not casual, he had wanted for any motive. Personal life was out.

'She lived with a guy; they were happy, planning marriage, kids; she used to room with another woman at Gant's Gully.'

'Julie Somers.'

'Right. What I'm saying, there was no jilted boyfriend in the background. If the guy she was living with had anything to do with it, I'm turning in my badge. I've known some grief in my time, but this was something else.'

'Was there nothing else it could have been?'

'Well, that's where we get a bit complicated,' he looked shifty, then shrugged. 'The hell with it. I'm not telling you this anymore than what you told me. The FBI got involved. I don't know how much you know about jurisdiction, but there was no reason for them to do so. On the other hand, if they turn up offering help, you don't tell them to get lost. Well,' he grinned: 'This town doesn't. The sheer extent of naval presence gives them a half-jurisdiction: anything could touch them.'

'So?'

'So they poked around and told me they thought it was a mugging and that's what they told my captain and that's how it got into the press and that's where it got left.'

'You were told to let it go?'

'Not directly. People are more circumspect these days, anyhow about anything that might look bad if it came out after. But they painted me into a corner and I didn't have enough to get out of it with. That's what I'm saying.'

We talked about the possibility of some kind of street drug development, a by-product of legitimate activity.

'Could she have been caught up in it? Stumbled on it? Been involved in it?'

'No way. This was one very straight lady. Time I finished investigating, I was half in love with her myself. And I'd seen the body,' he grimaced. 'You wanna see photos?'

I waved the offer away. I'm squeamish when it comes to dead bodies; even the ones I've put there; especially the ones I've put there.

I floated the thesis of another kind of drug. He considered this for a while.

'I'd have to say it's a possible, it works as a motive, and it fits with the Federales' interest, but what are we talking about here? Some sort of mass drug - chemical warfare? Poison? Lethal? Or some sort of individual drug? Where's it coming from? Who? More important, where's it going? Who's using it? For what?'

'Gee,' I batted my eyelids. 'I wish I could've thought of all those questions.'

He grinned again. I could see why he and Tim got along.

I told him about Julie Somers coming to England, and how she had reacted to my mention of Helen Thornton's death. He said:

'We talked to her. She didn't know anything. She was away at the time. It's a good life; the conference circuit.'

'Where?'

'Your part of the world; Galway, Ireland.'

Recalling her answer to my question about when she'd last been in England, I realised she hadn't lied, but she'd been less than fulsome with the truth. Nonetheless, it fitted with what Chambers had told me; also, it fitted with my first, spontaneous reaction to Boller's account. The Irish, the Irish: there's always room for the Irish. This was the only thing I held back from de Vries, not from mistrust, but because it was too vague, too unsupported. Idly, I asked:

'How come Chambers doesn't go to conferences himself?'

He shrugged.

'Maybe he likes to stay with his family. Some people do, you know.' Then I saw him remember something Tim had said. I knew what it was, because I hadn't told him. He said: 'Sorry. Thoughtless. It takes a long time.'

'Your wife's dead?'

'First wife. Leukaemia.'

'How long ago?'

'Six years. I've been remarried four years now.'

'You still miss her?'

He smiled thinly.

'How about every day?'

'How'd's your second wife feel about that?'

He stared up at the ceiling for a moment, then - as if on a casual whim but that was nothing such - pulled open a drawer of his desk and extracted a shoebox, which he pushed across to me. I looked at him to ask if he really wanted me to open it. He waved a hand to tell me to go ahead. Inside, a pack of photos, a bundle of letters, a silver chain and locket, three rings, a couple of buttons - one of them reading 'Love Is...Letting Your Partner Use The Bathroom First'. A copy of Leaves of Grass. I didn't open the letters and glanced only briefly at the photos. It hurt too much. One night, drunk, I had come close to ripping all my photos of Sandy out of the albums and throwing them away. Only the realisation that they were Alton's too had stopped me. I pushed the box back at him and said:

'She doesn't know, right?' Meaning his second wife.

'Right. Grief's like that. Eventually, you give in to it, or else you box it up and stick it in a drawer some place. You know?'

I did know but I didn't want to talk about it any more. I asked:

'Where're we going with this?'

'Both ends against the middle?'

'I go home, you stay here? You think there's something in it, then?'

'All there is to go on,' he shrugged. 'Keep in touch.' He put his carton away in the drawer and got up. He handed me a card, on the back of which he had written his home number. 'Have a nice journey home.'

* * *

I got back Sunday morning. Carson met me.

During the drive into town, she confirmed - as I had appreciated from the absence of either enthusiastic or abusive messages at the Treadway Inn - that there had been no developments on Dowell's disappearance. On the putatively plus side, no more members of Parliament had dropped dead either.

We took a detour to go visit Sheila and the kids. Alton was overwhelmed by indifference at the return of his devoted daddy. The children took their goodies into the garden to play with, compare, trade and destroy.

'One of these days he won't recognise you,' Sheila warned, as if she had no greater problem on her mind. 'When this is over, you're going to have to do some serious thinking, Dave.'

She shrugged. It wasn't an attractive gesture. She didn't look attractive any more. At a guess, she was catching a couple hours sleep a night. I knew from Carson in the car that she was still resisting all offers of official assistance and accepting not much more from family and friends. While Carson made tea, I said gently:

'You don't have to get by on your own, Sheila. It doesn't mean...' I knew what I wanted to say but not how to say it. I knew she was coping alone because she always did cope: for Tim, for the kids, even for Alton and me. She did so because Tim was the constant, the sheet-anchor, in her life; the moment she stopped coping, it would be like admitting he wasn't coming back.

'Shut up, Dave,' she snapped. 'You're a fine one to talk.'

I shrugged: a war with her I couldn't deal with this early in the morning, or rather, as it was in the States, in the middle of the night.

We sat around the table at which I'd found her that first day, as if time hadn't moved on at all. We were grim company. I was too tired to make jokes and Sheila wasn't finding the situation amusing. Carson said:

'Wally's coming over later.'

'Here?'

'Home.'

Sheila smiled bleakly.

'He's sweet. He telephones two or three times a day. He wants me to know how concerned he is, how much he cares, but he doesn't want to say so. So he rings up with this or that piece of innocuous information, and waits for me to tell him how I'm feeling, or how the children are. Then he grunts as if I'm wasting his time and hangs up as soon as he can, embarrassed.'

'What about Millward?'

'Doing everything we can, Mrs Dowell,' she mimicked. 'Is there anything we can do for you?'

'Find my husband?' I guessed how tart Sheila's answer would be.

'Doing everything we can, Mrs Dowell,' she repeated.

Carson continued:

'Wally saw a friend of his in Drugs.'

'And got?'

'Nothing. There's nothing going on that Tim was interested in. Nor did it start with any kind of tip on their part.'

'Would he know?'

'Yup. The computer's flagged so any outside enquiries show up. If Tim had made either a formal request for information, or plugged in to search the data on the QT, he'd have known.'

'What angle are they playing at the Yard?'

'Confusion rules? Ignorance *über alles*? Bang any heads they can get hold of? Search and seize whatever gets in their way? They've talked to your man in Newport.'

'De Vries? I know. He told me. Millward rang himself. Wanted to know what de Vries could tell him about Tim's movements in Newport.'

'What did he tell you he gave Millward?'

'Gant's Gully; nothing clear. Didn't mention their night on the Southern Comfort, though. Whoops, sorry Sheila.'

I scored something that might at a pinch have passed as a smile.

'That's all?'

'Yup.'

'Didn't mention you were over there?'

'Nope. Least, not that he said.'

'Nor according to Wally.' De Vries was playing it straight; I was not surprised, but it was reassuring to find my instincts were still in working order.

* * *

Nor had de Vries told Millward anything about Helen Thornton, Wally said when he arrived that afternoon. Least of all had the FBI been mentioned.

'How does that tie in?'

'Could be drugs; espionage... the Irish?'

'How did the Irish get into this?'

'I don't know that they do,' I admitted. 'It just seems an obvious connection. You've got British politicians being poisoned, whatever it is could conceivably come out of Gant's Gully, or anyhow out of the ocean, a lot of relevant ocean-life is floating around off the West coast of Ireland. Gant's Gully people to and fro.'

Carson asked:

'Couldn't it as easily be Muslims?'

Wally shrugged off the suggestion.

'I doubt it; it's not their style. Anyway, they don't do anything without publicity.'

Though I thought he was right, I toyed with it for a moment.

'Suppose... What they want is to put the government onto a knife-edge, an even sharper knife-edge than now. Maybe that's when they plan to go public?'

'You want me to prod SB. in that direction?' Special Branch. I shook my head.

'I thought you liked Tim.'

He frowned, struggling for something he didn't find easy to say:

'You take too much for granted, Dave. I want Tim back, you know that, just as much as you do. But I am a policeman, that's what I've spent my life doing, it's what I'll go on doing. I know you and Tim, well, you think you're both smarter than the whole of the force put together, and maybe you are, who knows, but he doesn't look that smart right now and don't expect me to see it the same way.'

I was being scolded. I reminded him:

'You weren't that complimentary about NDIU.'

'They're a special case,' he muttered, his expostulation exhausted. 'Anyway, if not SB, then who?'

I stretched my arms to relieve the tiredness in my muscles: all this travelling was wearing me out. There was more to come.

* * *

I decided to rule the Irish in or out.

For the first time in many years, I visited Belfast. The last time had been back when I was a law student and went over to be best man at a friend's wedding, back in the early 1970s. It was a Protestant wedding, though the couple in question had friends on both sides and she had for a time gone out with a member of a republican club. When I read out the club's telegram, it got booed. When I rose, I told them, at the instigation of the drunken groom:

'I'd been planning to make a long speech, but just before I got up a charming young man in a black beret asked me to tell you that, uh, you've got three minutes to get out of here.'

They didn't laugh.

I remember being shocked by Belfast at the time; it was hard to think of it as part of the same country, notwithstanding the proliferation of familiar images - post-boxes, telephone kiosks, post offices, shops. It looked more like news photos from the Middle East or some other war-ravaged city; a charred and scarred urban landscape. I remember, too, a strange, almost sensual reaction to the sight of soldiers patrolling with weapons at the ready or standing sentry outside police and army posts, the roads to which were littered with speed humps, not at that time a familiar London friend. Despite myself, a thrilled shudder: war comics, war toys, war movies, war noises.

I didn't have time for sightseeing or shock this visit. I needed to find someone, but had no current address, and all the obvious means of tracing him had turned up empty. I headed for Divis Tower, one of the tallest buildings in Belfast, at the interface between the Falls and Shankhill Roads, the final survivor of the Divis Flats complex, a Catholic stronghold now just as it has been before the rest of the flats had been torn down, as the only place I knew to start from.

I was looking for a man called Brendan Cunningham. He had been arrested in 1977 and tried in 1978. He caught ten years for his part in a conspiracy which would have earned him triple if it had come off, and if I hadn't worked as hard as I did ought still to have fetched him double. He didn't appeal: they can increase a sentence on appeal. He knew what I had done for him. He owed me. That's what he said when I saw him off from court the last day. To that extent, it was a long shot: during his time inside and since, he'd enjoyed plenty of opportunity to think up things that might've been said or done to get him off; that was the way it usually went, though Brendan wasn't usual.

Other than the rolling ocean, I did not really have any more cause for believing in the Irish connection than when I had talked with Boller. I did not even know if Brendan was alive, in Ireland or in any way active anymore. But to look for him around where the Divis had been, or to expect him to still be connected, were not long-shots. With his conviction, and the effects of ten years in a jail on the mainland, there were not many other places for him to go or things to do.

As we drove up, I began to despair. The anodyne streets and the bland housing that had replaced the Divis Flats proffered unrelenting anonymity. No one hassled me as I wandered aimlessly this way and that, asking occasionally if people knew him or where he might be. They probably thought I was a social worker or probation officer. With the spare weight I carry around, and my rasping, smoker's voice, they would not have confused me for police. Yet from the moment I stepped out of the cab, I felt the eyes upon me, as if they knew where I was going before I did.

I was about to give up and make my way back downtown when I was stopped by a scrawny kid of that indeterminate age that marks generational poverty:

'You're looking for Brendan,' he announced. 'I'll take you.'

I gulped and wished I had something to gulp with it.

'Where are you taking me?'

'Where we're going,' he answered lippily but accurately.

It was not far, just to a pub three or four blocks down from where he'd grabbed my arm. I was shown - half-shoved, still shocked - into the snug. Brendan was waiting for me. I would have recognised him anywhere. He was a small, wiry man, maybe five five or six, with long hair and a carefully shaped beard, once jet black but now entirely grey, a web around his eyes to house a family of spiders and yellow teeth where there weren't gaps. He looked a bit like Charlie Manson, but his eyes were considerably kinder. He was exactly my own age.

He grinned happily.

'Do I owe you money?'

We shook hands.

'How're you doing, Brendan?'

I remember the very first time I met him. It was at Brixton; he was on remand. It was my first visit to a high security prisoner. I was led along corridors and through gates I had not known about during my years in training and early qualification when Brixton was a second home for many of my clients, to all of whom I had to pay house-calls in order to take their statements and prepare their defences. The guards carried crackling walkie-talkies. The interview was conducted not in one of the usual rooms, but in a prefabricated hut, which had probably been erected twenty years before as a temporary measure but that would outlast the prison itself.

The barrister I had instructed was late. I went in ahead of him to get to know my client. He had been picked up by the police early in the week before and by my firm over the weekend. If memory served right, Sandy herself had been on call that weekend and had attended the remand at Willesden Magistrates' Court first thing Monday before passing the case over to me. We were surprised that the case was not transferred to one of the well-known Irish-defence firms: Brendan explained later that their notoriety had become counter-productive.

Just as I settled down across the table from him, a guard brought in his evening cocoa and a bun. For some reason, we mutually and tacitly decided to chatter aimlessly until he had drunk and eaten. We fell to swapping stories, even star signs, the way a couple of people becoming friends might do over a joint or a pint. We had been born but two days apart. I was struck then, and continued for many years to be haunted, by the notion: there but for fortune - a different place, different parents - could I have sat.

Those personal ten minutes, broken by the arrival of pomp and wig, had carried us through the lengthy trial, allowing us an occasional few seconds away from it all in the shelter of a shared grin or glance. I'd sent him a Christmas card for the next two years but when Sandy threw me out of the firm I didn't take his prison details with me and, besides, I didn't think I cared anymore. There had been no reason for any further contact between us.

'Do you want a drink?'

'Whisky,' he held up his glass and called out to the barman. 'On me.' He explained my own mysterious entrance. 'I was told someone was looking for me; I guessed it had to be someone from long back - the flats've been gone for years. I've as many enemies as friends from those days.'

However tenuous, however long ago, however ill-defined, however short-lived, there are some classes of connection that don't ever disappear. We toasted each other with genuine warmth.

'Are you still in practice? What was that firm called? Nichols. I remember her too.' He grinned sheepishly. 'About the last woman I got near for the next ten years.' Ten years had been the sentence, but with a recommendation against parole. 'You could say, I had a lot of reason to keep her in mind.'

I shut my eyes. I knew what he was telling me: that he'd wanked to the memory of my Sandy. If she was still alive, I might have gone back and told her and we would have laughed and maybe she would even have been a little turned on by it. Maybe I would have been, too, in some way I don't care to analyse. She was dead, and I didn't know how to handle what he said. The smart and manly thing to do was to ignore it. So I told him briefly that we'd ended up as a couple, had a kid together and that she was dead. If I did it to get a guilt-hold on him it was a waste of time:

'So're a lot of people,' he reminded me that soldiers took death with a pinch of salt. But he relented: 'I'm sorry. Tell me about the kid.'

'What do you say about a two year old who's well on his way to winning a Nobel Prize if he doesn't get distracted by the glitter of an Oscar?'

'I say a lot about mine.' He extracted a photograph from his jacket and pushed it across the table. His child was being held in her arms by his wife. Siobhan and Declan, he told me.

'Congratulations. I didn't know. Well,' I laughed nervously, the first round lost. 'I wouldn't, would I? Are you married?'

'Of course.' Republican women didn't have children out of wedlock. 'It's not so bad for the men,' he meant those who went to jail. 'It's the women I feel sorry for.' They came out too late to bear children. 'What do you want, Dave?'

'Information.'

His eyes narrowed, like he was sighting down an Armalite.

'What sort of information would that be?'

I explained that though still - or, rather, back - in the firm, I mainlined in private investigations. What I wanted to know was whether he had heard anything about a plot to kill British MPs. He laughed.

'No, though once upon a time I might have wished.'

'Are you sure?'

'No, not a chance.'

He got up to buy the next round.

'My turn.'

'No. I'm flush. I'm taken care of. You understand?'

He was telling me he drew an IRA pension in compensation for his years inside.

What he was also telling me was that he was still connected; he would know; it was, after all, as I had expected and the reason I had come.

'Not even some kind of, uh, unsanctioned thing?'

'Ah, well,' he admitted. 'There's people I can't answer for - like I said, as many enemies as friends.'

'Are we talking about the Real IRA?'

'You might be; I'm not, like I just said.' They were the enemy - he was old school IRA, the Provisionals. The Real IRA considered them traitors, and as much an enemy as the British, perhaps more. Curiosity got the better of him and he contradicted himself. 'What kind of thing are you talking about?'

'Poison? Lethal drugs?'

He looked at me aghast.

'The MPs that died?'

He might be receiving a pension but his mind wasn't retired.

'Is that possible? Some say they couldn't manage any kind of campaign like that?'

'Anything's possible; don't underestimate them - they're not fools.'

'Could you find out what there is to find out?'

'I might be able to if I had a good enough reason.'

I knew he didn't mean money. I could hardly tell him because the Prime Minister wanted to know. That left friendship. Maybe it hadn't been such a dumb idea to tell him about Sandy and Alton after all. Now all I had to do was tell him about the policeman's wife who'd been taking care of Alton since Sandy died. Whose husband was missing.

CHAPTER FOUR

Logically, I ought to have gone on to Galway. Instead, after an anguished telephone call from Ruth Binder at the office, I returned to London.

Nichol & Co was - incredibly - sixteen years old. Sandy and I had started the firm soon after we qualified, each of us too arrogant to work for someone else and fool enough to think we could work together. For the first few years we worked like maniacs. Most of our work was legally aided: either criminal legal aid or civil. A lot of it was small-time, volume crime and equally small-time landlord-tenant disputes, overlaid with domestic breakdowns and social security shortfalls. I did most of the crime. It got to me. As the cases we handled began to climb the ladder of success - some heavy crime, some political, dealing instead of using - I started to take some of my fees in trade; cocaine isn't declarable for tax, or to the partnership accountant, especially when it doesn't get resold. I didn't consider it declarable to my partner either.

In those days, we weren't lovers, though like most other professional partners we were closer - and therefore fought more - than any married couple. I don't fool myself it would have made any difference. When Sandy found out about my idea of practice, payment and pleasure, she kicked me out of the firm on no notice and halted my half-hearted law-suit with a less than half-share pay-off that didn't cover my debts to dealer or bank. After a long while wallowing in self-pity, I started to work from home as a private detective doing the things you don't read about in thrillers or see on the television: mostly process serving. It took until years later - as very different people in a very different space - to get back together, this time as lovers, the way we figured out with hindsight it was always supposed to have been.

Sandy never liked my investigating. Seemed to think it was dangerous. Seemed to want me to stay around. There was never any issue but that she would survive me. I was the high-risk number, boozing and smoking and chasing around like a maniac as I approached forty whom people occasionally shot at. Maybe she even had Alton as a way of settling me down. I know she toyed briefly with an abortion. It worked, though; the only case I took after he was born was Jada's, and even Sandy agreed there was no choice but to do it: unfinished business. In the interval, I returned to practice as a full partner.

Then the freaking bitch died on me and somehow she had gotten her way so far as I was concerned - stability, professional and personal, perhaps a smidgen of sensitivity to others - but she had forgotten to write an on-going part for herself. Yeah, sure, there are times I hate her. How could she do that to me?

Ruth's clamour for my immediate return was not without cause. I had failed to deal with a chain of correspondence from the Law Society concerning the change in our mandatory professional indemnity insurance following Sandy's death. Not to put too fine a point on it, they considered my track-record less alluring than hers and had demanded an additional premium which so annoyed me that I had tossed out each successive reminder. In consequence, we were wholly uninsured and therefore practising illegally. The urgency flowed from a phone call, during which we had been invited to specify what day this week would be convenient for the Law Society's appointed inspectors to descend on the office and take over the firm until a permanent resolution could be reached.

'Great,' I muttered down the line: 'Anything you can do?'

'I've done a bank transfer. I've spoken to Professional Purposes. They're prepared to hold off until next week if you'll go in and see them this. I've made an appointment for tomorrow afternoon. I'm coming with you,' she added, as if for some bizarre reason she didn't trust me to go there on my own and make the right reassuring noises. She was watching her partnership get thrown out with my bathwater.

Which was why, the next evening, duly chastened by the Law Society but about to be forgiven, I was at home with nothing to do when the phone rang.

'Mr Woolf? Dave?'

'Yes.'

'Julie Somers. Remember? We met just...'

'Sure, of course I remember. How are you? When did you arrive? Where are you calling from?'

She was calling from her hotel and had arrived the previous morning, a day after me, while I had been flying out again. Her conference was not due to start until tomorrow; she had enjoyed a couple of days seeing old friends and visiting old haunts - 'The one's that're still here' - but she was free next evening.

'Let me take you to dinner,' I offered. 'I'll come into town to meet you.'

'That's okay. I'll come up to you if you like. I really enjoy the tube.' Only a tourist.

I gave her my address and agreed a time. Before switching off for the night, I booked a restaurant on Upper Street, around the corner. Then I poured myself another drink, put on an Emmylou playlist and stretched out on the sofa, my free hand behind my neck, to ponder serious and weighty matters: did I want to or didn't I?

* * *

'How long are you over here for?' I asked as we sat on the patio.

The patio is one of the best things about the house. The garden is an odd shape. It used to be a riding stable, which accounts for the high brick walls around much of it. Looking out from the ground floor in the half-light, or casually during the day, all you can see is a fairly short, conventional garden the same width as the terraced house itself. But when you walk down the steps from the patio, you find a patch off to the left - maybe fifteen feet deep and the length of the next garden along - and at the end to the right a similar stretch behind two other gardens, ending at a substantial garden room. The patio is a sun-trap and often during the summer, or during a hot spell in the spring, I would sit outside with the external lights on, listening to music, drinking and reading well into the wee hours.

Julie's visit was a sort of first. She was the first new woman - as such - whom I had entertained in the house since Sandy's death, since we moved in. In honour of the occasion, or else in order to complete the betrayal, I made up a jug of Cape Codders, a drink Sandy and I had discovered in an American bar in the South of France on a working holiday together during the Pulleyne case, and for which I made the cranberry juice from punnets of cranberries bought at Christmas and stored in the freezer. It was and remains my sole exercise in original cookery.

'I'm not sure. I'm supposed to go back on Friday, but it's tempting to stay for a while. I've got some time coming.'

'Can you take it just like that?' I was growing more interested with each passing Codder. People are different on holiday; looser. In Newport, though friendly enough, Julie had still been the professional, save for the moment when the mask slipped and she had become Helen Thornton's bereaved friend.

'Oswald's pretty easy-going. Correction. Oswald's extremely easy-going,' she laughed musically. 'He's always had this thing about letting people go their own way. Most people, you know, they see research as a long, hard slog in the lab. Oswald thinks you need more time to cool out, feel your way forward, let it all mull over semi-consciously. It's why his programmes have been so successful, I think.'

'And they have?'

'Oh, sure. I mean, he's a real name. In the field, that is. No one's heard of him outside.'

'He struck me as a pretty nice guy.'

'He is. He's modest and supportive... Do you know anything about his home-life?'

'Nope.' I could listen to her for hours. I've long had a thing for skinny, as Sandy knew and resented. Skinny wasn't the word for Sandy: chunky, rather. For a while, I could almost forget what it was all about: Tim.

'So, his older brother was killed in Vietnam. Left two kids. The wife killed herself a few months later. He took the kids in, though at the time he was still in college and he and Maria - his own wife - had a baby of their own and not a dime to spare. Then his father died, so he took his mother in as well. He doesn't come from money, you know. And all the time, he's like building up this reputation, and in that sort of field you have to really work to make a mark, you know?'

I nodded. I could imagine.

'All of us, who were his students - I mean the ones he really took under his wing - he was like a father to us too. Did you know that almost half his personal staff at Gant's Gully studied under him?'

'Like Helen?'

'Right.' This time, she took it in her stride. Maybe it was the distance. 'We were a clique, a group, at J.H. Helen, Steve Conrad, Debbie Segal, Pat Hughes, Zeke Zeller, me. We used to fantasise about going on working together, being able to stay together. Except Steve and Zeke, we did; me and Helen and Debbie and Pat all ended up at Gant's Gully; all the women.'

'What happened to the others, the men?'

She frowned and flushed.

'Steve got into dope. Too much of it. What a waste. He was the brightest of us all, head and shoulders, you know. He was at Gant's Gully with us for a while. Did time for dealing. Died. OD'd.' Potted history.

'And the other one?'

'Zeke? Big money man: Wall Street. He was on the fringes of some of the more questionable deals people got busted for, though he skipped out of the switches just in time. He would,' she concluded without explanation.

'And you all studied under Chambers?'

'Yes.' She'd said enough. Not everything, I could sense, but as much as she felt comfortable with. 'Is that finished?' She pointed at the cocktail shaker. Because the home-made juice is so potent, it offsets the alcohol: I've never had a hangover from a Cape Codder.

"Fraid so.' I glanced at my watch. Half an hour 'till the reservation - five minutes' walk round the corner - add quarter of an hour safe to be late. 'I can make another; maybe finish it later?'

It wasn't a come-on or a ploy. I was so comfortable with her, I'd said it unthinkingly. She didn't respond either way, but confirmed she could help me out if I wanted to go to the bother. She followed me into the kitchen while I did the job. Lime juice, Belvedere, cranberry juice - and something I'm not going to tell about, so forget it; it's my drink. I even turned my back and hid it from Julie's view. In her honour, though, I allowed us fresh cocktail cherries, coasters and paper parasols.

Over dinner, she asked about Sandy and Alton. I gave her the edited version.

'Where is he now?'

'Alton? He's staying with friends; he stays with them during the weeks. I guess, well, I've got to sort something out soon, but when she died, they took care of us for a while and just went on taking care of him.' I laughed nervously. I felt nervous. I didn't know how to handle the subject with another woman. I was conscious of the fine line between telling her the tale with sufficient honesty for her to be able to read me right, and doing so with an eye to the sympathy that might tip her into something more.

'Good friends, huh?' She kept her eyes on her plate, carefully separating the flesh of her trout from the bones. I was eating duck with home-made redcurrant sauce. We were drinking a Chardonnay. The second bottle. For a slight woman, she could pack it away. We were compatible in the way that counted most.

'He's a policeman, would you believe.'

'A policeman?'

'Right. A detective.' I was still keeping up my cover as a freelance journalist, so I remembered to throw in: 'I met him on a story. We became friends. At the hospital, well, another friend of ours, a woman called Carson, she called him up. Sandy and I weren't married - I said that - it made it easier having someone around in authority. Tim... That's who I'm talking about... He came over. Later, he took me home. Carson took care of Alton for the night and brought him to Tim's the next day... Sheila - Tim's wife - fell in love with him. Everyone does.'

'I'd like to meet him.'

'Maybe you will. If you stay over the weekend,' I grinned wickedly.

She reached out her hand to cover mine.

'It's beginning to seem like a good idea.'

And I was beginning to feel guilty about how much I was deceiving her.

When we got home, we sat out on the patio to finish the jug of Cape Codders first.

* * *

I didn't fall asleep afterwards. Julie did but I couldn't. I'd broken the chain of solitude that stretched back to Sandy and I felt more alone than ever. The two times with Natalie hadn't counted: she was connected to before and what had happened between us was a part of it. Julie had nothing to do with Sandy or that time. With Alton away, the tie to Sandy seemingly cut, Julie returning to the States certainly within a week or so, what would be left? At about three in the morning, I got out of bed and went back down to sit on the patio in my dressing gown and bare feet. It was still warm. I didn't turn on the lights.

I didn't hear her behind me. I jumped when she placed her hands on my shoulders and bent down to kiss the top of my head. Then she fetched a seat-cushion from just inside the French windows where I kept them and joined me. She was wearing my shirt: it came down almost as far as her knees. I smiled, leaned over, placed my hands on the insides of her thighs and kissed her gently on the lips.

'Are you sad?'

'A little. A lot. I'm sorry.'

She covered both my hands with her own.

'Don't be. It's not something to be ashamed of. You're who you are, what you are. If I like you, that's what I like.'

'And do you?'

'Like you?' She chuckled throatily. 'No way. This is how I tell a man to get lost. Yes, I like you, Dave. Do you find that difficult?'

'A bit. You'll go back. This will have happened. I mean, oh, I don't want to make it into a bigger thing than it is, but it's pretty big for me. You do realise this... Well, I can't say it's the first time since she died, but the other one was a friend.' To distract us both, I said: 'I haven't told you about the club, have I?'

She shook her head, bemused. I explained.

'Alton is named after a man called Lewis Alexander Altonspritzer. He had a club down on the Old Brompton Road, near where I used to live. Earl's Court - South Kensington. You know those areas?'

'Sure. I lived on the Cromwell Road for a while. Then in Baron's Court.'

It wasn't surprising: they've long been centres of furnished, short-term accommodation. That was how I found a flat in the area. The difference was, I outstayed my welcome by at least a decade.

'Anyway, he was supposed to be Alton's godfather, but he died before Alton was born. Then I found he'd left me the club.' It was getting harder and harder to stay within my cover. 'Natalie - she's a friend of Carson who I told you about - she runs it for me. It doesn't make much money, but it doesn't lose it either. A couple of times after... Well, I was pretty smashed; I suppose she felt sorry for me; it was a mistake I guess. But what I'm trying to say is, she wasn't someone new; it was never going to be anything; it never could be; it was part of what had happened about Sandy is what I mean.'

I was getting myself into a bind. If Julie was going to stay into next week, now I'd told her about the club, how could I not show it to her?

'Penny for them,' said Julie.

I still couldn't quite tell her. I said:

'I'll make some tea.'

She nodded and, sensitively, did not follow me inside. When I came back out, she was not sitting on the patio. I was about to carry our mugs of tea up to the bedroom when I caught a movement at the end of the garden, half-way around the corner to the right. I put the tea down on the patio table and picked my way to where she was lying stretched out on the ground, her long, fair hair spread around her face like a frame, her eyes, though, faded and faint. The erotic impact on me was immediate and obvious. Her distant, detached expression did not change but she untensed her thighs so that they fell very slightly apart. I knelt down over her and unbuttoned the shirt. For her part, she reached out and pulled the belt of my dressing gown free. It was over in minutes and yet to this day I recall it as one of the most sensuous love-making events of my life.

* * *

We were still sitting on the patio as the light came up and I finished telling her the truth, including the tale of Tim's disappearance, why it had led me to Gant's Gully and what I suspected. She asked:

'And now? What do you think now?'

'What do you mean?'

'You've told me about it. What does that mean?'

I had committed the classic sexism: she wasn't just a woman I was sleeping with but also a highly qualified, research doctor, not only looking for but expecting to find the meaning behind each strain of an organism.

'I guess... Well, at least that you're not involved.'

'Nor Oswald.'

'Because?'

'Because you must think that to have told me,' she said calmly. 'You know what I feel about him.'

'Yes,' I answered slowly, because I hadn't really meant to go that far. Stack sexism on sexism: if she sleeps with me, she must have a greater loyalty to me than to someone she's not sleeping with. Or: 'It is just a professional relationship, isn't it?'

She scowled and slapped me - literally, but not hard - on the wrist:

'I told you about his family.'

I couldn't possibly, after such short acquaintance, be jealous, so I said:

'Does that mean yes?'

She couldn't help laughing.

'Yes. It's just professional. So?'

I shrugged.

'Nothing.'

She smiled benignly.

'You're all alike.' She didn't have to tell me who she meant. 'But it doesn't matter. You're not wrong to trust me.'

'Why not?'

She pulled her chair away from mine. Stared sadly off towards the sky. Didn't speak for nearly five minutes which is a very long silence between two near-naked people on a patio at dawn. She was unhappy. Struggling with something. A decision. Whether to reciprocate the trust. At last, she sighed and said:

'Because I don't think you're necessarily a million miles wrong.'

My heart started pounding; it wasn't from renewed lust. She was about to put my finger onto the link I'd felt was missing in her background account of herself and her life and work.

'Go on,' I instructed intently.

'I said Oswald let people get on with their own thing. Remember?'

'Sure.'

'And I told you about Steve, right?'

I didn't bother confirming.

'Steve went to jail for dealing. What he was dealing was a drug he'd developed on his own, a concoction he called Beam - as in 'beam me up, Scotty'.'

I smiled tightly.

'So?'

'So, the way it came about was blue sky time.'

'Blue sky time?'

'Blues skies is what it's called when you do research without a pre-determined purpose or end in mind. Just following where it goes.'

'And?'

'And maybe Beam wasn't all he happened onto.'

'What do you know, Julie?'

'Not a lot, not a lot more than you - maybe not as much. Something was going on around Steve when he died.' She opened her mouth as if to continue, then shut it firmly while she changed course. 'I thought - Oswald thought - he'd found something else, while he was at Gant's Gully, and maybe he was trying to pick it up again after he got out of jail. We tried finding out. When you turned up, Oswald made the association.'

'Come again?'

She arched an eyebrow. I laughed. It wasn't what I meant.

'Oswald made the association? Oswald made me?'

I was about to ask how when I recalled my slip about his bridge-playing hands. He hadn't bought my cover-up bullshit either.

'That's why he called you in?' When he stayed back to talk to his secretary.

'Right.' She didn't look happy. 'I'm sorry I didn't tell you.' I shrugged: I was still way ahead in deceit. 'We didn't know what you were up to. I mean...'

'Was I a goodie or a baddie?' Looking for the drug to destroy it or use it.

'Something like that. You see, before she was killed, Helen rang me. I was going to Galway so we couldn't meet 'till I got back. She was upset. She told me she wanted to talk about Steve. That she'd found something out. I know that's what she was talking about. I can't remember her exact words, but her meaning was clear.'

'So she knew too?'

'We all had an idea. Some of us took it more seriously than others. When Steve was high, he couldn't help bragging about what a big man he was going to be someday, rich and powerful, just like Zeke. There was a lot of jealousy between them. I told Oswald about Helen's call. That's, well, that's why the whole thing was on his mind, like it had come back to life - for the first time since Steve died.'

'Jesus, Julie, why didn't you tell this to de Vries?' I didn't tell her about the FBI leaning on de Vries to let it go.

'De Vries? Right. Of course. You saw him while you were in Newport,' she said dully. 'How much did you tell him?'

'More or less what I told you.'

'What could I tell him? Helen was upset. About Steve. It wasn't enough to justify the trouble that would follow. For Gant's Gully, for Oswald. Can't you see that?'

'And is that it? Just a suspicion about Steve? Was that enough to send you over here?'

'I was coming anyway. No, it's not all,' she added, suddenly but inexplicably angry. 'I don't want to talk about it anymore, not just now. Okay? Can you trust me on that? Please? It just isn't the time.' She was close to tears.

On any count, professional or personal, there wasn't a choice.

* * *

In the morning, after we'd both scored an unsettled couple hours half-sleep, after Julie had gone back to her hotel to change and attend her conference - agreeing to go to the club with me that evening - I rang Wadd and told him what I'd got - though not how - and rattled off to him the names Julie had given me the night before, including her own. He promised to feed them through all available data-sources, including NDIU Later, I rang de Vries, catching him in the morning as he came home from work, and gave him the same information.

Wadd had something for me too.

'Saint Thomas.'

'Saint Thomas? Hallelujah, Tim's got religion, he's gone into a retreat?'

'It's a hospital,' he snarled down the line. 'Next to County Hall. Right?'

'Right.' I had a vague image of it in my mind. County Hall is where first the London County Council and then its replacement, the Greater London Council, were located, until it was abolished in 1986. By the time London re-acquired its own authority in the form of the Greater London Authority, County Hall was a hotel and no longer available for local government. 'So?'

'So what was Tim doing there the day before he disappeared?'

'How'd you get this?'

'Pulled his home phone records. Followed the call through.'

'Millward think of this?'

'Nah.'

'So you got Saint Thomas? So what? Maybe he just rang there? Maybe he was sick?'

'He was there alright. And he wasn't sick that I knew of; besides, he has his own doctor, and we all have the force doctor.' He was dragging out his own piece of detection for all it was worth. I yawned loudly. He said: 'He went to see a Doctor Mallalieu.'

'Who is he?'

'She,' he corrected. 'Her name's one of those he was interested in.' In the file Doctor Kildare.

* * *

Doctor Mallalieu was a formidable woman. I was glad I had worn my suit for the occasion. I was glad, too, that she did not ask for ID. Wadd had made me an appointment through her receptionist as 'police business'. So all Mallalieu knew was that a detective was coming to see her and I was it.

Mallalieu was tall - five nine or ten. She was probably still in her thirties, but the way her greying hair was pulled back and her chin thrust forward made it difficult to be sure. Her gaunt face matched her lean body. I said:

'Detective Chief Inspector Dowell came to see you the week before last, Doctor. Do you recall that?'

'Certainly,' she snapped. 'I would hardly be likely to forget.' She was a real charmer.

'Could you tell me what you discussed?'

'What's this about, uh... Mr Woolf?' She had hesitated in order to try to recall my rank. Rather than risk admitting she had forgotten, she passed over it.

'DCI Dowell is, well, missing, Doctor.'

'Missing?' Her eyebrows raised like a schoolteacher to whom a student had just offered the excuse that he has mislaid his homework. 'You've lost a policeman?' she added scathingly.

'Something like that, Doctor.'

She shook her head, bemused.

'I'm afraid I really don't understand, and uh, I don't understand what it has to do with me.'

'DCI Dowell was working alone on a case, Doctor,' I explained, keeping my voice as deadpan flat as I could. 'He has disappeared. I am retracing his steps. If you could just tell me what he came to see you about, Doctor, it would be a great help.'

'Of course. I'm sorry. It, well, just seemed unusual.'

'This or him?'

For the first time, she permitted herself to smile, albeit only briefly.

'Both. A disappearing policeman seems unusual, and Inspector Dowell seemed unusual.'

'That's true. He is an unusual type of policeman. Why did he want to see you, Doctor?'

'It was personal,' she said. 'I mean,' she added quickly, flustered. 'Professional for me; personal for him.'

'He was ill?' Unlike in the States, there is no medical privilege in English law. Strictly, she could insist on confidentiality until in a court of law under subpoena, but only a doctor with something to hide would do so for other than the most intimate information.

'He thought he might be. He had been suffering from headaches, fuzzy vision, quite a lot of stomach pain, some other symptoms of what I told him I thought was stress.'

'Why did he come to see you, not his own doctor or the force doctor?'

'I am a specialist in the area of stress-related illness, Mr Woolf,' she clambered back onto her high horse. 'As for the force doctor, I would have thought that was obvious.' As I was supposed to be a policeman, I let it ride; I even managed to work it out for myself: what the force doctor knows, the force knows. 'His own doctor referred him,' she concluded, emphasising that medical ethics had been fully complied with.

'Do you mind telling me what you found out?'

She pursed her lips: this was going a little further than she felt comfortable with. I reminded her:

'DCI Dowell has gone missing. It could be a result of what you found out.'

'It's possible,' she conceded. 'He was certainly not in good shape. His doctor had carried out the usual checks: blood pressure, eyesight, urine analysis, blood test. Do you know what a hiatus hernia is, Mr Woolf?'

'Yes,' I said. I did too. Russel Orbach had once described it to me in great and distasteful detail - sketches and all - over dinner at Frederick's in Camden Passage.

'I would have described his symptoms as similar to those, but he'd already tested negative for it. He was vomiting a lot. Were you aware of that?'

I shook my head.

'What did you conclude?'

'Provisionally, as his doctor thought, stress. Severe stress, I would say. I had difficulty getting the test results from his doctor.' I wasn't surprised: you can't get what isn't there. 'I ran my own tests and not all of the results are back, but I would be surprised if it was anything else. How well do you know him?' She shot at me.

'Not well at all, Doctor.' I lied. 'He worked pretty much on his own, which is why we're a little bit lost about his movements. Why do you ask?'

She smiled again, though without warmth.

'All information about a patient is useful, Mr Woolf. Was he under a lot of stress?'

'What did he tell you?'

'He said there was nothing he couldn't handle; nothing unusual. Was that true?'

'As I said, I didn't know much about his work, but from what I've been told, I'd say so.'

'Personal stress?'

'Happily married, again so I've been told,' I repeated. I didn't think it opportune to mention my son: Alton could have driven Tim crazy; he often did me.

'Hm. Well, it can accumulate, take the smallest thing to trigger, something someone could normally take well within his stride. I would say...' She closed her eyes before choosing her words with professional care. 'I would say that if he was experiencing all the symptoms he described, and if I am right that there was no physical cause for them, it is not at all implausible that your officer has, well, reached some sort of crisis in his life, and if that is so...' Her voice tailed off. It could have been imaginary; it could have been something he was doing to himself.

'Did he make another appointment?'

'No. He was told to ring in for the results of the tests and make an appointment then.'

'Did he? Ring in, I mean.'

'No. He wasn't due to do so for another week.'

'Which is when you'll have all your results back, right?'

'That's correct. And now I suppose,' she grimaced, 'you are going to ask me if you can see the results when they come back?'

'That's correct too,' I smiled, though I had no intention of bothering; I was more interested in how she answered.

'I shall have to give that some thought, Mr Woolf. Why don't you give me a call towards the middle of next week?'

'Fine. Thanks. You've been most helpful.'

I was still digesting the information she had given me as I worked my way towards the exit. I was so deep in thought I almost did not see Margot McAllister as we passed in the corridor.

'What are you doing here, Margot? Visiting constituents? Disaster victims? Germs with a vote?'

She managed a tight smile.

'Routine health check. I missed last year's, but with what's been going on, well,' she laughed nervously, 'I thought it best to comply.'

I shook my head in confusion.

'Comply?'

'MPs are supposed to have a health check once a year, here.' I nodded; it was news to me. 'In fact...' She glanced pointedly at her watch.

'Listen, Margot, did you think any more about my suggestion? To meet Jada and Frankie?'

'I thought about it,' she admitted. 'I feel, well, ambivalent, but Horace - funnily enough - he thinks it might be a good idea. Probably wants to meet Jada,' she smiled.

Popstars and politicians. They have a lot in common and they tend to be fascinated with one another: the grass is always greener.

'Come on Sunday,' I suggested. 'This Sunday. Lunch.'

'I... alright,' she said suddenly. 'Alright, then. Now I really have to go.'

Only after she went did the thought occur to me: who the hell was going to cook? I could hardly serve continuous Cape Codders; Natalie invariably went to visit her parents on a Sunday; and Carson, well, she cooked like an angel - the angel of death.

Then I had an idea.

CHAPTER FIVE

Before I met up with Julie to go to the club, I called in to see Frankie and Jada, to set up Sunday and persuade Jada to do the honours in the kitchen. It was a long time since I had a visit with them. Sometimes we bumped into each other - out shopping or just walking - but that didn't count. We'd been hot and cold during the time since both Orbach and Sandy had died. At the beginning, there was some mutual dependency, especially since Jada had forward commitments ahead of her new responsibility for her half-sister. Later, as her commitments settled down and she reconciled herself to a less active, less high profile career, the two of them had tended to retreat into their tiny new family unit. The strongest tie between us was Alton: if she was prepared to marry someone much younger, Frankie and my son would one day stroll into the registry office together.

Frankie answered the door. Just like she had the first time I came to the house, in answer to Orbach's summons. Unlike on that occasion, however, she was pleased to see me and hugged me without being asked, calling down to the kitchen:

'It's Dave.'

'Can I come in?'

She took me by the hand and pulled me inside in case I changed my mind.

Jada was cooking. I sat down in the kitchen. Frankie - blessed child - brought in my bottle from the living-room. It wasn't the bottle that Orbach had bought when I started to work for him, and that I had finished off the last night he and I were together. It wasn't even a distant cousin. But it looked a lot lower than when I had last been in the house. I studied it while Frankie fetched ice. That girl was going to make someone a perfect wife. Matter of fact, maybe she should marry much older instead.

'Do you remember Margot, Frankie? Who used to live with Russel?'

There was no embargo on mention of him. Until Frankie was old enough to read her sister's autobiography - something Jada was already struggling to put off - there was no connection in her mind between her parents' death and Orbach.; even then, there would be no link to how Orbach had himself died, something the book did not cover not could do so because even Jada - whatever suspicions she might have had - had not been told. Only two people still alive knew for sure: Carson and I. Then there was Tim. He 'knew', because he knew me and could guess and maybe I'd given him a few clues, though not ones that would stand up in court, but had he really known, for sure? And was he still alive?

'I think so.' She prodded her nose, her eyes alight with laughter. I laughed too.

'Right. Did you ever meet her, Jade?'

'No. I've seen her picture.' In the papers. 'Why?'

Her voice was cold; like she was angry at me.

'Why, kid, I thought you might like to write a song about her is all,' I drawled softly, to say I was picking up on it.

She swung around, her eyes aflame.

'What do you want, Dave?'

Frankie shrank back. Even though she'd lived with Orbach for a good portion of her life, she still hadn't learned how to handle sudden, domestic aggression.

'What's up, Jade?'

We both looked at Frankie.

'Go into the garden, Frankie,' Jada said.

'Go into the other room, Frankie,' I said.

'She's not your child,' Jada snapped. 'Do as I say, Frankie.'

Confused, Frankie withdrew without argument.

'What's up, Jada? What's this about?'

She turned back to the sink in which she had been cleaning vegetables. She didn't answer for a while. I let her take her time. It was something I'd learned about her. She was - whether in song or on the page - a wordsmith. She liked the way words worked. She liked it best when she chose the way words worked instead of allowing herself to be dragged along by them.

'Why didn't you tell me about Tim?' she asked without looking around.

'Ah.' I can be a wizard with words too when it suits.

'I saw Carson in M & S.' There was a number of supermarkets nearby, including a Marks and Spencer.

'So?'

'So she told me you were working on a case; she told me Tim had disappeared.'

'And you're angry? Why?' She knew Tim, but not well; just from around the time Sandy died and once or twice since. She knew Sheila better; she had taken Frankie to visit Alton in Ealing.

'I don't know,' she admitted unexpectedly. 'I just am. You tell me.'

Sometimes I almost forgot how young she was. Sometimes, too, I forget that - almost as much as Frankie - she looks upon me as some sort of surrogate parent. I felt sorry for them if I was the best they could do.

I thought about it for a while before I managed to put it into words.

'You feel excluded. Like, it was a very big thing we all went through together, and now I'm going on with, well, something like it on my own?'

'Maybe. Is it?'

'Is it what?'

'Something like it,' she sighed as if I was too stupid for words.

'It's not connected,' I said. 'It's just a case. I do cases.'

'Just a case?' she expostulated. 'Tim's missing? Just a case?'

'What is it with you, Jade?'

She cleaned the sink of carrot peelings and plonked the mess into the brown recycling bin on the counter. Then she rinsed and dried her hands and came to join me at the table. She picked up the bottle and topped my glass up. I protested.

'I don't want any more. Yet.'

'I do,' she shared it with me.

'I thought someone had been at it.' I remembered when Jada didn't drink at all: it seemed like a long time ago; it wasn't.

'Do you mind?'

"Course not.'

It was sort of cosy, sharing a glass. I understood now.

'You're jealous. Of me?'

'I think so.'

I laughed hollowly. Who'd be jealous of me? She had everything going for her. Fame, fortune, friends, beauty and brilliance: a life ahead.

'You're lonely?'

'Bored, I think.'

'I thought you were writing a new album?'

She shook her head.

'Blocked. It's... I don't know,' she sulked. 'What's to write about? I should write an album about Frankie?' I'd taught her Jewish. 'I wrote a song about Frankie,' she laughed. 'But I don't think it's a whole album.'

She was too young. She didn't have a wealth of past experience to draw upon. She'd tapped the well dry too soon. Her first and second albums had been hits, but there hadn't been one since. Her book had been a hit, but how could she follow a book called Where I'm Coming From if that was where she had stayed?

'I thought there was another part in the offing?' It had been mentioned the last time we met in the street.

'Maybe. Maybe not. I don't know if it's what I want to do. Early mornings, have to get someone in to look after Frankie, I just don't know.'

'Do you see anyone? Boyfriends?'

She snorted.

'Yes, right. Guys my age love going to the zoo.'

'I'll take Frankie. I mean, I'll take her in the evenings more.'

She shook her head.

'It's not about the time, Dave. Are you staying to eat?' She brought the heart-to-heart to a sudden end.

It was far earlier than I ate my evening meal and I hadn't been going to do so, planning on eating at the club later with Julie. I said:

'Sure.'

* * *

Sunday lunch was something of a tourist treat for Julie: she was going to meet a popstar and two members of Parliament. On much the same basis, Carson said she'd claim it as overtime. Alton, however, was unimpressed. Julie came with me to Ealing to collect him: despite her anxiety, Sheila, too, seemed to fall before her elfin charm.

To show willing - and perhaps to demonstrate domestic ability - Julie pitched in to help Jada both with the shopping on Saturday and the cooking Sunday morning. I got to look after the youngsters, which meant keeping an ear open to make sure Alton didn't beat up Frankie too badly. Also, I had to choose the wine. Hard life.

Until the last minute, I wasn't sure Margot and Horace were going to show up. Politicians tend to find themselves otherwise engaged at times most people have nothing better to do than to entertain them; it impresses no end to think of our great legislators grinding over the wheels of power into the dark hours and through the weekend. But once Margot had made up her mind to do something, as she had made up her mind to re-establish contact with Frankie, it became as serious a commitment as, say, to vote during a three-line whip.

Fortunately, it was another glorious day. We could eat out on the patio. It was a little cramped around the table but less claustrophobic than it would have been in the dining area between the living-room and the kitchen. Margot was never one for small-talk and was apparently happy to sit by while Horace regaled us with tales from the battlefront in Whitehall. He was either no respecter of state secrecy or else very good at creating the impression of confidential candour. Despite myself and my indifference to politics, I was caught up in it.

Julie too.

'How big a difference if you lose the by-election?'

Horace snorted. Even his snort had a Scots accent.

'We started this Parliament with a majority of eleven. We'll be down to five. It'll only take three more to lose overall control. And there's plenty more than three marginals left.'

'Like mine,' Margot interrupted. Her constituency was somewhere in the north-east corner of the country.

'Like yours,' he confirmed. 'You should see Ted Farlowe's analysis of the odds,' he sighed, meaning it was the last thing any of us wanted to see.

Julie asked:

'Who?'

'Ted Farlowe. He's the PM's political assistant. You wouldn't know him,' he said, probably not intending to be as patronising as he sounded. 'Not a great lover of your country.'

'I don't know,' Margot said. 'Didn't he spend some time at Harvard?'

Horace shrugged.

'Were you at Harvard, Julie?'

She shook her head, smiling slightly to conceal a frown.

Horace would not be distracted from his theme.

'Anyway, we're desperate,' he admitted. 'Jada, come and campaign for us?' he added tipsily.

She smiled shyly, eliciting a look of sympathy from Horace until - as I guessed she would - she reeled him in.

'I don't think you can afford my fees,' she said, sweet as meringue pie.

Margot laughed at the expression on her husband's face.

'It's a different generation, Horace.' She turned conspiratorially to the rest of us. 'Horace thinks we're still in the sixties when everything was free and it wasn't necessary to make a living.'

I got up to pour more wine for the adults. Frankie, busy feeding Alton, demanded some for herself. I caught a grudging concession in Jada's eye and wasted a splash. I didn't mind; it wasn't expensive wine. Margot was on mineral water again.

'Ach, go on Margot, relax a little, won't you?' Horace didn't want to go home pissed on his own.

'Just a little then,' Margot did as she was bid. 'In the same glass, please, Dave.' She meant for me to mix it with what was left of her water. More waste.

The sun was having a funny effect on her hair; it seemed almost dark, brown more than red. Julie frowned again as I commented on it. Margot said:

'No, it's gone like that in the last few days. I don't know why; it's never happened before. I suppose it's better than going grey.' She sipped her wine distractedly. 'That's why it's so necessary to be careful,' she returned to the subject of the elections, brushing aside my trivia. 'Neither Bob nor Malcolm could be described as careful, could they, Horace? Nor Maureen.'

If she meant to conceal her point, she wasn't doing a very subtle job of it. Horace guffawed and raised his glass in a toast to her. Bob, Malcolm and Maureen had all been black-belt boozers.

'That's the trouble with the middle-classes; they can't hold their liquor.'

Margot sighed good-naturedly.

'That's not what the Mistress Mallalieu said.'

'Mallalieu?' I queried. 'Doctor Mallalieu?'

'Yes,' Margot was surprised. 'Do you know her?'

'I've met her. Is that who you went to see the other day?'

'She sees all of us. Stress is her subject.'

'Yes, of course.' I was disappointed. I'd momentarily been excited by the coincidence but now I thought about it, it was obvious.

Jada asked:

'Who's Doctor Mallalieu?'

Horace answered.

'The Mistress Mallalieu is the tyrant who really runs the country. She has medical charge of the Members of Parliament. Sees us all once a year. If, that is,' he hesitated for effect, 'if we go. I go,' he declared proudly. 'Every year.'

Margot laughed.

'I missed last year,' she explained for the benefit of the rest of us. 'That's what he's getting at.' She leaned over the table and chucked her husband under his ample chin. 'Such a sweetie.'

It was all well-intended. I guessed I was witnessing the closest thing they had to a row. On its way back, her hand paused to pick up his glass, neat wine not spritzer, from which she drank with bravado.

'See, I can hold my drink too.'

Frankie had grown understandably bored with the grown-up chatter and now led an uncharacteristically but helpfully taciturn Alton into the garden, handing him down the patio steps like a pro. We all watched, unavoidably affected: one double and one half orphan.

'A bad report from Mallalieu can cripple a ministerial career quicker than an ill-timed leak,' Horace continued. 'She tells us what to eat, not to drink or smoke, when to sleep, how often and whether to make love. Of course,' he added, 'no one pays her the blindest bit of attention.'

'You don't,' Margot reprimanded affectionately.

Her eyes held his. The other three of us watched their love with a pleasure similar to that with which all five of us had watched Frankie and Alton descend into the garden. Her eyes held his without wavering. He began to frown. He asked if she was alright. Her eyes held his. Julie - not without medical experience or qualification - stretched out a hand to touch Margot's arm. Jada half-rose without knowing why. Her eyes held his.

Of everyone there, I was the one with the most relevant experience and the first to spot the familiar mantle in descent. Her eyes held his until, prevented by the arms of the patio chair from falling to the side, she toppled onto the table without a sound. His eyes, horrified, held now to the vacant space which announced not one but two forthcoming by-elections.

* * *

Nothing spoils a Sunday afternoon so much as someone dropping dead during dinner. Jada dialled for an ambulance but we knew from the outset that Margot was lost. Horace looked like he was about to lose it too. He sat there, aghast, struggling between shock, manly resolve and an untoward display of emotion. Julie took it most detachedly. For the first few minutes,

Frankie was wholly unaware of what had happened. We could hear her in one of the garden recesses lecturing to Alton:

'And then you've got to bring him some ice.'

For all my familiarity with death, I was badly shaken. Margot was, in my eyes, still associated with Orbach: for a moment, it felt as if, from beyond the human pale, he was still reaching into my life.

Out of habit, I stretched out a hand to take the cordless phone from Jada on her way to the back of the garden to take care of the children. I was going to ring Tim: that's what I always did when someone died on me. As I realised that I couldn't, reflexively I said to Jada:

'Take them down the road.'

She nodded: she didn't need telling twice.

Julie and I stood between the now uncontrollably sobbing Horace and the late Margot McAllister to shield them from the children's view as Jada hustled them, protesting, across the patio and into the house. I waited to hear the front door slam before picking up the phone to dial Wally's home number.

'Why are you calling me,' he complained. 'What can I do?'

'Oh, hell, Wally, I just want someone to take care of things, you know, from my end.' If there were entanglements like police or press.

He grunted and hung up without committing himself, though I knew he'd come.

The ambulance arrived within ten minutes of Jada's call. Still stunned, Horace followed his wife's body outside and accompanied it to the hospital. She was being taken to the Whittington, which I'd normally say was a fate worse than, if it was not a comparison no longer available. As the ambulance men slid the stretcher inside, a small crowd of residents already gathered to watch, more of them looking out of their windows,

Horace asked me to ring Boller on his private home number, which he gave me.

'He'll arrange what's necessary.'

First, I checked on Julie, who was, to occupy her hands, clearing away the patio table, her face distracted and distraught.

'Are you alright?'

'Yes, sort of. I'll make some coffee, shall I?'

'Please. Look, I'll understand if you want to go somewhere, be on your own.'

'Do you want me to go?'

'No, of course not.'

I held out my arms and she tucked her tiny body against mine and we hugged for warmth and reassurance and to remind ourselves that we at least were still alive.

Then I made my call.

'Margot McAllister has just died. Another heart attack, I suppose. She and Horace were having lunch at my home. It was very sudden.'

There was no reply for a long time. I could hear him breathing. He said flatly:

'Damn.'

I could imagine what vexed him.

Then he recollected himself.

'It's terrible. She was a good friend. She was young.' But he couldn't keep his mind off the true agenda for long. 'They've all been too young.' To die. 'What are you going to do?'

'I don't know. I think I've been getting somewhere. Just not fast enough.'

'Hurry up, Woolf, hurry up, damnit,' he hissed.

By the time we finished talking, Wally had arrived. Julie had led him into the kitchen where they were drinking coffee: she had only made enough for two, and they were them. She got up to make more but I waved her away: I, too, could use something to do with my hands. From the attention he was paying her, she had made another fan. Idly, I commented:

'If they lose Margot's seat, they've only got two to go before they're out.' Or at best as impotent as only a minority government can be. Then I said:

'Some sort of killing drug that leaves no trace, is that possible, Julie? Would that fit with what you and Oswald were worried about?'

'It could.' She wondered aloud. 'Injected? Maybe when drawing a blood sample?' Without saying the name, she was talking Mallalieu. 'It's possible. It's not unprecedented, though once a drug has been identified, it's usually possible to find it. When people talk about untraceable drugs, what they mean is that it's unknown. Because it's unknown, no one is looking for it, they aren't running tests for it.'

'You're saying?'

'Unless you know what it is, or what's in it, you won't be able to establish if it's there. Not if we're talking something new. Obviously, if it's a compound of something familiar, the familiar chemical or substance will show up, and then the only question is what it's been mixed with to achieve the effect. A regular toxicology screen covers maybe fifty-seven or fifty-eight possibilities, which is like next to nothing, you know. You only need to know what they are to avoid any compound that will trigger a response. A first-year student knows that.'

I had noticed before how clipped her tone became once she began to pronounce on her subject. Wally asked:

'Could that sort of research come out of Gant's Gully?'

'Perhaps,' she confirmed for him what she'd already impliedly admitted to me. 'We do a lot of experimentation with toxics.'

At my suggestion, we went back out to the patio. It was not, I grant, the sort of conversation one would particularly want to be overheard by neighbours enjoying the weather in their gardens, but in Cloudesley Road most of them went away for the weekends and no attention had been attracted by Margot McAllister's decision to skip dessert. I carried out with us the bottle of sparkling Crémant blanc which I had been about to suggest we move onto but for it. There was no point in wasting it. I also carried the phone out with me: I can't hear it ring from outside otherwise.

'Let's flow with it,' I suggested, meaning that I was going to try and follow it through. 'Start with the development by Steve Hilton of a lethal drug, presumably extracted from some kind of sea-life or plant. Let's say there's a line, somewhere, somehow, to the Irish. Now let's think what's going on that end. What I picked up in Belfast, there's still real, active fury about the way the IRA have gone into government. What if the Real IRA has a drug, and is taking down enough MPs to cause the government to fall? How'm I doing so far?'

Once upon a time, the idea would have been so bizarre I wouldn't have dared voice it; in recent years, though, we had become used to the notion - killing drugs used by Russia, by supermarket blackmailers, by terrorists, by spouses who didn't want to pay for a divorce, by children pissed with their parents because they'd been grounded; the list was endless.

Wally was counting on his fingers:

'Four.'

Julie's eyebrows arched into a question-mark.

He explained.

'Four hypotheses. Four unproven, non-credible, over-imaginative hypotheses in one over-long sentence.'

I protested.

'How do you know how many sentences I made?'

Julie said:

'I don't want to think that what Dave's said is right, obviously, for at least as many reasons as four. But the first part of it makes some sort of sense. I think, maybe to begin with Steve wasn't doing anything with it, thought he'd make his millions out of Beam. Then he gets busted for Beam, does time. Maybe he changed a lot in jail; I suppose everyone does; I never saw him afterwards. Maybe he met people, maybe he turned into someone who could do that, develop a drug that killed.' She was hiding something she wasn't about to share. She continued tangentially: 'I don't think he could have before, but, well, I suppose I wouldn't want to think that,' she admitted, referring to her long-term friendship with him.

'What about Irish connections?' I asked. Not a distinctly Irish name amongst them: Thornton, Hilton, Hughes, Zeller, Segal - or Somers. I didn't bother with Chambers: I knew he wasn't Irish.

She shook her head.

'It wasn't where we were at. It was qualify, have fun while we're doing so, preferably without catching AIDS, and get a good job as soon as possible. Greed is good. Oh, hell, I don't mean we were money, career bores - except Zeke maybe - not while we were still studying. We were all in medicine or related research; none of us expected to be the new Alexander Fleming. I suppose you could say that we cared about what we did - as much as you sixties people.'

Wadd held up a hand in horror.

'I'm not that old.'

I never took it as an insult.

'But everything's relative. The remnants of Reaganite ideology had us in its grip. That didn't mean we followed it blindly, or even at all. But what we thought and did and wanted still had some sort of relationship to it. Am I making any sense?' she asked unexpectedly.

I thought about England. I thought about the youngsters I knew, including a lot of left-wing lawyers. They cared, they thought they cared, they thought they cared as much as we used to. But their idea of caring, the notion of what commitment it called for, the measure of what they were foregoing by abandoning the conservative route, was very different from us - and fell a long way short.

'Yeah. Sort of. Where're you going with this?'

'Just that for myself and the others, we didn't have such strong views on things like Ireland; not strong enough to want to do anything about it, anyhow. I mean, what you're talking about has to be Weathermen, Baader-Meinhof, Black September, Red Brigade, that sort of thing.'

In an earlier case, I'd encountered 'that sort of thing', as she put it, but predominantly historically, the only current activity represented by an anachronistic, solitary offspring, left bewildered in the jungle long after everyone else had gone home from the war.

'Real IRA's pretty current,' Wally reminded us pretty unnecessarily, helping himself - but neither of us - to another glass of wine as he did so. 'I'm driving,' he explained contrarily.

The phone rang. It was Jada, asking what to do about Alton. I asked her to hold onto him for a while longer, then we'd pick him up and take him back to Ealing. That was a thought.

'What do we tell Sheila?'

'Never mind that,' Wadd grimaced. 'What do I tell Millward?'

We were still pondering when the telephone rang again. I responded with my usual enthusiasm.

'Yeah?'

'Mr Woolf?'

'Yeah.'

'Hold on a moment; I have a call for you.'

I could hear what sounded like scuffling in the background. A car door slam? A voice saying:

'It's Timothy. Do what they say, David.'

More scuffling; the first voice again.

'You know the routine, Mr Woolf. You do as we say or that's the last you'll see of Chief Inspector Dowell.'

'That's a threat already?' I asked.

The dial tone was not amused.

* * *

I recounted the conversation verbatim while it was still fresh in my mind. Wally wrote every word of it down. Julie looked ashen.

'How could you? How could you?'

'Easy, Julie. Two things. First of all, Tim told me to do nothing they said.'

She looked confused. Wally explained.

'Nobody calls him Timothy, nor does Tim call him David.'

She didn't look convinced. I said:

'It's a standard technique for contradicting the instructions of a captor, taught in all the best hostage schools; taught by Tim, too, some of them.'

'Even so... You didn't wait to hear what they were going to tell you.'

'It's a question of control. If I gave in to them at once, then all I could do would be to follow where they lead and hope to get lucky, hope they'd slip up. If they've got Tim a prisoner, if they're the same people we assume they are - responsible for the deaths, connected to Mallalieu...'

Wally snapped his fingers.

'That ties in; your visit.'

'Right. It wouldn't take a lot to find out there's no Woolf in or around Tim's work - other than me; there're politicians who know, which means it's virtually public knowledge. Anyhow,' I continued my explanation to Julie: 'they've gotta be good; the chances of a slip up on their own terms are remote. Now I've thrown them; they're going to have play me differently, they're not so sure anymore how to gauge my reactions. They'll ring back, and soon, before we have time to put a tap on this line. They want something or they wouldn't've rung at all.'

She stretched over and touched my hand.

'I'm sorry. For doubting you, I mean. I think, well, just it's amazing you could think of all that so quickly.'

I preened visibly, declining to mention - as I saw Wally eyes speculating - that I'd only thought of it after, as a way to justify my automatic, flip response.

The phone rang.

* * *

It took little effort to establish that each of the deceased had, like Margot McAllister, kept an appointment with the austere Doctor Mallalieu within a day or two of his or her death. Margot was the one with the lengthiest delay: six days, Monday through Sunday; the others lasted between one and three days. It took not much greater effort to conclude that the doctor merited full-time surveillance. To my chagrin and regret, I was unavailable for the latter - incredibly boring - task because I had met her: Carson was the lucky soul who enjoyed the opportunity to follow her wherever she went, so far as practicable.

The doctor's schedule did not lend itself easily to surveillance. In addition to her sessions at Saint Thomas, from which there was a number of exits, she had a practice at 144 Harley Street, which backs onto and connects up with the London Clinic on Devonshire Place, providing an exit either way and an additional foot-route onto the Marylebone Road as well. Mallalieu drove between the two locations and to her home in Belsize Park. She lived alone: if there was a lover in her life, she did not see him - or her - frequently. When at the hospital, most of her work was in the room in which I had seen her, but there were also a few inpatients who she visited on the wards. Carson outfitted herself with a white coat, a clip-on photo-identity card and a stethoscope which I was praying she would resist the urge to use. Just how far could our indemnity insurance be stretched?

Meanwhile, Millward needed side-stepping. We badly needed a tap on Mallalieu's telephones. The security services could have put one on with no questions asked, at any rate not until someone else got pissed off about his pension and published his memoirs. But they remained off-limits until we were more certain what we were dealing with. Boller had, however, left to me how to handle the police, short of any reference to him, my relations with him or his suspicions. Gee, thanks.

Monday lunch-time, Julie out on a photographic mission to capture what was left of her former life in London before it was replaced by modern architecture, Wally and I hammered the subject into the ground outside the Crown across the road from my house.

'If Millward were to tell the truth,' Wally said during the first round, 'he'd admit he's just about given up. If it wasn't a policeman, he'd do so. Obviously, he can't admit he hasn't got a clue where to look or what to do, but that's the nub of it. Whoever we're dealing with here is either political, so heavy that no one dares to whisper, or entirely unconnected to the constituency.' The criminal constituency.

'Makes me feel almost sorry for the guy.' We were sitting on a lot of information he could have used, and probably made much more of, though at physical risk to Tim - if the phone call were to be believed - and political risk to the Prime Minister. The second call had not added greatly to the first.

'Very witty, Mr Woolf, we're all laughing out loud, especially your friend. I'll be in touch again. When it suits me.' He was wise to my trick.

'Save your pity,' Wally now said, referring to Millward. 'He's a prick.'

'How's Sheila doing?' He had seen her the night before when he returned Alton. We had decided to say only that as a result of a call, we were certain Tim was still alive. That was why Wally took Alton back, so he could lie convincingly that he had not taken the call.

'Well as can be expected. Angry, I think; more than anything, angry.'

'With?'

'Tim.'

'Yeah. That figures. What else did you tell her?'

'That we had some ideas; not what they were. She was alright about that.'

It wasn't disinterest but an expression of confidence.

'Can you get a tap onto Mallalieu's lines without telling Millward why?'

'Not easily. What if we feed Millward Gant's Gully, but nothing this end?'

'And link it to Mallalieu?'

'That's what I was thinking.'

'He could make the connection. He may be a prick, but he can't have got to Commander if he's a complete fool.'

Wadd snorted derisively, telling me not to believe it, and got up to fetch another pint.

'You?'

'Sure.'

I thought about Wally's idea while he went in to the bar. Millward would only make the connection to the MPs if what we fed him was a killer drug. Not if we fed him Beam.

'Is it enough for him to get a warrant?' For a tap.

'Not normally. But in this case, I think he'd go without one. He has nowhere else to go. He'll have to pull in Drugs, though.'

'It'd still be quicker than, uh, you arranging something?' Something unofficial and illegal.

'Sure.'

'Do it. Lay it off on me. Tell him I went to Newport.'

'What'm I going to say about why?'

'Say Sheila told me.' Wally was not supposed to have told me the time of day but they couldn't discipline Sheila or suspend Tim's pay on account of her actions.

'How do I get you back to Mallalieu?'

'Say you don't know, didn't ask, forgot. That's credible.'

He yawned with theatrical boredom.

'He'll want to see you.'

'Yuk.' On æsthetic grounds, not professional. 'Okay. I can handle that. I'll talk to de Vries to back us up. I've got another idea, too. phone tap doesn't give us other conversations?'

'That's right. That's why they're called phone taps,' he scored smugly.

'I think I can get a bug into Harley Street; Saint Thomas' too.'

'How?'

'Jada at Harley Street,' I grinned.

Jada certainly had the contacts to provide the necessary equipment: we'd used them before. She had the status to claim to be susceptible to stress. She was also itching for something to do.

'Carson at Saint Thomas'; if she can't find a way, she isn't worth her pay.'

'You actually pay her?'

'Ask her yourself; see how many unbroken bones you walk away with. If you can still walk.'

* * *

By arrangement through Horace, the autopsy was adjourned long enough for Julie to attend; her credentials had to be confirmed first. This didn't ill-suit me: the Law Society inspectors were into the office for the next few days and I had to attend full-time and long into the evenings explaining what I understood of our accounts and files. They were not impressed but I found it interesting: I was learning more about how the business ran than Sandy had ever cared to confide in me.

Apparently bored once the autopsy was over, results of tests she caused to be run not yet available, Julie made her own way to the club and came home with Carson. Carson was making a real effort. They seemed to be becoming chums. I felt a pang of inane jealousy. I didn't want Julie to be a part of the family; I didn't want to establish a framework around her that involved others; I wanted her for me. It didn't seem possible that it was only six days ago that we had first slept together: we hadn't spent a night apart since.

'She's a very boring lady,' Carson said of Mallalieu. 'Either that or she's a night prowler.'

'Which you're not into finding out?'

'Actually, yes. Millward's turned friendly now he thinks Wally's on his side again. He's given over some men to help. Makes it look like he's doing something. She's also a very covered lady now.'

I was surprised about Millward and it didn't fit, but I couldn't work out why, so I asked:

'Jada?'

'Friday morning. Harley Street.'

'St Thomas'?'

'Yeah. I'll try tomorrow.'

'I'm tired. I'm going to have a bath.'

I poured myself a substantial shot to take upstairs with me. I didn't look at Julie. I wanted her to follow of her own accord. I was settled into the bath with my drink and an ashtray balanced on the laundry basket when she did so. She sat on the loo, cover down, as I had sat once or twice before, watching her while she had bathed.

'Tough day?' she asked.

'Tiring. Not so tough.'

'Anything new?' On Tim.

'A possible. Brendan rang; he's coming over tomorrow or the next day.'

'He's the guy you went to see?' I hadn't given her the name.

'Yeah. Ex-client.'

'You get lucky, don't you, Dave?' I grinned and stretched out a hand, which she took. 'That wasn't what I meant,' she laughed.

'I know.' I hooked my neck onto the end of the bath to support my head. 'I do and I don't. It's a much, much smaller world than people appreciate.'

'What world's that, Dave?' she asked softly.

'The world of power, I suppose is what I mean. Politics perhaps. There's been a political strain - small 'p' - in all the cases I've been involved in, meaning they've been cases where, well, the establishment, the grey men who hold the reins, have an interest. Judiciary, lawyers, freemasons, MPs. What I'm trying to get at is, where I've worked is where people with power or trying to seize power are active.'

'This Real IRA?'

'Sure. It's not about blowing up a UVF or UDR part-timer in front of his children in his home. It's not about knocking off soldiers on patrol. It's not about bombing Harrods, or even a club in St. James. It's a power-play to which things like that are peripheral, a little public pressure, a reminder the game ain't over till it's over, an invitation back to the table.'

'And your Brendan, he's a power broker too?'

'He was in the lion's den, Jule. The lion's den isn't crowded either. No, but you're right, I am lucky. Not the way you meant: lucky by chance. But lucky - if it is lucky - because the places I've been and the people I've met are where the power-action is. That's all.'

'I guess,' she sniffed. 'If you can call the Prime Minister powerful,' she added mock-snootily. 'Are you still tired?'

'Doesn't look like it.'

But we lay in bed side by side talking instead. Downstairs, I could hear Carson moving about, putting herself and the house to bed for the night: the room she slept in was directly beneath my own, though while I had an en suite bathroom, she had to use the one on the ground floor, a flight down. Julie said:

'She's something special.'

'Yup.'

'And she's very fond of you.'

'Yup.'

She rolled over to watch my face, resting her head on her elbow, her tiny, thin body barely touching mine. Between us we made up the right contents of a double bed:

'I'm not sure why. I'm not sure why I like you, Dave. I'm not sure what I'm doing here, either.' She pre-empted any flippant response. 'I mean in London, with you, in the middle of all this. You come stumbling around Gant's Gully, trip over me, pick me up and stick me in your pocket to play with later...'

'Is that how it feels?'

'Yup. I'm not complaining, Dave; I'm just confused.'

'Join the club. 'Course, I could say the same about you: you popped over to London and picked me up easily enough. There's a lot you're not telling me, isn't there, Jule?'

'Yes.'

'Why?'

'I'm not sure. I'm not sure where you're going with it. I'm not sure our interests are the same.'

I pondered this for a while.

'You mean Gant's Gully? Oswald?'

'Some. But... Well, the others, too. I mean, Pat and Debbie, and Helen.'

'Helen's dead; she doesn't have any interest.'

'Doesn't she?'

'Julie, I don't want to pressure you, but my friend's out there somewhere - Sheila's husband,' I reminded her about Sheila because they'd liked one another. 'If you know anything, anything,' I stressed, 'which might help me find him, you have to tell me.'

She rolled onto her back and stared up at the ceiling.

'I don't know anything, Dave, anything that would help you find him. That's true. I promise.'

I wished I could believe her.

I wished it even more when I awoke in the morning to find she'd gone.

CHAPTER SIX

The next day, Wally called me in to meet with Millward. I took a taxi to the Yard; parking's impossible, legal or illegal. The interview was with Millward, today in plain clothes, a uniformed, ranking policewoman and a DCI - same rank as Dowell - without a name, a roly-poly, red-faced, jovial-looking man with blow-dried bouffant hair which added three inches to his height: no Wadd, no one else, no junior officer to take notes. The absence of the latter, and the mix, put me in my mind of my midnight visit from Boller, Black and McAllister.

'I told you to keep your nose out of this, Woolf,' Millward went straight onto the offensive before I had a chance to sit down and make myself comfortable. He did not offer me a cup of tea. I deduced he didn't like me.

'No. No, you didn't. I mean, I agree it was the sort of situation where that's what you might have been expected to say, like, if you'd read the script closer. I'll even go so far as to agree that you meant to say it. But you didn't say it, I assure you.' I delivered the speech with the earnestness of a villain caught red-handed trying to persuade him I was on my way to Lost and Found with the loot in a bag marked Swag.

'Don't play smart with me, Woolf,' he snarled.

'Now that is in the script,' I answered, nonchalantly lighting a cigarette without asking permission, blowing smoke in the direction of the No Smoking sign. I waited to be told to put it out. None of them did so.

People who don't have a lot to do with the police rarely realise just how influenced their speech is by television and thrillers. It is a section of society subject to disproportionate fictionalisation and dramatization: more, even, than doctors or journalists; a lot more than lawyers; and, did you ever watch a TV show about an accountant, a management consultant or a book publisher? After a while, bombarded by Hollywood's and Elstree's idea of how they ought to talk and behave, they give in and copy it.

The woman interrupted this exchange of banal insults to introduce herself.

'Mr Woolf. Detective Chief Superintendent Gooch, NDIU. That's...'

I nodded to say I knew.

Neither she nor Millward introduced the DCI.

'Obviously, we're very interested in what you told DS Wadd, especially as it didn't coincide with any information of our own.' It was a designedly generous admission, intended to elicit my respect for her candour. Momentarily forgetting that what I was supposed to have told Wadd about Beam wasn't at all true, I was unimpressed: as an occasional taxpayer, it's my money that pays her salary; she ought to have known. 'I was hoping you would run through it again, for us.'

'Sure. It's not much. There was a guy called Steve Hilton, studied at Johns Hopkins in Baltimore, went on to do research, ended up at Gant's Gully oceanographic institution outside of Newport, Rhode Island, developed a chemical cocktail he called Beam, did time for dealing it, now dead. The information I have is that he maybe went live again before he checked out: which information relates to a body also went dead not so long ago called Helen Thornton. Finger points at maybe Annette Mallalieu did a side-line in them here; first got onto them for medical use...' This was also a cocktail: a mix of information and imagination.

'How?' Millward snapped.

DCS Gooch looked pained: we had one thing in common.

'Call de Vries in Newport. He'll give you the, uh, dope.' He would if he stuck to the promise that he had made on the phone the other night.

'In writing?' Gooch asked pertinently.

'Nope. Gant's Gully has navy connections; you don't make a fuss around it unless you've got it sewn up.'

'Why did he talk to you? Why didn't he tell me any of this?' Millward asked.

'I've given you both answers,' I said, though I didn't expect him to appreciate it. 'Because official it isn't, and because I'm not official - though as he knew - and as he was happy to respect,' unlike Millward: 'I am Tim Dowell's friend.'

'Did he give you Mallalieu?' Gooch asked. She was far shrewder than Millward though that wasn't difficult.

'I got her from Tim's doctor.'

Gooch flashed a look of contempt at Millward: it would have been as easy for the police to find, and quicker. I didn't tell her the police had found it: I might yet need Wally for something trivial.

Millward said:

'It's not much of a connection.'

'You've been going along with it.' By providing surveillance additional to Carson's.

Detective Chief Superintendent Gooch said:

'We're acutely aware of the problem of legitimate research, Mr Woolf. I mean, as an enforcement problem. Let's face it,' she shrugged her shoulders in resignation, 'there's a generation who grew up believing through their adolescence and student days that there was nothing wrong with drugs, at least non-addictive drugs. Why should some of them not have found their way into medicine and drugs-research?'

'Which isn't exactly highly paid,' I concluded for her. 'Sure. I knew a few of them. I went to college with some of them. Hell, if I could hold a test-tube upright I'd probably be one of them. So what?'

'So until something comes onto the market in sufficient volume to get out onto the streets, we are not going to know about it in development or wholesale distribution. It's kept within a closed community.' Yet another one.

'Which is why you're prepared to pick up and run with it this time?' And swallow the allegation against Mallalieu without choking.

'That, and because it is all we have got to go on in terms of DCI Dowell,' she admitted.

'We?'

'Yes, we. The NDIU has an interest now.' Now I'd given it to them.

A slice of action was all Tim meant to them, to be fought over like the last piece of pizza.

'Why did you go to Newport, Mr Woolf?'

'Because he'd been. That's all. I had to do something. You know the feeling?'

She smiled.

'Yes. I do.' She paused then trashed my answer. 'It wouldn't be, by any chance, that you had a little more than that to tempt you to make such a long and expensive journey, would it?'

'How could that be, Superintendent?' I batted my eyelashes to satirise my innocence.

Millward interrupted.

'We know you and Dowell worked together.'

'He had a habit of showing up in the middle of my cases, and not coincidentally either, as I'm sure you're aware. But work together puts it a bit strong. More like the puppet master and the puppet. Anyway, so what?'

'The Commander could be suggesting that DCI Dowell had already confided in you before he disappeared...' She hesitated. 'Or he could suspect that DS Wadd has been a little too, shall we say, candid with you - the way he might think DCI Dowell might have been if he was available.'

'No to both. But so what if either was true?'

'Then you and I would probably put the same information together the same way, wouldn't we, Mr Woolf?'

I laughed.

'Whatever I say, you'll take as an admission of one or other of your options.'

'It's not a game, damnit, Woolf,' Millward said testily. 'Dowell's missing. Doesn't that concern you? He's supposed to be your friend, you know.'

'Where are we going with this, Commander?' I asked.

The Chief Superintendent and Millward exchanged a glance. He asked, suddenly sounding relatively pleasant:

'Where does Julie Somers fit into it?'

I went hot and cold. My first thought was Wadd. My second, that they had already talked to de Vries who wasn't sticking to the agreed story. My third, that they had me under surveillance too.

'She's from Gant's Gully. I met her there. She was over for a conference; she's been a useful source of information. She stayed with me for a while.'

'We know,' he said smugly.

'How?'

'I don't have to tell you that, Mr Woolf.'

'I don't have to talk to you, either, Millward. I'm a lawyer and what I know is what I know. This isn't the States where you can yank my licence, you know.'

'There's no reason for Mr Woolf not to know,' Gooch continued to calm troubled waters: soft cop, hard cop. 'After DS Wadd passed on your information, we ran the names through the computer for recent arrivals. That's all.'

'How did you know she was staying with me?'

'We didn't,' Millward said smarmily. 'Until you told us.'

I smiled thinly. I'd used the same trick often enough myself.

'How come I don't get the feeling we're on the same side here, Millward?'

For the first time, he delivered an answer that was neither unduly aggressive nor untrue.

'Because you're holding back on me, Mr Woolf. Aren't you?'

'Is there anything else, Commander? Superintendent?'

'I have some questions, sir,' the DCI spoke for the first time.

'Do you also have a name?'

'Gregory, sir. Detective Chief Inspector Gregory. Special Branch,' he added. 'And, for what it's worth to you, also a friend of Tim Dowell's.' Lying shit: Dowell didn't have friends in the police any more than I did.

I knew less about Special Branch than I ought to. I knew, of course, that they were the British political police, and that most of them carried guns most of the time. I knew they had taken back command of the Anti-Terrorist and Diplomatic Protection Squads. I knew they played by few rules. I knew that all of them had to sign the Official Secrets Act. I knew that, like most specialist outfits, their principal priority was to bring problems within their purview for no greater purpose than to preserve their power. I also knew that Tim reserved his greatest contempt for them.

'Shoot,' I said unthinkingly.

'I'd like to ask you about your trip to Belfast last week.'

'Did that show up on the computer, too?' I asked.

'Something like that, sir. Would you be willing to tell me why you went there?'

'No.'

'I, uh, could of course keep asking that question for a long time, sir,' he said mock-apologetic.

'PTA?' The Prevention of Terrorism Act permits the police to hold suspects - used to be Irish nowadays mostly Muslim - for a prolonged period without taking them before a magistrate. I wasn't sure how long, but I was damned if I was going to admit my ignorance to them. I laughed: 'For a visit to Belfast? Waddaya going to do? Arrest the Queen next time she pops over to look at the troops?' Periodically a Royal or similar dignitary is air-lifted into the province for a couple of hours' photo-call to prove we aren't scared, the impenetrable wall of heavily armed troops notwithstanding.

'Who did you see while you were there, Mr Woolf?'

'Uh, no one who'd mean anything to you,' I smiled sweetly. When he didn't smile back, I added: 'Haven't you forgotten about professional privilege?'

'I think I must have, Mr Woolf. I must remember to look it up, or better still, consult the lawyers - sometime in the next few weeks when I have a spare moment.'

'Oh, come on, Gregory, this is bullshit. What's this about?'

'Ve chust follow orders, Herr Voolf,' Gregory said in a stage-German accent that wouldn't've fooled a monolingual Mandarin.

'Whose? Millward's?' I tossed my head in the scowling Commander's direction.

Before Millward could respond, Gregory shook his head.

'It doesn't matter, does it? You'll end up telling me, so why don't you stop wasting time with the comic routine and get on with it?' Comic routine? Me? He had a nerve. 'Where is Tim Dowell, Woolf?' Gregory snapped suddenly.

'Wha...? You think I know? How's about you tell me?'

Millward said:

'I'll tell you what I think, Woolf. I think you know where he is. I think that's why you went to Belfast. I think this is Irish. I think they've got him, and you know it, and that's what you went to Belfast for.'

'Yeah?' I turned back to Gregory. 'There's a question-mark on the end of that, sunshine. Tell me what we're talking here, Inspector?' I demoted him one grade; I hoped it was the beginning of a downward spiral that'd bottom out with his departure from the force. 'I'm party to a kidnapping? I'm negotiating? You want to fill me in what's on your mind?'

'You tell me.'

'Ah, fuck it. You know the relationship between me and the Dowells. You think I'm going to have something happen to Tim? Get real, will you.' I was bored.

'Stranger things have happened.' With this I could not argue: if blood ties could turn as evil as I had witnessed in a number of cases, then why not the more opaque relationship I had with the Dowells? 'We want the name of the person you went to see in Belfast; we want whatever you have. It's that simple,' he concluded, almost apologetic in manner if not in intent.

I thought about it for a moment.

'Let's get it dead straight. You're saying that unless I give you everything I know, you're going to keep me banged up here under PTA? Is that right?'

Gregory nodded. Millward looked pleased. Gooch looked worried.

I crossed my arms and told him to go fuck himself.

* * *

They came back for me an hour later. Millward himself fetched me. I was led up to the tenth floor. I guessed why about a moment before I met the man himself. I was ushered into his expansive office, invited politely to sit and offered a whisky.

'Southern Comfort?' I inquired without much hope.

'Uh, sherry?' Dunlop offered.

The Metropolitan Police Commissioner was a much smaller man than I had imagined. Neat and thin, compact. He had more medals on his uniform than hairs left on his head. He wore thick, horn-rimmed glasses. He had a mean face, like he probably checked his wife's housekeeping accounts. I don't know why I was surprised, but to my surprise he was smoking a cigarette.

'Oh, alright, twist my arm - some more,' I added, meaning I'd had my arm twisted already, not that I wanted more sherry.

Dunlop nodded to Millward. At last I realised what the Commander did for a real living. He was the Commissioner's butler. I noticed he did not pour himself a sherry; once I tasted mine, I appreciated why: it was foul. Dunlop said:

'I apologise for the delay, Mr Woolf. I had a number of telephone calls to complete before we talked.'

'You ever think about just asking someone nicely if they'd awfully much mind hanging about, instead of banging them up without a by-their-leave?'

He shrugged.

'Habit, Mr Woolf. You mustn't forget,' he smiled pleasantly: 'When I was a bobby on the beat there was much less of the polite liberalism than today.'

'You want to talk, talk.'

'Yes. Who are you working for, Mr Woolf?'

'Sheila Dowell. Me. My son. Tim's kids.'

'Have you established what he was working on at the time of his disappearance?'

'Have you?' I wanted him to lie to me first.

'I've known all along.' I should've guessed he'd disappoint me.

'Him?' I tossed my head vaguely in Millward's direction.

'I, uh, have given the Commander as much information as he needs.'

I thought about that for a while. It was pleasingly circular. Dunlop knew about the Parliamentary deaths as an issue, because the Home Secretary had spoken to him. Wadd had told me that whatever Tim was working on was under direct report to Dunlop. I had guessed that Dunlop had put Tim onto it. Dunlop had given Millward 'as much information as he needs'.

Until I knew how much that was, I couldn't tell how much trouble Wally was in...or I.

'And how much was that?' I asked.

Dunlop frowned.

'In all seriousness, Mr Woolf, I'm contemplating a charge of interfering with the police in the conduct of an investigation.'

'Yes,' I worked it out now. He had been trying to find out from other sources what I knew and from whom: from the government, maybe from America too. No one was talking to him. So he was threatening me instead, knowing that if pushed I'd have to play my ace card - if, which is what he wanted to find out, I had one. The problem was, I was fairly sure he wasn't bluffing. I said: 'Can we talk privately?'

He didn't hesitate.

'Thank you, Mr Millward,' he dismissed him.

'Your men must love you,' I said.

He smiled again, much less pleasantly than before.

'This is my last job, Mr Woolf. One becomes Commissioner; one can usually stay as long as one wishes - it's very difficult to displace a Commissioner; one retires from the force. Unlike you, who appears to have no one to whom to answer, I've spent my life until now following someone's orders.'

'Margot McAllister was a friend; she died in my house.'

'But why was she there to begin with? That's what's been puzzling me.'

'You remember Mr Justice Orbach?'

'Of course.'

'His ward lives down the road from me; I play a little part in her care. Orbach used to live with Margot. She wanted to see Frankie - the child - again. That's all. It's nothing suspicious. And, uh, it'll check out.'

'Well,' he said sarcastically: 'I can see why you didn't want Commander Millward to hear that.'

'Why don't we do it this way? I know what you think'. That I was working for Boller on the MPs' deaths. 'I'm not in a position to confirm it. But I'm not denying it. Okay?'

'How far have you gotten?'

'Pretty far. Mallalieu's the link. But I think she's just a tool. Bust her now and I doubt you'll get enough out of her. The rest of the jigsaw includes Gant's Gully, and maybe the Real IRA or anyhow some kind of Irish; there may be some answers in Baltimore. And, uh, there is one thing I haven't mentioned: I've spoken to Tim.'

He gawped. It wasn't a pretty sight. He lit a fresh cigarette without offering me one. That was alright. I don't like English cigarettes anyway. I read someplace that they're more carcigenous than American cigarettes. Something to do with the way they are processed. The same thing that gives English cigarettes that cloying, dirty-ashtray smell and second-hand taste in someone else's mouth.

I ran through the two phone calls, omitting only to mention that Wally Wadd had been in the house at the time. He said:

'You've got a lot of nerve, Mr Woolf,' to have kept it to myself. But he said it admiringly, not critically.

'Seems to me we've both been keeping our information on a tight leash. How much have you told Millward?'

'As I said, enough. That Dowell was looking into the deaths of the MPs for me. For me,' he stressed, meaning he had been loyal to the Prime Minister's concern. 'Which is why he came back to me once you mentioned Mallalieu.' Which was why we had been given the surveillance assistance: not my half-baked story.

'Though,' he added: 'That was a name he should have brought up long before.' Without warning, he threw at me: 'Wadd?'

'Wadd? Oh, yeah, Wally. What about him?'

'I told Dowell Wadd would have to go back to normal duties after this matter was concluded; it'll take a long time to bring him back into the fold.'

'Why bother? You've never succeeded where Tim's concerned. Maybe you'll get two for the price of one.'

All the time we were talking, he was thinking. He said:

'I'll assign DS Wadd to liaise between you and the Yard, formally. Alright?' I nodded. 'And you keep in touch with me. Let me know what you need. Alright?' he repeated.

'Why?' I asked simply.

'Not for favour,' he brushed aside the inference that he was sucking up to the P.M. 'As I said, it's my last job on the force.' Rather, to show his contempt for his colleagues and, in particular, Commander Millward.

* * *

I found Carson in the lobby. It wasn't by arrangement, but she knew where I'd gone and had begun to worry. Ruth Binder was along for the ride.

'Are you going to tell me what this is about?' Ruth demanded as we drove back to the office.

'How come you managed to park?'

'Did you ever see anyone try to stop her?' She tossed her curls backwards in the direction of a quietly seething Carson.

'Why's everyone so angry at me?' I complained.

'I don't know why she is,' Ruth got hers in before Carson could take over the airwaves. 'I know why I am.'

She waited to be asked. I asked. She said:

'I know you think I and James and the others are a bunch of idiots, Dave, but in case you've forgotten, we're supposed to be your partners.'

'Salaried,' I reminded her.

'Not if you weren't dragging your feet on the negotiations,' she contradicted me.

'Me? I thought it was you guys?'

She pulled into the kerb and switched off the engine. In the mirror, I caught a grin on Carson's face. I scowled back at her, which only made her grin more broadly. Ruth swivelled around in the driver's seat so she could look directly at me. She said:

'You've got to make some choices, Dave. We're fed up. We're fed up trying to run a law-firm with a senior partner - only profit-sharing partner - whose idea of a hard day's work is to drift in at eleven, take a liquid lunch from twelve to three, and fall asleep in the office until it's time to go home. That's when you bother to show up at all.' I started to protest but she waved my objections aside. 'We're also fed up with a senior partner who spends such little time working as he does behaving like an overgrown schoolboy acting out fantasies of growing up to be Dick Tracy, lumbering the staff with duties that don't come anywhere near their job descriptions, rendering us all vulnerable to acts of violence and disrupting the entire routine of the office. I mean, don't you ever stop to think how we feel about it all?'

I didn't come back with a flip answer, or any. The honest truth was that it had never occurred to me to ask how any of them felt about it.

'I, uh, don't want to go into a whole spiel about what this last year's been like for me: you know all that. You also know I haven't been doing any investigating either until now.' I meant in place of law. 'I'm sorry if I haven't been considerate of your position, and James'...'

'Or Neil. We could have kept him if you had given the slightest indication that you would actually have given a damn.'

I flashed at the back seat: Carson was supposed to have run that kind of interference for me. She shrugged.

'I tried. I also tried talking to you about it, Dave. You just haven't been hearing.'

Southern Comfort coming out of my ears.

'You know what this is about, Ruth?'

'A bit. Your friend Tim Dowell's done a runner. I don't know who you're working for, though,' she added, meaning that she minded not knowing.

'The Prime Minister, actually,' I said dryly. I could trust Ruth: professional privilege applied.

Ruth's eyes widened.

'This is true?'

'Yes, actually,' I repeated. 'And I know it sounds weird. Look, I have to get through this the only way I know. Can you and James, well, carry it all a bit longer and as soon as it's over, I promise we'll sit down and talk? Either I'll pull out of the firm, or I'll pull out of investigating. Okay?'

'What does pulling out of the firm mean?' she asked, her eyes agleam.

'You get it. You and James. Okay?' I repeated. Everyone wants something. Like Sandy said, they were lawyers. What else should I have expected? Charity? Concern? Help?

I waited until we were back at the office for my confrontation with Carson. She, too, was feeling left out.

'I hardly get to see you,' she complained. 'Last night, you didn't talk to me for ten minutes.'

'I was tired. I'm tired now, too'. I didn't expect it to deflect her, and it didn't.

'Sure. I could hear how tired. You were talking to Julie for long enough.'

'I thought you liked her?'

'I do,' she sighed dismissively. 'What's that got to do with it?'

'She was a pretty good source of information. Besides...'

'Yeah, yeah, I know. She was the first woman you've got off on since.' Natalie was still a no-go topic. 'Just how far do you trust Ms Somers, anyhow? Now she's gone.'

I shrugged.

'A lot less than when she hadn't. What're you telling me?'

'Oh, just something Wally mentioned when I saw him at the Yard.'

I waited. She waited. I sighed. She sighed in imitation, saying she knew me as well as anyone and if I wanted to play games she could too. I gave in first.

'Please.'

'Only that when Julie Somers was at school here, one of those schools for the children of American expatriates, she got picked up at a demonstration.'

'Over?' I asked wearily, suspecting the answer that was coming.

'Ireland,' she trumped. 'Some glitch in the Good Friday agreement.'

It wasn't much on its own - a teenager on a protest. But it didn't jibe with what she'd said:

'Just that for myself and the others, we didn't have such strong views on things like Ireland; not strong enough to want to do anything about it, anyhow.'

* * *

Broody, stuck, perhaps unconsciously hoping in vain that Julie might show up, I went down to the club. Natalie joined me for a meal.

'God, I'm hungry.'

I grunted.

'Dave, you're all over the place,' she announced calmly, as if telling me I needed a haircut. She held up a hand to forestall my protest. 'I know, I know, you've had it rough. I do know, you know; we all do; you've laid enough of it off on us; we've all had to live it too. I gotta tell you, we're getting kind of tired of it, bored too.' It was payback day. 'The way you're going at this Tim thing, it doesn't make a lot of sense.'

'Everyone's an expert now?' We talked dialect on our own.

'More expert than you seem to be right now. This is good,' she noticed what she was eating. 'I run a good kitchen,' she said with proud satisfaction. Then she decided to co-opt the thought into her conversational direction. 'I run a good club.'

'So?'

'So that's okay. I'll run a good kitchen and a good club for a good boss who leaves me alone and gets on with his thing and what he's doing is something pretty good too.' She didn't mean 'and' what he's doing is good, but 'if'. 'Yeah?'

'Has Ruth been in touch with you today?'

'No.' She knew who I meant: office outings had been to the club since I inherited it. 'But if you're saying what I think you're saying, I'm not surprised.'

'Look,' I fought back. 'I know I'm getting nowhere fast. But, you know, there isn't exactly a lot to go on, and what there is I dug up, okay? You know? Me - not Wadd, not the police, not...' I remembered in time that Natalie was not privy to who my client was and was not supposed to be. 'Not anyone else,' I tailed off lamely.

'That was two weeks ago,' she snapped. 'Almost,' she corrected to pre-empt my doing so. 'Since when did you sit on a case for two weeks? 'Specially this. Huh?'

'I don't know where to go anymore,' I admitted. 'I'm waiting for something, someone.' Like a phone call. 'I wouldn't've been hanging out so much with Julie if there was anything else to do.'

'Bullshit.' I pushed my steak away automatically. 'You make things happen, Dave. That's your style. You don't wait for them to happen. It's chicken-and-egg. Things aren't happening because you're not paying them any attention.'

'Great. I need a lead and you're giving me analysis?'

'I'll give you a lead,' Wally said from behind.

He let himself into the booth without a by-my-leave but not without difficulty: a bulky man, Wally Wadd. The first time I met him, I asked Tim if people became policemen because of their names or whether their parents gave them the names so that they'd become policemen. He never did answer. I sized Wally up curiously, debating whether I dared ask him directly, and decided against.

'Lead? As in lead part, dog-lead, leading counsel?'

'Something like that.' He wasn't in a mood for jokes. 'Just out of idle curiosity, what would you say if an SBDS,' - Special Branch Detective Sergeant - 'just happened - happened,' he stressed, 'to mention to me that a sometime Provo soldier - one who'd done a ten-spot in this country - was found a few hours ago with a hole in the back of his head?'

I didn't say anything. I was thinking of the photo of the little boy Brendan had shown me just a few days before. Natalie - and Carson and Ruth - were right: it was time for me to get a grip on myself and on the case. Before anyone else I knew got hurt. I asked:

'When did it happen?'

'This morning. Seems he was on his way to the airport. Had a ticket to London in his pocket. They bush-wacked his car.'

'They?'

He shrugged.

'Real IRA, loyalists, out of left-field loonies, who knows?'

'I've got to ask you, Wally, you know that.' I didn't have to spell out what it was I had to ask him.

Natalie got up to leave us alone; if Wally was going to admit he'd snitched, she didn't want to hear it.

'No, I didn't give anything up. Not where you'd gone, nor who you'd gone to see. I didn't have a name either, remember?'

'I've been thinking about that. You didn't need a name, did you? I'm going to Belfast, I'm going to see someone, I'm not going to have the internal IRA phone directory to play with, am I? He was the only important one I defended. That'll be on file, won't it?'

'Sure. SB files at least. Tim's, too, of course.'

'Which you can operate,' I reminded him.

'Fine. Right.' He wasn't angry. The other way round, he'd have asked me. 'I'm playing both sides of the street. Make you happy? I mean, perhaps you should stop trusting me, you know, you're so careful who you trust, you've got so many people you can trust.' I wasn't the only one growing irritable under pressure from his friends.

'Sarcasm doesn't suit you, Wally; not as well as Tim wears it anyway. How's Madam Mallalieu?'

Joni - I'd always assumed she spelled her name the Mitchell way - came to clear away. I asked:

'Bring a glass for the sergeant and how do you spell your name?'

'Whatever way you want and a glass of what?'

I groaned: even the hired hands were smart-asses.

'Beer,' Wally placed his own order: he was more likely to get served than if I did. 'Can you do a steak sandwich?'

'Sure.' She gave him the smile she ought to have given me if she wanted to keep her job. Then she stuck her tongue out at me to make fourply sure I got the point. Fourple? It's one of my immigrant grandfather's expressions. During a business deal, he'd swung around to someone and said: 'Whatever he's paying you, I'll double it, I'll triple it, I'll fourple it'. I still can't use the word quadruple without feeling disloyal to my origins.

'Madam Mallalieu is ice-cold, about as ice-cold a surveillance subject as she seems to be every other way. Myself, I think she knows we're watching. Oh, and yuh, the Grim Lady Gooch?'

'I vaguely recall.'

'She says you're talking shit. This Beam thing lasted about two minutes in the States and never got over here.'

'How come?'

'The first few batches were okay, the ones Hilton made up. While he was inside, someone tried to trade in and a few buyers checked out, if you catch my drift.'

'So? Hilton got out; maybe he started over?' It's what Julie had suggested.

'Nah. Wasn't out long enough before he died, Gooch says. He went back to Baltimore when he got out, hung around a few weeks, went home to a place called Oxford, in Maryland, where he came from: small town, little more than a village really, across the Choptank River from Cambridge if that's any help to you. Oldest working ferry in America, according to the guide book. Means sweet FA to me. Drugs overdose.' As I'd been told. 'Could be suicide, could be accidental, nothing to suggest outside assistance.'

Joannie - if she wasn't interested in me, she couldn't enjoy the blessing of a sixties' spelling - brought Wadd's sandwich and beer.

'On the house,' she said.

'Hey,' that was supposed to be my line; it was my house.

'Natalie told me to tell him; she said you'd be too cheap.'

I sighed exasperatedly: where'd you get staff nowadays? how'd you make a profit?

'But you can leave a tip,' she added, addressing Wadd.

'Ta v'y 'uch,' he muttered with difficulty, his teeth stuck in his steak. At least they hadn't used the good meat.

* * *

I attended a memorial service for Margot. I like to think I would have done so regardless of any recent involvement with her but it's probably untrue. I hate death ceremonies worse than almost anything except hospitals.

It wasn't a funeral. For one thing, she was going to be cremated once all issues surrounding her death had finally been disposed of; for another, there were no prayers, just speeches and reminiscences before a gathering in Westminster Hall, the only bit of the original House of Commons to have withstood Hitler's bombs, around which the building had been re-created. It is where Parliament used to be held a few centuries ago. It is where they held the trial of King Charles. Thomas More, too.

Horace had sent me an invitation. It was my house from the wings of which Margot took her final bow. Boller made a speech of course. How could he not? The proceedings were being televised, though only a few seconds would be shown on the evening news and I somehow doubted they'd run it during Parliament Today, even if it would be more interesting than the usual drivel.

One thing he announced was that the by-election was being called at once. Margot, he said, would not have wanted her constituents unrepresented a moment longer than necessary. What he meant was that there had been adverse comment in the press on past efforts to postpone by-elections in order to put off the reduction in his majority. The Leader of the Opposition spoke briefly. The current director of the lobby group she had once led made a speech, as did a representative of her women's group. I kept waiting for Orbach to show up to grab the microphone but it was Horace who spoke last.

'Thank you all for being here. I know it's made a great difference to me, and to Margot's family, to see so many of her friends present to share this time with us. Margot...' He hesitated, as if reconsidering his notes. 'Margot loved life, but she wasn't afraid of death. She loved her independence, too.' He was picking up on something the woman from her group had said. 'But she wasn't afraid of commitment either,' he concluded defiantly. She had been his, not theirs. 'She loved, I think most of all, the feeling she had at the end of the day - usually tired, usually much later than she would have liked to be able to relax - that she had spent a full day, a useful day, a day without waste. Some people have described Margot as a workaholic. It's not how I think of her; her work was her purpose, and it defined her, and she was happy that it should be so.'

He paused, then continued.

'We should all be glad of that. Glad and grateful. There are very few people who can look back and count with such confidence the number of concrete benefits they brought to the community. Benefits is the right word, too,' he laughed lightly to tell us it was a deliberate pun. 'Her lobby career promoted and protected a range of benefits that brought daily sustenance not to hundreds, not to thousands, but to millions of people, for years on end. That was her first cause, and she never abandoned it: in Parliament - dare I say it in present company, regardless of who was in power - no one could seek to attack the welfare state without risking her wrath. She inspired the respect of friend and political foe alike: she had no enemies other than political.'

I stopped listening after a while. I hadn't made a speech like it for Sandy nor would anyone do so for me. At the end, the gathering sang a socialist song from a printed sheet and I made my way out of the Hall without waiting for them to finish.

I sat down in the main lobby. Ted Farlowe, the PM's political assistant, had introduced himself to me and said he wanted a word. He was in his early thirties, with lank, oily hair that could've benefitted from a gallon of Head and Shoulders, wearing a light, cotton suit and casual slip-on shoes, with the personality of an oyster and so fat I needed wide-angled eyeballs to see all of him at once. He led me to the reception in a committee room on the first floor. Within minutes, the air around us was heavy with opinion and argument on every subject under the sun except Margot.

'The trouble with Margot,' Farlowe said conspiratorially: 'Was that she didn't drink enough. This world we live in...' He waved a hand airily - and, I suspected, already a bit tipsily - around us, but it was his world not mine: 'That's how these people unwind, all of them, and if you don't keep up with them then you're out of tune with them for at least three-quarters of the waking day.'

'Horace was teasing her about it at my house. Just before...'

I stopped to remember, and to allow the realisation to sink in. I'm not a scientist. We didn't yet have the autopsy results. But I now knew how the drug worked. Margot had survived her visit to La Mallalieu longer than the others. I made a bet with myself: notwithstanding how little she drank, when the full autopsy report was returned, it would have some rude things to say about her liver.

I didn't say anything to Farlowe. I still didn't have his measure. Without telling me what he had wanted to speak to me about, he had been drawn away during my reverie. I saw Horace, standing alone, holding a glass he wasn't drinking from, everyone too embarrassed to talk to him, like he had a contagious disease. I knew the feeling. I hadn't seen him to talk to since he had clambered into his wife's ambulance. As I approached, I saw that his eyes were glazed over. He wasn't drinking in public, but he was doing a lot of it on his own. We shook hands.

'Thanks for, well, taking care of things that Sunday, Dave.'

I shrugged: I could hardly have done less; though it was warm during the days, it got cold at night and someone might have asked questions if we'd left the body where it fell.

'How're you coping?'

'I cope,' he said gruffly. 'That's all.'

I didn't remind him that I knew. Something I'd found out at the time, it doesn't help hearing others got problems too. One or two people I was vaguely acquainted with had lost partners or someone they'd been particularly close to. I avoided them like the plague. I didn't want to hear about their grief, how they knew what I was going through. Whatever they thought, they didn't know how I felt. My grief was different; it was mine; their love hadn't been ours.

'If you want someone to spend some hours with some evening,' I offered.

'Thanks. How are you doing?'

'I don't know. Getting somewhere maybe. Maybe not. Nothing I can talk about yet.'

He gripped my arm.

'But you will tell me, when you can, when you've got something, you will tell me?'

I unravelled his fingers.

'What would you do, Horace?'

He smiled grimly.

'What do you want me to say? That I'll kill whoever it was?'

'If there'd been a someone for Sandy, I would have,' I said flatly and without hesitation.

'Would you? Would you really? Yes, I suppose you would. I almost forgot: you've done it before; one more wouldn't hurt. Is that it?'

I'm not sure what I would have answered if someone hadn't joined us. I recognised her face from the papers, but couldn't put a name to it. As she drew Horace to one side, he turned once, looking straight at me, as if he was waiting for my answer.

Farlowe was free. I gave him the eye. He came over, a fresh glass in his hand. Unusually, uncharacteristically, I was one of the few people not drinking heavily. I asked:

'What was it you wanted to tell me?'

'I have a message for you.'

'From?'

Despite his fat face, he smiled thinly.

'The message is that the Real IRA has nothing to do with it.'

'Does that mean they know who does?'

He shrugged.

'If they do, they're not telling.'
'Nor anyone else, it looks like,' I muttered.
Nor was he listening anymore: nor anyone else.

CHAPTER SEVEN

Metal plaques inviting the public to 'Toss One In' were attached to wire trash-baskets in the streets. In some parts of London, they would have ripped the plaques off the bins and done so. 'Baltimore: The City That Reads' was printed onto the slats of wooden street seats marked 'Reading Zone', as well as on numerous other signs and notices.

What was I doing there? I was doing what I did best, and that Natalie had reminded me was how I did it: making things happen. I belong to the bull-in-a-china shop school of detection. I was banking on finding people still around who knew Chambers and, hopefully, who had known Julie's class-crew.

Carson came with me. We arrived at Washington National on Sunday afternoon. By arrangement, Luke de Vries was due down the next day. He was using the open file on Helen Thornton as his excuse: accompanied by the absence of a direct order to leave it alone. The case was febrile; even his bosses would not want it to look like they'd let it go. It was time for a pow-wow. Only Wally was missing.

Advance warning that we were going to have difficulty finding accommodation arrived when we couldn't rent a car; everything was pre-booked. While I was still arguing at the third desk, Carson, in a fit of inspiration, bought an Inn Guide at the bookstore, reasoning that if Baltimore had been invaded by conventioneers, as we were informed, it would be the larger, more expensive, chain hotels which would be full first.

We ended up at a place called the Shirley House. It was a friendly, folksy sort of establishment made up of a couple of town-houses joined together, with entrances on two streets at right angles to one another, where we'd be able to enjoy a sherry that evening and communal breakfast the next morning with other guests, but without soft-drink machine, room-service or a liquor licence. They had only the one room available, though when we were shown up to it we found it was more like a suite with its own bathroom and sitting room as well as the bedroom. There was, however, only one bed.

'I guess we aren't going to bump into Julie, anyhow,' Carson said, tickling a thought association I could only tentatively acknowledge. Neither long hair nor lustrous hide of her had been seen since she left my house.

After we checked in, a little spaced but not at all tired, we strolled aimlessly and circuitously towards the Inner Harbour district, beneath the tall, thin Citicorp Building that dominated downtown, past the Clarence Mitchell Junior Courthouse, until we came to the National Aquarium, outside of which we watched the dolphins in the pool and - at Carson's insistence rather than mine - took an unguided tour of the USS Torsk, a WWII submarine so small the crew hardly had room to store their iPods. We followed our noses back to Pratt Street, pausing at the Holocaust Memorial on the Community College Campus, until we found ourselves in Little Italy.

The area was replete with gentrification. Most of the houses were renovated and re-fronted. On the corner of Albermarle and Stiles, we ate ice-cream and drank coffee at a place called Vaccaro's. Carson ordered a dish of biscotti e armaretti, those little almond biscuits you get with coffee in an Italian restaurant instead of After Eight mints or dusty chocolate truffles. The café was less than half-full; I guessed it was time for Last Mass. Carson scoffed greedily until I said, in my best Godfather voice:

'Show some respect for your stomach. You want it should make you an offer you can't refuse in the middle of the night?'

She burped gracelessly.

I watched her affectionately:

'You got as much class as me, kid.'

'Whole lot more. Oh, uh, yeah, and don't call me kid,' she added pointedly; it was something Sandy used to say to me.

'You're the only one can get away with that,' I said.

'You don't show it much anymore.'

I frowned. I was confused.

She didn't explain. There was a sudden tension, not unpleasant, that it took me a little time to identify. I let the surprised expression on my face ask the question for me.

'Why did you bring me with, Dave?' she answered with a question of her own.

'Maybe what you said the other day, feeling left out. Now that Millward's covering Mallalieu, there wasn't anything else for you to do. Maybe there's more to do here than I can handle on my own. Maybe I just wanted company. Maybe I don't know. You going to tell me?'

She sat up straight in her chair and studied me curiously.

'What Ruth said the other day was right. You don't think about what anyone else's feeling, do you, Dave?'

'Why now, Cars?'

'Why not? You don't get to choose the time,' she replied in a spoiled tone.

I shook my head in genuine and profound confusion.

'We're working Tim's disappearance is all.'

She snorted; her snort is the most loaded I've ever heard. I reached across the table to take her hand.

'Let's let it go, okay?'

'Sure. Whatever.'

That evening, we got pissed on Miller Lite and after dinner liquors at a cavern-grill on Pratt Street just around the corner from the hotel. It was only nine thirty when we went back, but two thirty in the morning in London. In the sitting-room, I pulled out a flat half-bottle of Southern Comfort I'd bought at Heathrow for the hell of it and held it up in invitation. She nodded reluctant agreement to take it warm. For one day, we were on holiday. Anything went.

There was only one comfortable armchair, so I straddled an upright.

'I did know about Natalie, you know,' she said, opening her agenda.

'I assumed so.'

'I didn't mind,' she added defiantly. 'Or about Julie.'

I waited patiently. If I had trouble handling women generally, and Sandy especially, I never even tried with Carson. Nor, so far as I knew, did anyone else. That was where Carson was at: she handled herself. She said:

'You don't know everything about me.'

'I never claimed to.'

'No? But you've acted like it.'

She was saying I took her for granted, and I did.

'I want things too.'

'If I knew what, it'd be easier.'

'Who said it was supposed to be easy? Who said I know what I want myself?'

She reached inside her blouse to scratch an itch on her shoulder. It was oddly erotic. I was glad the way I was sitting concealed the effect it had on me. It might have hidden the sight but it didn't hide the thought. She said:

'No.'

Despite myself, macho pride asserted itself.

'I didn't ask.'

She smiled sweetly.

'No?'

I laughed out loud. I don't know why I ever try lying to her. I said:

'For what it's worth, I agree.'

'Why?' She asked unexpectedly.

'Why what? Why do I agree?'

'Yes, that.'

'I don't know. You tell me.'

She got up and stumbled towards the bathroom.

'Because it's not worth wasting time working it out,' she cut me down as she shut the door behind her.

'Gee, thanks, kid,' I said, too quietly for her to hear.

She wore a t-shirt to bed, which made it worse because I could see her nipples through the thin material which was more tantalising than if she'd been naked. I kept on my jockeys, which didn't conceal anything. I thought that was going to be it, but when I rolled away from her to go to sleep, she pulled me around to face her. She was lying on her back. Without hesitation, invitation or permission, she reached inside my underpants with one hand and with the other took my own hand and placed it firmly between her legs.

'That. That's what I want.'

Feeling embarrassed, it was what I wanted too.

* * *

Luke de Vries arrived in the morning as scheduled, and met us - also by arrangement - at ten thirty in a Burger King just off 33rd Street, between Memorial Stadium and the main Johns Hopkins University campus. He was accompanied by a chubby uniformed woman he introduced as Baltimore Police Sergeant Carmen Lovell. She said she was pleased to meet us like she meant it. I was still a bit spaced, no longer from the journey but from the booze and the psych-battering of the night before. Luke explained.

'Carmen suggested meeting you. Figured it would be easier if you had any problems.'

I translated this as she wanted to inspect us and decide for herself just how much damage we were likely to do before she ran us out of the state. De Vries' own contact with her was for the same reason as when Tim had called him up to announce his presence in Newport: professional police ethics.

'I wanna see I got this right. You're working a Newport murder you think dates back to time at J.H.?' she pointed at de Vries. 'That right? And you're working a policeman got kidnapped in England you think dates back to time at J.H., that right?' she pointed at us.

We all nodded soberly, as if it wasn't as crazy as she'd made it sound. She shook her head.

'You got a whole lot more going on than you're telling me about. That right?'

We nodded again.

'You think people gonna talk to you?'

This time only I nodded, adding:

'They usually do. People get curious about a PI; they want to say they met one, they want to know what we do, how we do it; the only way is to find out is to appear willing to answer; after that, it's downhill, they're on the hook.'

She crossed her arms beneath her ample Latin breasts, over her ample stomach, resting her left elbow on the forward-pointing handle of her ample service revolver. I'd never seen it before in real life, only in westerns: a cross-body draw.

'I'm thinking maybe I oughta tag along for a while?'

Luke flashed me a look that said not to argue. Carmen grinned.

"Sides, it's easier to park.'

It was not only easier to park, but to open doors. By lunchtime, we were reading screens: staff and students. After a while, we bored Lovell away, agreeing to catch up with her again and report at the end of her shift, and - a bundle of print-outs in de Vries' greedy grasp - made our way to the campus cafeteria to eat and talk.

'This is what we've got,' he waved the print-outs. 'There's a bunch of middle class kids who are studying here: Segal, Somers, Hughes, Zeller, Thornton. Hilton's the odd one out. He's black, he's poor, but he's way the smartest of the set. They come together as a group here: the only prior link's between Segal and Hughes, they're both out of Chicago but there's no identifiable connection - could be just coincidence; I don't figure it for much difference. They've got majors and classes that overlap: pre-med, biology, marine biology, toxicology, chemistry. Scientific stuff. They take classes and seminars with - among others - Oswald Chambers. Hilton - as you might expect - is Chambers' favourite son; lot in common, background-wise.'

He shuffled the print-outs, then extracted a notebook from his briefcase, flicking the pages until he found what he was looking for.

'Here's an interesting tit-bit I got from the officer on Hilton's bust in a call the other day. Didn't count for anything at the time, but Chambers was scheduled as a witness for Hilton but didn't show for the trial.'

'Witness to what?'

'Hilton tried to claim he was doing legitimate research.'

'Was he still at Gant's Gully?'

'Not by then. He quit almost a year before.'

'How did the defence run?'

'Said he was free-lancing, following his own ideas,' de Vries grinned. 'Which was true: just not what he meant by it.' He sipped his milk from its red and white carton through a straw.

'But Chambers was originally going to give evidence?'

'Hilton's lawyer said. Chambers was in England at the time.'

'At University College Hospital?' I remembered him telling me. Suddenly, it clicked: 'Mallalieu. She was there at the time?' The information was in Tim's file: I'd overlooked it. I didn't feel smart.

'Right.' He'd got to the same place.

'How did they link?'

'Heart drugs, Chambers; heart stress, Mallalieu. Yeah?'

'Yeah,' I groaned at my stupidity. Julie would have known her name: one more lie by omission. 'Go on about Hilton.'

'Way I see it, Chambers and Hilton were close; father-son, teacher-student. Hilton went bad and Chambers kissed him off. Hilton figured the old man would still come help in his time of tribulation and, uh, trial, for old acquaintance and all that. Chambers gave him the finger.'

'How do the others fit in?'

'They don't - not obviously, anyhow. But there is an additional connection. Julie Somers' brother.'

'She has a brother?'

'At the time Hilton was busted, Neil Somers was his roomie.'

'Where were they living?'

'Cambridge.'

My ears pricked up.

'That's across from where he came from, right? Oxford? Across the River uh...' I couldn't remember the name of it. 'Across the river, anyway.' I'd looked it up on the state road map we'd bought.

'Choptank,' de Vries laughed at my efforts to show off. 'Wrong Cambridge. Not Cambridge, Maryland, but Cambridge, Mass. Neil was enrolled at MIT.'

'Doing what?'

'Computer science.'

'Which tells us what?'

'Nothing. Except maybe this: before Hilton went home to die, he was living back with the brother for a while.'

'Where?'

'Here. Neil Somers was employed by the hospital - here - at that time. On computers. Medical record programmes. One other thing: he and Pat Hughes had a side line - clowning, amateur and local, but extremely good apparently; probably could've gone pro if they wanted.'

'Great. That's all we need. A clown. Where's he now?'

'That I don't know yet. Not at the hospital, anyway.'

'Is Chambers all we got so far as Mallalieu is concerned?'

'No. There's Helen Thornton,' de Vries said promptly. 'She went to London the summer Chambers was there, partly vacation, partly to work with Chambers at the Hospital. She was still here at the time.' Meaning J.H. 'She stayed with Mallalieu.'

I cocked my head to one side in acknowledgment at his discovery of the connection.

'Did you know she was gay?'

'Mallalieu?'

'Yup.'

It was interesting for one reason only: if it was known that Mallalieu was gay, in those days it might well have stopped her getting her Parliamentary position. It was, after all, a massively sensitive post, well open to abuse and - in turn - its holder to blackmail. At any rate, that was - until forced to change direction mid-stride - the way the security services, which would have vetted her for the job, had always treated homosexuality, male and female.

'How'd you get that?'

'Pat Hughes told me,' he said apologetically. 'I went back to see her.'

'Back?' I was being dumb. 'Right: from when you were looking into Thornton's death?'

'Yes. She said that Thornton had spent some time in London, but I didn't think anything of it at the time. I had no reason to follow it up.' With hindsight, it was tempting to ask why not, but it would not have been fair: the police can't run down every aspect of a murder victim's life as far back as it goes. 'I only remembered it a couple of days ago. I saw her yesterday - no, Saturday - and asked if she knew where Thornton had stayed.'

'Was Chambers' family with him?' Carson asked.

'Yes. But I don't think he'd have let Thornton stay with him anyway. Oswald's two-by-four,' he said. 'Stand up guy, straight arrow.'

'You're convinced of that, aren't you?'

'Yup. Everything I see says maybe they connected through him, or collected around him, but there's nothing puts him in the frame.'

I was confused about Julie. I had trusted her. When she had walked out, I did not automatically assume the worst. Now, too much was coming to the surface for me to ignore: Chambers-Mallalieu; Mallalieu-Thornton; Julie-Neil; Neil-Hilton. She could prove the most expensive of my sexual encounters Tim Dowell had ever paid for. Carson was not enjoying similar thoughts, but had the grace not to rub salt into the wound: she, too, had taken to Julie. Luke leaned back in his seat and waited for us to re-join him.

'Tell us about Segal and Hughes. They're still at Gant's Gully?'

'Yup. Segal's married to a navy officer. She only works part-time now, had a kid last year. They live in the old part of town.' Newport: the old part was that which lay between where Dannie and Lucy lived up by the Redwood Library and the East shore where the harbour, the expensive shops and the Treadway Inn I'd stayed in were. Wooden houses, no two of them alike or even painted the same colour, a hundred, two hundred years old and a few of them even older. It was, I had a vague memory, what we would call in England a Conservation Area.

'Segal's a Jewish name. You got Jewish navy officers?'

'Not that I know of. His name's Maxwell. Sound Jewish to you?'

'What else you got on her?'

'Rich, very rich. Family money. Did a lot of travelling when she was young. Got into a scrape in Europe. I suppose you might say literally.'

'Meaning?'

'Her father had a lot of influence. The Irish may have title over Chicago politics, but they're mortgaged at Jewish banks. Well, I don't know how true that is anymore, but it used to be that way. When she was younger, she found herself pregnant in Dublin. Instead of doing the sensible thing - flying to England or somewhere else with legal abortion - she had a back-street job that got a bit botched, though from the fact she had a kid last year not too badly. Anyway, the Consulate got involved and straightened it out at her old man's request.'

'Why didn't she go somewhere else? Can't have been difficult; can't have taken any time, either.'

Luke shook his head. Whatever files he'd scoured for what he'd given us didn't delve any deeper. It was beyond me too.

Not Carson:

'She wanted the father with her,' she said flatly, firmly, bitterly.

'So?'

'So he wouldn't go with her to England, or maybe anywhere - or couldn't.'

I exchanged a glance with de Vries. He said:

'So that's what she's for.'

I didn't bother with a smart-ass answer. I would have said I was proud of her but only if she first promised not to knock me down for patronising her.

'What else?'

'On her?'

'Sure.

He shook his head to say it was all he'd found.

'What about Hughes?'

'Ah, well, she's a real Madam Mystery. Patricia Olwyn Hughes. You'll never guess her ethnicity.'

'What's the mystery, or was that it?'

'Lot of missing pieces, missing time. Bit like your Mallalieu: no private life to pin down.'

Carson delivered another of her meaningful snorts.

'You think, if a woman doesn't have a lover there must something wrong with her. What does that make me?' she added.

'Don't tempt me,' I muttered as de Vries chuckled.

'For another thing, she's very loaded.'

'I thought you said they all were.'

'They weren't poor, but that's not the same thing. She has a coast-house outside Newport, must be worth two-three million clear. Yeah, her parents are well off and that's what she said when I asked her, but I've made a couple calls to Chi and I'm sceptical that's where it comes from. The father's a lawyer with a bank. Okay, he doesn't take home a patrolman's pay, but there's five children, he's still alive, he doesn't have assets in that league.'

'Grandparents, something like that?'

'Hell, no. The paternal grandparents had nothing; on the mother's side, her grandfather was a New York cop; Catholic family.'

'Maybe grandpapa was on the pad?'

'Yeah, sure, all cops are. The only honest cops are private, right?'

'Do you know any more about Thornton?'

He shook his head.

'That's what I'm doing this afternoon. I've got a session booked with her student counsellor. What about you guys?'

'There's a handful of people worked with Chambers. We'll split them between us, see what we come up with.'

We arranged to meet at four, back at the cafeteria, leaving us a couple more hours before we were scheduled at the station with Carmen Lovell.

* * *

'You were wrong about one thing,' I said cheerfully when Carson arrived. 'You want a coffee?'

'Sure. I'll get it.' She, too, was unusually good-natured. 'Another?'

Once she returned, she asked:

'What was I wrong about?'

'Not bumping into Julie Somers.'

'You saw her?'

'Nope. But she was here.'

'When?'

'Friday.'

'Why?'

'According to Professor Christiansen, to say hi and did he happen to know where her brother was.'

'Hm.'

'What's the matter? You don't believe it?'

'What doesn't she believe?' Luke asked, lowering himself onto the bench beside me.

I told him.

'She also dropped in to say hallo to Marianne Cohen - the counsellor I told you about.'

'It's a conspiracy,' Carson contributed. 'Say hi to everyone; kill 'em with courtesy.'

Luke frowned.

'Ms Cohen said she seemed depressed. She wouldn't admit it; claimed she was just visiting, looking for her brother, but she said that was her style, bottle it up. She was the least open of the group: the one that kept most to herself.'

'What else?' Carson asked.

He flipped open the ubiquitous notebook.

'Thornton was another odd one out. Cohen counselled all the women in the group. That was pretty standard then: women for women. Hughes, Segal, Somers - very ambitious, intense was one word she used, maybe angry but she never knew what at; a sort of universal anger - not uncommon in students. Segal was a bit older: that works with time off to travel in Europe. Thornton was different. A real sweetie, Cohen's description. She hung out with the others, followed them, but didn't fit in, though she thought she had a relationship with Hilton for a while, and then couldn't let go of it when it was over.'

'Did Hilton have scenes with any of the others?'

'Possibly Segal. Segal was the most promiscuous. Hughes and Zeller were the closest, but she didn't know if they were an item. They weren't a wild group sexually. Cohen said: too focused for that.'

'Focus on what?'

'She thought politics.'

'That's a direct contradiction from what Julie told me.'

'So?' Carson asked snidely, misunderstanding the reason I shook my head as I said:

'So it's probably true. Ties in, too, doesn't it, Luke?' With Ireland, an Irishman who couldn't or wouldn't travel to

England and another one who had more recently tried to do so and didn't make it.

'I think so,' he confirmed quietly. 'What did you guys get?'

I told him about my talk with Professor Christiansen. He was originally Chambers' teacher, later his colleague. He had been reluctant to talk about him behind his back, but I had been able to use de Vries' name. He said it was nothing new for Chambers' students to form a clique around him. The man had charisma, charm and talent. He called him a good scientist but a great teacher, a genius at inspiration. He said that if he took yearbooks for those periods when Chambers had taught at the University, he could probably place several groups around the country who had stayed in touch with one another, many of whom could have found themselves working together, or set out to do so.

He was emphatic that Chambers had no political edge. He was not bitter about the death of his brother. As a successful black man, he had sought to encourage others. If there was any bitterness in the man, it was focused on Hilton, the only one of his sometime protégés to have turned sour. He was not in the least surprised that this particular group of students should have gone to work with Chambers at Gant's Gully: they had been at the college during the crucial period of Chambers' own evolution as a marine toxicologist and they would have participated in his research. He had only known them personally at a distance:

'Except for Zeke Zeller. I knew him a bit better.'

'Breadhead?' Julie had said so but it might yet be true.

He smiled.

'I haven't heard that expression for a few years. But, yes, sure. That's how I knew him. Even then, he was into making money. He put together a consortium to buy up a couple of inner city housing tracts; Oswald put in some money; so did I.'

'And?'

'And we all did very well out of it. The boy had a sixth sense for money, the Midas touch. Both tracts were brought into urban redevelopment programmes within a year; we doubled our money on one of them.'

'The other?'

'Hell, the consortium wanted to sell. We were just academics out for a quick buck or two to help pay for a new car, put a kid through college, a porch on the back of the house, a vacation in Europe. He held out, persuaded us to hang on. And he was right, of course. Have you been down to the Inner Harbour district?'

'Sure.'

'Don't know if you noticed. There's a big block of condos, stacked, layered, I don't know what you'd call it.' I nodded. I remembered. I had been impressed: I could imagine living in one. He concluded: 'We found ourselves owning half the land. I'm not even going to tell you how much we made.'

I remembered Julie talking about Chambers' poverty.

'Must have made a big difference to some of you?'

'Oswald, you mean? Hell, yes. When I first knew Oswald, I used to fix our seminars just before lunch and then insist he eat with me. I don't think he ate otherwise. You know about the family he had to support?'

'What about the students Zeller was close to? Did they share in his good fortune... Skill?'

'I don't think so. I think it probably put something of a distance between them. The impression I got, though, he was always a little apart from them, apart and ahead. He was the leader: leaders always have a slightly strange relationship with their...well, followers,' he concluded lamely.

'And that was about it for Prof. Christiansen,' I wrapped it up for Luke and Carson. I had made a couple of other calls, but without any information worth relaying. 'Carson?'

'Oh, well,' she batted her eyelashes: 'I can't compete with you big boys. Me, I only got the story about a doctor from London who had such a bad crush on one of the students here who she'd met during the vacation she came over to see her and ended up in the hospital with an overdose and a bill she wasn't insured for. It's a great background for someone responsible for the health - including stress-related health - of every Member of Parliament, wouldn't you say? Something she'd really want to put on her CV, you know?'

* * *

Carson was still filling us in on her source - a laboratory technician who used to work for Chambers and who freely admitted she wouldn't have minded taking Helen Thornton's place in Annette Mallalieu's arms - when we were interrupted by Carmen Lovell.

'Hi.'

Luke glanced at his watch. We weren't late for meeting her. She was early. She sat down, expelling breath with a whoosh. We didn't need telling she had some news for us. Her face said it. All we needed telling was what it was:

'One of those names you were looking at - Somers, Julie Somers?'

'Right,' de Vries said. We let him do the talking, cop to cop.

'Found in the Holiday Inn this pm.'

We also did not need telling what she meant. My immediate, irreverent question, which I did not voice, was how had she managed to get a room. Luke asked:

'Homicide?'

'Suicide.' Seemed like Marianne Cohen was correct when she assessed her as depressed. 'Here,' she handed de Vries a sheet of paper. 'It's just a copy. You want to translate it for me?'

Carson reached across the table and picked it up, skimming it once before she read it aloud.

'This is where it all began so it might as well end here. I was a student here. I'm enclosing my i.d. and the telephone number of my parents. It sounds trite, but I want to say that I love them and I'm sorry for the hurt this will cause. If there was any other way to unravel it all without hurting them even more, I'd take it I know. I loved my brother, too, for too long; he's a clown in more ways than one. There have been a lot of people hurt. Too many. It wasn't funny, Neil. I should have stopped it sooner. That's why it's my fault.'

Carson looked up and said softly.

'Words look a little blurry here?'

'Yup,' Lovell said. 'She was crying. Drinking, too. Heavily.'

'That figures,' I contributed obliquely.

Carson continued to read slowly.

'I haven't got much longer. At best, a few minutes more. The police should also contact a police detective in Newport, RI, called de Vries. He'll want to know about this. I know who killed Helen Thornton and why. Steve Hilton's death was murder too, but this isn't. I know this isn't making much sense, but it's as far as I'm prepared to go. De Vries is in touch with a man in London called Dave Woolf. I just came back from there. Tell him I don't know where his friend is. If I knew, I'd say. Tell him too I'm sorry I walked out on him. Tell him we weren't a lie; he'll know what I mean; I wish it had been a different place and a different time; I wish I could do it all over. The main thing to tell him is that I wasn't honest about what tests to run during the autopsy but I'm making up for it now.'

Carson had read ahead and finished off to the accompaniment of her own gentle tears.

'It's coming. I felt it. It's coming. I'm glad. It's coming. I couldn't stand it when I saw Margot McAllister die. That's when I knew what I had to do; it's just taken me a bit longer than I thought it would. It's....'

After a lengthy silence, Carmen Lovell asked:

'You want to start telling me about it here, or down at the station?'

* * *

Washington National serves both Washington DC - in addition to Dulles International - and Baltimore.

Luke dropped us off before he drove into the capital. He had an appointment at the FBI. It was time to find out what their interest in Thornton had been. Besides which, the interstate threads made it federal. Too many people were involved to continue to contain it on our own. Carmen Lovell had insufficient interest to risk jeopardising her career by keeping anything quiet; her superiors none at all. I figured de Vries was relieved he was being forced into the open. For the time being, it was agreed not to tell them about England's legislative losers other than McAllister. If her own autopsy lived up to Julie's advertisement for it, however, the rules of the game would necessarily change. Margot would have to be re-autopsied: for the first time, we would have direct evidence to connect Mallalieu.

Carson and I were taking the shuttle up to New York to try and see Zeller. We'd go home from there: de Vries could cover Newport - and an interesting re-interview with Segal – and, so far as it proved relevant, Cambridge, Massachusetts. We drove in sombre silence, each of us with a different set of confusions. If we'd come to Baltimore to make things happen, they'd happened; more than we had sought, expected, intended or, in one respect anyway, wanted.

We were at the police station until nearly nine o'clock, after detouring past the hospital, where I was asked to confirm that Julie was who her note claimed. It was a less gruesome experience than I expected: I watched on a screen as an attendant pulled the sheet back from her face and, as soon as I pressed the buzzer, replaced it. It was her, but there was something different. I had to ask them to heighten the colour contrast to spot it: just as I had commented on Margot's hair being darker the day she died, so too was Julie's.

There was an APB out on Neil Somers. The police had found his house, but not him. He'd fled in a hurry, leaving behind clothes and personal belongings, but no identification or passport. A neighbour confirmed a visitor over the weekend who fit Julie's description. Whatever had passed between them would unlock the mystery, but until he was found her suicide note asked more questions than it answered.

Julie's name had not been released to the press and would not be for the time being. Part of our job - Luke's and mine - was to stretch that time being. Luke made about fifty phone calls securing support for this tactic, and put one through to Wally Wadd so I could bring him up to speed and find out what was happening in the UK.

'Got the autopsy results on McAllister...'

'Yeah, I know, nothing in it. Put a hold on the body. We'll have more in a couple days here. It'll have to be done over.'

'Mallalieu took a trip over the weekend. Paris.'

'Great: as soon as the bugs were in. And?'

'And by the time the formalities were complete to pin a French tail on her, she'd gone to ground. Rented a car is all I can tell you.'

'Is she back yet?'

'Nope.'

'What about Tim? Nothing?'

'Not quite nothing. You got a call on your answering machine. Too short to trace.'

'What're you doing, Wally? Did you break in?' Tim used to do that before he had a key, break in whenever it suited.

'No. Jada called.' Jada had a key, as I had to her house. We shared a window cleaner, and took turns to let him in to each other's place. Also, it gave each of us an option if we got locked out. 'Smart girl,' he added.

'Why?'

'She took the tape out after she listened to it, to prevent it being recorded over.'

'Okay.'

'Said it was the last warning. Said they didn't want to kill Tim. Said they didn't need to unless you made them. Said it wouldn't be long now. Said not to get any closer.'

'When was this?'

'Jada isn't sure. She picked it up Sunday night. You got a number for a woman called Jane, wanted to know if you'd go sailing with her next weekend?'

'Why? You wanna sail?'

'No. Her message was the one after. I want to know when she rang.'

I gave him the number, adding:

'Tell her no way. She nearly killed me last time,' I said.

We didn't waste the Baltimore PD's money saying good-bye.

'The autopsy, Dave?' Carmen Lovell reminded me where we'd left off.

'Right. She killed herself with the same stuff that's been killing the others. What she's saying is, if we look close enough we'll get the answer.'

'Where'd she get it from?'

'That's the whole question, isn't it? If she had it all along...' I didn't finish the sentence: the implication would put her in the middle of the frame. 'Or else she got it from the brother.' I still wasn't sure what that spelled.

'We're looking, we're looking,' Carmen said, irritated and frustrated.

'Shit,' Carson contributed. 'It's a hell of a way to pass on a message.'

'Most suicides are just that,' Carmen said morosely. 'Messages to people left behind. How do we get it, if we don't know what to look for?'

'Chambers, I'd say. If we've got to gamble on anyone, he's it.' I exchanged a glance with de Vries, who nodded agreement.

'I'll call him, get him down tomorrow. You'll meet him?' Lovell copied.

'Give him a couple of pointers,' I said. 'One, it's triggered by alcohol and I'd say destroyed by it to leave no obvious traces in the body itself; instead, look at the hair, analyse it, that's where he'll get the answer.'

They all gawped. Carson snarled:

'Since when did you know anything about bodies? Anything else, I mean,' she added quickly.

'Remember all those books you made me read?' I smiled sweetly.

De Vries said:

'We're going to have to do something about this Hilton guy. Unless he was cremated.'

'I'd leave that until you've finished up with Julie,' I suggested, trying not to stumble on her name and the image of her tiny body on a slab at the morgue being cut into small slices. I didn't envy Chambers: she was his friend too. 'It's getting easier, though. There's only Segal, Hughes and Zeller left.'

'Of the original group. You're forgetting Mallalieu, Neil Somers, the connection between them and what it's all about.'

The way we'd pieced it together earlier ran a political cell comprised of or within the Johns Hopkins set, Irish-connected, using their scientific skill to achieve an end way beyond bombs.

'Fine: two each. You get Segal and Hughes; we'll take Zeller, and then go home for Mallalieu.'

'While I go for Neil,' Carmen chipped in. 'For the time being.'

But not that night.

Luke dithered between eating with us or with his new cop colleague. Carson decided for him.

'I want to talk to Dave.'

There was a personal side to Carmen Lovell's news for which there had not yet been any time. Julie was less than a week out of my bed and still wedged in my mind. We ate at the Washington Grill, the same place as the night before. We were not interested in experimenting with food. I wasn't interested in food at all.

We steered clear of her until we'd put a few beers away. Carson picked the moment and the way into it.

'You don't have to put the two together. I don't think you should. I think that would be unfair to Sandy.'

I nodded.

'Yeah, that far I got for myself. In my head.'

'Not in your heart, huh?'

'Stomach, I think. Hey, you had the right idea last night: anything more and you'd probably be freezer meat.'

'Cheers, chuck,' she held up her glass. 'Here's to cold cuts. It wasn't your fault, Dave. Neither was.'

At the hospital, I'd told Tim:

'It's my fault, Tim. You know?'

'I know. I got it on the wire hours ago. As an accident of course. One thing's got nothing to do with another, Dave. There's no connection.'

'Wrong, Tim. I'll tell you how it is. I've been playing God, playing with death; this is his message back telling me who's really in control. Get it?'

'She's not dead, Dave. Don't give up hope.'

But hope was merely a way of bridging the time between love and death.

'This is different,' Carson said as if she had been listening. 'If anyone was trying to play God, she was. Why'd she get next to you?'

'I doubt it was for my sex appeal. I don't know. I still can't accept she was involved. I mean...' Carson waved away the explanation. That Julie was 'involved' in one sense was beyond argument; I meant I couldn't accept she was criminally involved. 'She was a strange woman. I knew something was troubling her all along. I should have pushed it harder.' I hadn't because I hadn't wanted to alienate her - for the most selfish reasons.

'Forget it, Dave. You're torturing yourself. You're running out of guilt about Sandy, so you want someone else to feel guilty about.'

I met her eyes. Her words were harsh but her eyes were tender. She was challenging me to cry for Julie. I wanted to. It doesn't matter how short love is; the only question is how deep. If you get to a certain depth - however quickly, however short the time you hold your breath down there for - it's with you forever.

'You liked her too, Cars. So did Nat... So did Sheila... So did Wally...'

'Don't make it more than it was, Dave. She was a body in the right space, that's all. Like you were last night.' For her. 'Like I'll be tonight,' she offered, as if inviting me to share some of her French fries.

'Is that all there is, Cars? Bodies, time and space?'

'What do you think, Dave?'

'I want more,' I said fiercely. 'I did that one, for years on end, more years than I want to remember. Sandy wasn't a body, damnit, Carson.'

'Well,' she softened. 'Maybe it's what you make of the body that counts then.'

I thought about it. There were a dozen conversations going on at once. I repeated:

'I don't want any more bodies. Where does that leave us?'

She looked down at her food, pushing it around her plate like it disgusted her. When she looked up, her eyes were swimming.

'You'll have to be gentle, then, Dave. Can you do that?'

Like I said, when we drove to the airport, we all had our confusions.

CHAPTER EIGHT

We had not called ahead to make sure of Zeke Zeller; it might have spoiled the fun. Instead, he spoiled ours. He was out of town and his secretary did not know when he would be back; nor, so she said, did she have any idea where he might be contacted. We had to kill a day in New York before we could catch the overnight back to Heathrow, to arrive as last time - with the additional hours on the clock - first thing in the morning: it would be Wednesday when we got home. After ringing Wally to tell him when we'd get in, and learning that Mallalieu had not yet re-emerged, we used the opportunity to do some sightseeing and shopping. Though most everything was as available in England as in the States, I still liked buying stuff in America.

The only seats available were club class. For the extra cost, we ought to be getting a share of the airline. Still, it gave us access to the business lounge, from which I made another call to England, this time to Ted Farlowe, to forewarn him I'd need to see his boss ASAP. It had occurred to me during the day that Boller might be a little busier than my average client or contact. I was wrong. Before I got a word in edgewise, Farlowe was breathing fire at me.

'Where have you been?'

'America. Why?'

'I've been trying to reach you. He wants to see you. Where are you calling from?'

'America,' I repeated, adding what time we'd be back.

I'd never travelled anything but cattle class before. Though not enough to justify the price, the difference told. We got a pair of spacious seats on our own.

I still wasn't sure what we were doing: it was like we were playing at lovers. When all the lights were off, and the movie had finished flickering, we curled up facing one another, each of us with one knee tucked between the other's legs, whispering, occasionally kissing without pressure or particular passion but with curiosity and contentment.

Wally didn't meet us at the airport. Just about everybody else did. Millward was present in person; so also Gregory; they glowered at each other across the customs hall which their police passes had permitted them to penetrate, to save them waiting with the hoi-polloi at the crowded barrier. That was where we spotted Farlowe as the four of us emerged: Gregory on my side, Millward making sure Carson didn't do a runner either. I thrust out my hand at Farlowe.

'Ted, nice to see you,' as if he was an old friend.

Farlowe took in my companions with a raised eyebrow. I introduced them by rank. He might have been a political assistant but he was not totally devoid of wit. He extracted his

House of Commons identity pass and, enjoying the moment of power, trumped them.

'The Prime Minister would like to see Mr Woolf. Right away.'

Their internecine hostility dissolved in the face of this open attack by the common enemy. Neither of them spoke at once. Eventually, Millward released my elbow and sighed.

'It would be most helpful to the police if you would call on me later in the day, sir,' he said to me sarcastically. 'At your convenience, of course. Sir,' he repeated to make sure I got the point that he had no respect at all either for me or for my new minder's employer.

Before we parted, I asked them:

'Want to tell me why you're here, gents?'

They could hardly refuse to answer, which was not necessarily the same as telling the truth. Millward said:

'I have a Detective Chief Inspector missing, sir, in case you've forgotten.'

'Did you hear about Mr Cunningham, Mr Woolf?' Gregory contributed, as if he hadn't arranged for me to be told.

'How did they know the flight?' Farlowe asked as he led the way to his car.

'Could be Dowell's side-kick; all the info he's been piling up is getting a bit heavy for a DS to turn a blind eye to.'

Carson shook her head.

'I doubt it. Didn't you say they had you down for Belfast? And got Julie's name off a flight list easily enough?'

'Maybe, but it doesn't say how they knew where I was.'

'Caught you on the way out,' she concluded convincingly. 'Then kept computer-watch for a return booking.'

I hate it when she's ahead of me.

'Julie? That's Julie Somers, the woman who went to the McAllister autopsy. You know the autopsy's produced nothing?'

'But the next one will,' I promised, with more conviction than I could be certain of.

'What next one?' He stood by his car, keys to hand, without unlocking the door, shocked. I gestured to him to let us in; we were tired, we wanted to sit, we wanted to get moving. After he'd done so, he repeated, marginally more in control of himself: 'What next one?'

'Hers,' I said tightly. 'Somers'. It should have been carried out yesterday; we should have some results before the end of the week.'

'She's dead?'

Like I said, not totally devoid of wit.

He only just managed to stop the car before he would have smashed through the automatic barrier without paying.

* * *

We did not talk any more about the case on the way in. When I asked Farlowe why Boller wanted to see me in such a hurry, and why he had suddenly been prepared to reveal the connection between us in spite of his previous promises of denial, he avoided answering. As we drove into the Cromwell Road, Carson, without warning or explanation, asked if Ted would mind dropping her at the club on the Old Brompton Road instead of taking her on with me to Downing Street: it was hardly a detour at all. To my surprise, I minded. I didn't want to go on home after, alone to an empty house. I said nothing, but turned to look at her enquiringly. Her face was expressionless.

* * *

Boller looked tired as he hovered over me, thrusting a scaly paw across the solid oak desk, his chin pointing at the top of my head.

We had been admitted by a policeman and were ushered inside by a uniformed flunky who reached for my battered, suede hat with distaste and ignored my leather jacket, t-shirt and jeans. I - not Farlowe - was searched for weaponry and wire by a besuited detective from Special Branch. Finally, I was asked to wait a pro-forma ten minutes in the panelled lobby lined with old masters on loan from the National Gallery by a surprisingly amiable secretary in her mid-forties while Farlowe went to wash his hands or see his boss.

I ought to have felt overwhelmed by this, my first visit to Number Ten, but didn't. It was no grand or large building; the policeman on the door was not armed; there was only one Special Branch man; the secretary could have been anybody's. There was no pomp or ceremony; it was all on such a small scale.

Boller came straight to business.

'There's been a development, Mr Woolf.'

There'd been many, but I suspected that none of mine were the ones he had in his mind.

'I've come to the conclusion that I can no longer keep quiet about this matter.'

I did a double-take.

'That's a bit of a volte face; last time, you could kill to keep it quiet.' Not the best metaphor, but he got my meaning.

'Perhaps I've come to the conclusion that the lives of my friends and colleagues are too important to risk any further.'

I pulled a face. He couldn't possibly mean it.

He smiled bleakly.

'Ah, yes, your scepticism about politicians. I don't actually have to explain myself to you, Mr Woolf, do I?' Before I could answer, he continued: 'It doesn't matter. I shall tell you anyway. I would not like you to get any impression that might alter your opinions. Last night, one of my colleagues came to see me. He had been warned to postpone his appointment with Doctor Mallalieu, but wanted to explain that he had intended not to bother anyway. Had other things to do, in the time he has left.' I caught his drift.

'How long?'

'Three to six months. And, yes, he has a losable seat, which is why he had been specifically warned. So, you see, Mr Woolf, it looks as if they are going to have their way after all.'

'I see.' I saw: the only way to avoid it would be a massive sympathy vote, which in turn required him to release the true story. It would have been a gamble if he still had a choice. Without a choice, it was a shot at staying in power; not a good shot, just a shot. 'What about Tim Dowell?'

'How does it hurt him?'

'Once they know we're onto the truth, they'll also know we're getting close to him.' I explained about the phone message Wadd had picked up with Jada's assistance.

'They cannot have believed that the police were not close in any event.'

'Men like Millward do a fair imitation.'

'I'm sorry. It cannot affect my decision.' Pretty much what Millward had said. 'Naturally, I would far rather have some proof; naturally, I shall still be trying to get it.' Naturally.

'You know what makes me so bloody angry, Boller?'

He was taken aback, though I was unclear whether by the curse or the use of his last name.

'What?'

'The fact that I've got you the proof you want.'

The penny finally dropped for Farlowe.

'Of course, the autopsy on Julie... uh... Julie Somers.'

'What did you find in America, Mr Woolf?' Boller asked excitedly.

I thought about telling him to piss off but he was, after all, my client, so I summarised rapid-fire.

'About as much confirmation as one could expect without catching them red-handed of a plot based on a group of people who studied together in Baltimore and later worked at Gant's Gully in Newport, Rhode Island. That there is a killing drug, the make-up of which we will probably know by the end of the week, which is likely to enable us to point the finger at Doctor Mallalieu. That Doctor Mallalieu is missing, and so is a man called Neil Somers who is evidently central to it all, and whose sister Julie's body is providing the evidence of the drug to make up for her failure to do so using Margot's. What we don't know yet is why: there are distinct Irish threads, including an informant killed on his way to see me, but it's still short of a full explanation.'

I continued:

'If Mallalieu turns up again, and the evidence is in from the States, the police are going to have to act. It's far too compelling, and they'd have to explain themselves to our transatlantic cousins, who'll want her for themselves - at least to talk to her.'

The Prime Minister rubbed his hands together in glee. I didn't offer to shake either of them as I left.

* * *

Jada had bought in a pint of milk. I made a cup of tea before listening to the messages which had come in after the one about Tim. My sailing friend, Jane, had rung back rudely about someone she referred to as my assistant, who I took to mean Wally. There were two callers who had hung up without leaving a message but after the tone, so that they registered on the message-counter without bringing any joy or light into my life. There were three calls from Ted Farlowe, now overtaken by events. There was a call from a woman with what could have been an Irish accent, but she said only that she would call again, too briefly for me to decide. There was no message from Carson.

I went down for my customary post-Atlantic two hour stint, unbroken by any further calls, relieved that Boller, with unexpected encouragement from Farlowe, had ultimately decided not to take me off the case. Not yet. If I was going to find Tim, I needed all the influence I could muster. I awoke to the sound of someone moving about. It was probably burglars, but I didn't care so long as they left my CD collection. In the end, curiosity got the better of me and, slipping into a dressing-gown just in case Jada or Frankie or both had let themselves in, I went downstairs to find Carson in her bedroom piling into her suitcase the clothes she normally kept at my house.

'What the hell's going on, Cars?' I asked weakly. 'I thought... Oh, hell, I don't know what I thought, but whatever it was doesn't fit this.'

She put down a stack of underwear and crossed to the door.

'Hi,' she said, sliding her arms around my waist and kissing me lightly on the lips. 'Did you have a good snooze?'

I was doubly confused: her tone was caring and her body too. Before I knew it, we were making like it was a month since we'd seen each other, wriggling to get her out of her clothes, falling back across the room without letting go of one another and onto the bed, barely missing the edge of the suitcase, finishing what we'd started during the night on the plane.

We were still lying there, waiting to regain breath so we could talk and Carson could explain why on the one hand she was coming on like a long lost and on the other like an imminent ex- when the phone rang. I took the call stark naked downstairs in the dining-area, where the cordless receiver resides and recharges.

'Is that Mr Woolf?' It was the Irish woman who had said she would ring back.

'Yup.' I tried to conceal my anxiety: for all I knew, she could be one of Tim's captors.

'My name is Siobhan Cunningham,' she said softly, almost like someone frightened to be overheard. 'I'm, I was, Brendan's wife.'

'Oh, God, I was so sorry to hear about him. Where are you ringing from?'

'I'm in England,' she half-whispered.

'What are you doing here?' I was excited: Brendan was no virgin; he knew about taking precautions; I might yet find out what he had been coming to tell me.

'I need to see you,' she answered.

'Of course, sure. When, where?'

'I'm frightened,' she added.

'I understand. Look, tell me where you're calling from, I'll come and get you.'

'You mustn't be followed. There mustn't be any police. I'll meet with you this evening. Eight thirty? Promise me you won't tell anyone.'

'I promise,' I said with my fingers crossed.

'I'll meet you then.'

'Where?'

She hesitated. I suggested:

'There's a pub, the Three Johns, White Lion Street, N1.' It was not far from my house, but not so near anyone keeping a watch on me would be likely to spot us by accident. She wasn't the only one scared: I preferred playing on home turf. 'Could you find it?'

She confirmed she could manage and hung up quickly as if frightened the line might be tapped or traced.

During the call, I had been vaguely aware of Carson coming down to use the bathroom, returning to her bedroom, creaking again on the stairs. As I hung up, I cried out enthusiastically.

'Movement, Cars. That was Brendan's widow.'

I heard the front door bang loudly behind her. By the time I'd grabbed some clothes, she was no longer in sight on the street. She had flown. Just when I needed her most.

* * *

Wally came by to see me, explaining that he had gone to the airport to meet us but had spotted Millward. As caution was the better part of keeping his job, he'd turned right around and come back to London.

Current scuttlebutt spoke of somewhere in West London where arms and a hostage - presumed to be Tim Dowell - would be found. My visit to Belfast, followed by the death en route to see me - as it was accurately premised - of Brendan Cunningham, had convinced the police of the Irish connection, leading to a war of attrition on the fringes of the London republican movement that squeezed out this titbit. On the authority of the Commissioner, mega-man-hours were being thrown into the search. The possible involvement of the Real IRA put Special Branch in charge of the case. Until this morning, the police had been under instructions to keep the press out of it; during the day, the press had arrived on the scene, clearly well-informed. I knew by whom.

Wally said:

'West London's a meaningless phrase that could encompass everything from Kensington and Kilburn out past Heathrow almost to Slough.'

'You got any mates in Dublin?'

'I know a few names. Why?'

'People you trust?'

'Irish?'

'Racist.'

'They're white,' he protested.

'So're Jews.'

'You rest my case.'

'Well?' I gave up waiting for an apology.

'Maybe one or two,' he mumbled. 'What do you want?'

I gave him the Segal abortion and a date. I wanted daddy's name in case de Vries couldn't con or beat it out of her.

'What about Mallalieu? Still no news?'

'They found the car. In Switzerland. Near Lucerne. Her entry is confirmed. No departure. No trace of her. The moment we get the revised autopsy results and they find her, we can claim her.'

'What about the others?'

'FBI says Neil Somers probably got out to Canada Sunday evening, Monday morning. They're running names out of Canada but so far zilch.'

'Zeller?'

'Got back home yesterday evening. Said he'd spent some days up in Newport with Pat Hughes. De Vries says she confirms. They've all been sweated a while, but nobody's giving anything up. Trouble is, they're too middle class to hassle without more to go on. Where does Zeller fit in?'

'Mister money-bags. Tell the FBI to get the IRS to play games with anything Zeller has a stake in. Also Zeller to Hughes as a source of her income.'

'And Segal?'

'I'm guessing she's the prime connection to Ireland.'

'Not Julie Somers?'

'Ask her yourself.'

'I'm sorry about her, Dave.'

'Yup.' I didn't want to talk about it. 'How did my Heathrow reception committee get there? It was Gregory as well as Millward. Do you know about that?'

He shook his head. I also gave him an account of my meeting with the Prime Minister, to explain the sudden interest in freedom of information. He scowled.

'Bastard.'

'Gee, surprise me. You going near the Yard?'

'Can do.'

I took a ride. I didn't tell him about my meeting that evening. I don't think I actively mistrusted him but I was running short on the blind alternative. I thought I'd be able to catch up with Carson in time to provide me with cover and make sure I wasn't followed from my house.

* * *

As it was Millward who'd asked me to come in to see him, I went to see Gregory. This time, he saw me in his own office and offered coffee. He promised there was neither poison nor truth-drug in it so I accepted.

'Why did you come to see me, Mr Woolf?' I took as read he knew I had not yet seen Millward.

'Millward I can figure. He's got a copper missing, he's got the job of finding him; I'm running around like a blue-arsed fly; he's sure I'm onto something and not telling him; Dunlop's given me his seal of approval; he spots me leaving the country; hell, he ought to be there when I get back.'

'That doesn't answer my question.'

'Sure it does. I'm here because I don't know what you're up to. You and Millward didn't look like you'd come to the airport after spending the night together. Why were you scanning passenger lists for me? You'd been told to lay off.' By the Commissioner.

He leaned back in his swivel chair and laced his fingers behind his head.

'I know it's not much about Dowell.'

'How?'

'I have, well, more contacts than the average copper - like Mr Millward,' he sneered, depriving the man of his rank.

I remembered something else Tim had once told me, during the Disraeli Chambers case.

'Special Branch. They're not really part of the police, in the way the public'd understand. They're an institution all on their own. With their own purposes to fulfil. What they deal in is international.'

I struggled to put it together for myself. If I let him tell it, I'd get an edited account with less than ten percent real beans, which would influence my thinking despite myself. My way would either be entirely wrong or pretty close to the truth. He helped me out.

'You were in Baltimore. The woman Julie Somers committed suicide; I'm told the autopsy had more people in attendance than centre court at Wimbledon.'

'That, I presumed, is what Millward knew and wanted to talk to me about.'

'Not all of it. Not the autopsy.'

'Right. The FBI were there?' I presumed they declared their hand after seeing de Vries.

He nodded his head slowly, smiling all the while.

'Them and others.'

'DEA? No, that would go to NDIU. IRS? No, they'd go to Fraud, they're the only coppers can count.' I couldn't think of any other acronyms. 'Homeland?' Homeland Security.

He yawned theatrically.

'Took you long enough to get there.'

I digested the information slowly, with the remainder of my coffee. It hurt. It was a dimension that had not occurred to me. I spoke slowly.

'Whatever was under development at Gant's Gully was known about. It was authorised? Semi-authorised? That means Chambers knew? Hilton didn't develop it; he stole it?'

'Getting warm. Actually, it didn't exist, in the sense you mean. Chambers was asked by the US Navy to follow up a line of investigation, to see where it went. He subbed it to Hilton. At the time he quit, Hilton claimed it had gone nowhere, produced some evidence that appeared to prove it. When he was arrested for the other kind of drug, however, suddenly he asked to see Chambers and claimed that he'd lied. He wanted the charges dropped. He wanted Chambers to make a deal for him, with the government, Department of Navy.'

'His lawyers said Chambers was going to give evidence for him, that he'd been doing legitimate research, but never showed for the trial?'

He shook his head.

'No. That's what Hilton told them, in order to keep open his line to Chambers. His lawyers weren't involved; they weren't told anything about it. If Hilton told them, he would be hurting his own cause: the whole thing depended on secrecy. The only people supposed to know at Gant's Gully were Chambers and Hilton.'

'So what happened?'

'Here's where it goes queer. Chambers told the Navy Department he didn't believe Hilton. There was a Mexican stand-off. Hilton wouldn't spill word one to prove his point, because the moment he did he was unnecessary and he was paranoid enough to think he wouldn't live to trial.'

'That's paranoia?' It sounded like common sense to me.

'Maybe.' He shrugged. 'Chambers persuaded the Navy Department to tell Hilton to get lost. For a penny-ante drug-dealing bust, but for Chambers they'd probably have gone for a deal on spec. Chambers was, they said, more than a little bit hinky.'

'Where was Chambers at in all this?'

'Chambers wanted Hilton inside doing time, and no killing drug on the outside.'

'But according to him there was no killing drug?' I challenged.

'Right. The Navy Department bought that, just about. There was little they could do: Gant's Gully had both the technology and the know-how. If they tried to go elsewhere with their ideas, they would end up doubling the number of people who knew about it and doubling the risk of a leak. Better no one should have it than anyone else. It all goes to sleep while Hilton does his time. And what time? Three-to-five out in one.'

'Is that suspicious?'

'No. The dope-drug was never big, and people didn't start dying of it until after he'd been sentenced. Theoretically, they could have brought him back on a murder charge, or manslaughter, but there was no evidence he'd actually manufactured the later versions of it that caused the deaths. You've got to remember, with most designer drugs, no two batches are ever alike.'

'You said it goes to sleep while Hilton's inside. Then what?'

'Then two things.' Hed ticked off a finger. 'First off, Hilton's dead. Big sighs of relief all round.'

'Does that mean what I think it means?'

'Not so far as I'm aware.' He understood I was asking if the American government was implicated in it. 'Everything's cosy, until about a year ago.' At which point in time, I seemed to recollect, Neil Somers had jumped the Johns Hopkins Hospital ship.

'What happened then?'

'The American government get a whisper that Chambers has opened it up again at Gant's Gully, this time using the woman Thornton.' He ticked another finger. 'The whisper went Thornton to Segal to her husband.' Who was Navy and at Newport. 'At that point they bring the FBI into it.' This I already knew, though I didn't tell him so.

'How did the CIA get involved? They're only supposed to act abroad.'

'Supposed is right. The FBI brought them in through Homeland Security on the basis that it governed classified material. We're talking what could class as a military secret and that's always ambiguous.'

'Here too?'

'Smart chap.'

'CIA to MI5 to you?'

'MI-who?' he confirmed.

'What were the CIA looking for when they told MI5?' I began to understand why the English service was commonly abbreviated to what I had hitherto always regarded as the somewhat pretentious shorthand 'Five'.

'Well, follow it through from the other end. The Yanks know Chambers has gone back to the drawing-board.'

'Diving-board, actually.'

He ignored me.

'So far as they can tell, Chambers and Thornton haven't yet come up with the answer by the time Thornton buys it.'

'And that's not them either? Right. It wouldn't be. Not if they thought she wasn't yet there.'

'But Thornton got killed. What does that tell them?' He quizzed me like a school-teacher.

'That someone else is in the same market and didn't want the competition, which suggests they now know Hilton wasn't lying. Which means they're looking for the competition. Which takes them in the same direction I ended up at: groups who get their point across to an ever-eager public by whacking off whoever's handy.' Like the Real IRA.

Without rising, he bowed courtly, to acknowledge that I had finally put it together if not the way it was, then at least the way he wanted me to read it.

'Who got Tim going in the same direction? You?'

'No. That's one of the questions I would have asked you this morning.'

'Moi? What are the others?' Dopily, I skipped his use of the past tense.

'I said would have asked. The other question would have been who was getting whacked out with it, to use your terminology.'

'But you're not going to bother now, are you?'

'No.'

'Because between our encounter at the airport and my arrival this afternoon, you had a telephone call?'

'Yes.'

'Which miffed you because you'd say it should've been your brief all along?'

'Chief Inspector Dowell has no affection for Special Branch. I expect you know that.'

'I think it went a bit further than want of warm feelings. Loathing is one word that comes to mind; disgust, distaste... You want me to go on?'

'I think I have your point. What would your guess be? About the first question, I mean.'

'Tim didn't need anyone to tell him. He worked it out for himself.'

'That would be my answer, too, along with my admission that his feelings about us are not necessarily mutual.'

He was confiding his respect for Tim. I hoped Tim didn't get to hear about it before we found him; he might not want to be rescued.

'You're saying no one here came to the same conclusion?'

'No one here,' he stressed. 'Not in my office or command.'

'But elsewhere? Yes, of course. MI5. They wouldn't care about that, would they?' The government brought down. 'I mean, they might even like the idea. That's what Boller thought.'

'I wouldn't like to think it was quite that bad. Anyway, they could justify it on the ground that as soon as it became public knowledge, obviously everyone would go underground. They wanted to get their hands on the drug.'

'To give back to the Americans?'

'Who knows?' Yeah, right.

'And now?'

'Now, they still want to get their hands on the drug.'

'As do you?'

'I want Tim Dowell found, alive.'

'I'll buy it,' I agreed to believe him for the time being. 'Millward? How come the lost love?'

He shrugged.

'No mystery, Mr Woolf. The man's a bumbling incompetent, that's all. I thought you would have worked that out for yourself by now.'

'I did. Last question: why are you talking to me?'

'Where did Julie Somers fit in?'

'I don't know.' I gave him the same answer I gave Wadd. 'Ask her.'

'That's the point, Mr Woolf. If you and I had been on somewhat better terms during our last encounter, I might be able to.' She might still be alive.

'Thanks. I really needed someone to remind me.'

* * *

I couldn't raise Carson: she wasn't at the club, she wasn't at the office, she wasn't anywhere else I could think of. Natalie herself was inaccessible until early evening, well past the time I should have left home if I wanted to take the precaution of checking out the Three Johns before my meeting was due, as well as lose anyone who might be tailing me. Nat, too, when finally I reached her, swore she didn't have a clue where Carson might be, even when I stressed I needed her professionally. Because I had expected to be able to find her in due course, I had not bothered to track down Wally. I couldn't leave a message either: now that Special Branch had in effect taken over, I had little doubt that - if not previously - I was now as bug-riddled as a New York tenement. Depending how quickly they got around to it, they might even have Siobhan Cunningham's call that morning, but the timing was unlikely.

I was troubled that I was unarmed. In recent years, both American-authored and indigenous thrillers located in England have played fast and loose with how difficult it is to carry in this country. I had learned why during a lecture on the subject which I had attended as part of an earlier investigation; Raymond Chandler's edict - if plot lags, bring on man with gun. The reality is harder to bear. I carried a gun in my first case; I bought it illegally; I used it ineffectually; had it not been for a common interest in keeping events under wraps, I could have done time for it. In my third case, too, I had been equipped with a gun, similarly illegally, but the stakes had been so high - and the going so rough - that Tim had been prepared to turn a blind eye.

I had no sources of supply left. Both previous guns had been provided through the club, by Lewis and Malcolm respectively. If either of them had still been alive, I wouldn't own the club, and it would yet be frequented by the sort of people who could find me a weapon. As it was, the side-effect of Natalie's culinary reforms had been to elevate the nosh beyond the average villain's taste-buds. If I got into trouble, I'd have to hit back with kiwi-fruit sorbet.

Because of my fraught and failed efforts to contact Carson, I was ten minutes late. Cunningham had waited. I recognised her from the photograph Brendan had shown me. Politely, she held out a hand. She was a handsome woman, not yet thirty, wearing flat-heeled, calf-length black leather boots not designed for the country, and a skirt that was a little too tight for her thighs.

We talked about Brendan for a while to get comfortable with one another. She told me how she'd corresponded with him while he was in jail and how he had come to see her when he got out. She told me how frightened she had been of him, despite his letters, and how shocked she was to find such a gentle man on her doorstep. She told me what a hard time she had given him, refusing to settle for anything less than everything for nearly two years until he had worn down her resistance and wooed her into marriage. She told me:

'I hate those two years now.'

I said:

'I lost about twelve years making the same sort of mistake.'

'The funny thing is,' she confided, 'I have a weak heart; it's in the family. Even though, well of course, I knew the sort of risks he'd run, it always seemed as if he'd outlive me.'

'How's Declan?'

'Too young to understand, thank God.'

She was matter-of-fact and dry-eyed about her loss. It was not indifference but conditioning.

'How much do you know?' I asked her.

'Not much. That's usual.' So enemies - Brits, Prods or erstwhile allies - could not torture partners for information. 'I knew he'd seen you, he couldn't keep quiet about that; he was excited about it. Seeing you again after all these years; that you'd come looking for him to ask his help. He spent the rest of the day on the phone. Went out that evening to see someone; told me he was going to come over to see you. That was all.'

'All?'

She smiled nervously.

'No, not quite all. He left this in... In a special place he knew I'd look.'

It was an envelope, marked with my name, address and phone number. I frowned, thinking of who else might have found it. She understood.

'It would never have been found by anyone else.'

'Have you opened it?'

Her eyes shone.

'Certainly not.'

'Why did you bring it over? You could have sent it. Wasn't it dangerous for you to come in person?'

'Perhaps. But,' she smiled: 'my passport is in my maiden name.'

It struck me how rarely one heard the expression these days; it was pleasingly quaint.

'Still,' I insisted.

'Still? They killed my husband. I don't know who they are or why. I only know they didn't want you to get this. I'm presuming, if they didn't want you to have it, it'll help you find out who they are. Do you see?'

'Oh, yeah, I see.' I smiled back at her asking in a stage-Irish accent: 'And is it yeself or meself as is to pay them back for it?'

'I don't care, I really don't care who does it.'

Just as long as it gets done.

Carson came in on cue.

'You're clear,' she announced calmly.

'Not quite,' I corrected. 'You're here.'

Siobhan sensed she was an ally, even if only of sorts.

'Siobhan, meet Carson. She's Australian,' I added as if that might explain most of the confusion. 'She works for me, I think. But don't ask me how she got here,' I added, looking pointedly in her direction.

Carson sniffed.

'You think you're the only detective?'

I waited patiently.

'I overheard the name of the pub on the phone this morning.'

I played the conversation back in my head.

'But not what time we were meeting.'

'Nah, I watched you leave.'

'Great. I was looking for a tail, I don't even spot you?'

She shook her head, smiling excessively sweetly the way she does when she knows her next remark will annoy me.

'Oh, I was at Jada's all day.'

It wasn't the time or the place to ask what the hell she was playing at. By now, both Siobhan and I were equally confused.

'Drinks?'

We each held up a glass; Jada held out her hand for the money.

'This is business.'

'She's sweet,' Siobhan said once Carson was out of earshot. I told her Carson would probably kill her if she overhead. She said: 'You don't just work together, do you?'

'Do you always notice things so fast? Do you always say whatever you see?'

She shook her head.

'I was a teacher, until Declan. You have to be observant when you've a classroom of thirty-five children to keep an eye on, and half of them spend the evenings patrolling with an Armalite. And I'm sorry I said anything... It just made me think.'

'Are you going to open that or sit here and prattle all night long?' Carson asked as she sat down, neatly managing to avoid sloshing the envelope with the only drink she spilled - mine.

'Prattle probably,' but I picked it up and, a little nervously, slit it open with a thumb-nail that needed trimming. Ladies and Gentlemen, the winner of this year's Oscar for Off-Screen Violence is...

CHAPTER NINE

Joe Leahy.

I shuddered: I knew the name.

I pushed the envelope away from me as if I could make him go away too.

* * *

'Joe Leahy,' de Vries whispered into the phone as if frightened of being overheard.

'I know.'

'You know who he is?'

'Oh, yeah.'

'They're holding back the autopsy results, you know that too?'

'No one told me, but I worked out they'd have to. Where's Chambers?'

'No one knows. Gone to ground. Or kept under wraps.'

'How'd you get Leahy?' I was impressed; I hadn't expected him to score, which was why I'd prompted Wally to put out his own feelers across the Irish Sea to discern the identity of the Segal seed man.

'Sweated Segal.'

'Sweated?'

'Husband didn't know about it.'

'That's how, not why you had to.'

'Only the loyalty factor. She's long out of it. Whatever it is. But Leahy was who.'

'Even then,' I sighed. 'He's been around all these years, and no one got next to him. She did. How?'

'I couldn't get any more. She's more frightened of him than her husband.'

'I don't blame her.'

'Be careful, Dave.'

'How much more can you do?'

'Depends.'

'On?'

'Whether I want a pension.'

'Like that is it?'

'Yeah. And, uh, Dave, I'm sorry, but I've got kids, you know?'

'Yeah, Tim too. But, well, I understand.'

'If I can... Well, if I think I can, you know.' Get away with it. 'Hope you find your man, yeah? Let me know?'

'Yeah.'

'Take care,' he repeated.

* * *

'Joe Leahy? Fuck.' Wally didn't often swear. 'He's way out there: splintered from the Provos with the Irish National Liberation Army, splintered from the INLA with the Irish Socialist Vanguard, splintered from ISV with the United Ireland Army. He's even too far out for the Real IRA, so they say. On the other hand, I heard a rumour he sometimes freelances on contract; you know, non-political. '

'Fascinating. We find Tim with a bullet buried in his head, it's important it was political or just business?'

He shuddered:

'He's got a gaggle of former and current republicans to call on, whatever the job; quite his own army. What else did your friend have to say?' Brendan Cunningham.

'Nothing. That was it.'

'Helpful,' he growled sarcastically.

'Yeah, right, let's really slag the guy off; he probably stage-managed his own death just to annoy me.'

* * *

'Joe Leahy?' Farlowe plucked lumps of dandruff out of his oily hair. 'He has no influence left; he has no political agenda to serve. I don't believe it,' he said flatly but somehow hollowly.

'Sounds like you know him pretty well?'

He flushed.

'I know of him. I know my job.'

As before, I was kept waiting for a few minutes before I was allowed in to see the man, though this time Farlowe was kept waiting with me.

I didn't need to see Boller to tell him about Leahy: a phone call would have served as well, or a post-card with a second class stamp. What I did need to see him for was to ask him:

'Can you unlock the autopsy results on Julie Somers? Better still, find out where Chambers is?'

He leaned back in his chair.

'Joe Leahy?' he asked, rolling the name around in his West Country burr, speculating how the information fit into his campaign tactics before deciding whether or not to help. It put a whole new perspective on the game.

* * *

'Joe Leahy,' Sheila said quietly. 'Yes, I recognise the name. What does it mean, Dave? I mean...' What does it mean for Tim's chances.

'It's, uh, well, not good news, Sheila.'

She nodded. That much she'd worked out for herself. Carson took her hand.

'It doesn't necessarily mean...'

'You don't know, Carson. None of us does. Please, no empty reassurances. I'm not sure...' Sheila's voice cracked. 'I'm not sure I can handle them.' She began to cry. 'I'm not sure how much more I can take,' she admitted. As if she'd almost rather hear he was dead than continue in suspense. She must have lost twenty five pounds in the last couple of weeks.

'Is there somewhere you could go, Sheila? Would you like to come back home with us?'

'I can't,' she shook her head. 'The kids. The phone.' Tim might ring.

'They can come back with us. Or... Mary?'

'I don't know.' She was tempted. 'She could take...' Not Alton, too.

'That's okay,' Carson said. 'We can take care of Alton. You could if you come back with us.'

I frowned.

'No.'

Carson looked at me in surprise at my objection. I shrugged. 'Sorry. It's just...'

'Dave's right, Carson. It's too dangerous.' Sheila saw at once: she was Tim's wife.

'Jada? Frankie would love it.'

We left it that Sheila would think about coming over to stay for the remainder of the duration.

After Siobhan Cunningham left us the night before, as depressed and as terrified by the name as any of us, perhaps even a little more so, Carson came back home with me. Not until we were safely inside did I get to ask what game she was playing.

'Not a game, Dave. If we're going to explore it - us - I need some distance. I don't want to slip into living together without thinking about it. That's all. Jada said I could use their spare room for a while.'

'Why not stay at the club?' I asked. 'Half your things're there anyway.' And Natalie was her best friend.

She glowered at me.

'You can be so thick sometimes, Dave.'

Because I also owned the club.

'Are you going to Jada's now?' I asked defensively.

She laughed and came over to the sofa on which I was sprawled out.

'Move over. No, I'm not going there; not if you ask me to stay, that is. See? That's the way people do these things. Geddit?'

'Will you stay?' She waited. I added the awful, unnatural word. 'Please?' We snuggled up. She felt good. I felt comfortable. Despite the news Siobhan had brought, I felt safe.

'Yes, I'll stay. Now,' all brisk and business again. 'Tell me about Leahy.' But she didn't move away to where she'd been sitting before.

In part because she was Australian, and in part because she never followed politics or read the newspapers closely, she did not know Joe Leahy as much as might be expected.

Joe Leahy was one of those names Irish parents frightened their children with to get them to go to sleep or to behave. Originally a bomb-maker, he had shown even greater ability as a planner and had taken part in many of the major operations both in the Six Counties and on the mainland. For all I knew, he had played a part in the case for which Brendan got caught, though his name was not one of those expressly referred to. As Wally said, he had split off with the INLA, for whom he had performed as star assassin. When the ISV was formed, he was in its inner cabinet; in the UIA, he was the leader.

It was impossible to gauge accurately how many people he had killed, especially if Wally was right and to his political notches could be added a few straight commercial shoots. So far as I was aware, for the last several years he had engaged in no bombing activity, or public-target terrorism, only individual murders with bullets. An Irish politician here, a traitor there, an old foe or, just as likely, a new friend. Although he had never mentioned him to me, I had no doubt he had been personally known to Brendan.

I would have said, before I heard about Segal, that Leahy would never be found in public, meaning anywhere outside a tight circle of - temporarily - trusted cohorts. To stay out of sight and the clutches of the police throughout the Western world for as long as he had managed took an enormous amount of continuous caution. I didn't know what Segal had going for her in those days, but I wished I'd had the opportunity to find out for myself. Also, I wanted to know just how involved she and Julie were with Irish politics, though a demonstration over the details of the Good Friday agreement hardly made Julie a mass-murderess. Hell, I'd gone to pro-Irish demos myself back in the day.

'Who's he hooked up to now?' Carson asked, rolling off the sofa and landing on the floor with a thump. 'We're too old for this sort of thing - well, between us, too big.' Kneeling beside me, she undid one of my shirt buttons and stroked my belly tenderly, though saying, as usual, something contrary. 'You need to lose weight.'

'You know the best way to do it,' I laughed without answering her question and without having an answer to her question of who Leahy was hooked up to now.

* * *

The phone rang in the middle of the following night, following the day during which I'd seen Sheila and the Prime Minister. I was exhausted: for the third or fourth night in a row, Carson and I had sat up talking until dark o'clock in the morning, as if, now we were proper lovers, we had to go back to the beginning and discover each other all over.

The caller disconnected as soon as I picked up the phone. Then a sharp rat-a-tat-tat at the front door. I flew downstairs, still struggling into my dressing-gown: if they were going to shoot me, I didn't want to be found naked. Not after what Carson had said about my weight. On the inside doormat lay a page torn out from a street map of London: the next page over from where I live. A red dot marked the spot. A circle formed with a coin containing two straight, ruled lines out from the centre told me the time. I didn't bother handling with care: if after that much trouble to avoid handwriting identification they'd left fingerprints, they were going to be a whole bunch easier to catch than I anticipated.

I had ten minutes to get dressed and get there. I memorised the spot and thrust the page at a sleepy Carson, rasping for her to call Wally as I pulled on a pair of jeans.

At that time of the night, there was little traffic on the roads and I was only about three minutes late. I glanced around: no one obvious. There was a pair of free-standing phone hoods on the corner, one of them for cards, the other for cash. The cash one rang. I grabbed the receiver. Tim said:

'I get to tell you I'm okay. That's all.'

'Sheila's fine, Timothy, they're all holding up fine.' I remembered to use his full name, in case they'd already taken the receiver away from him.

The same voice as before said:

'I'll pass the message onto him, Dave,' telling me both that it had been and that they hadn't been fooled. 'Now we've got a message for you.' He hung up.

At the same time, I realised I had heard but paid no attention to the sound of a car starting up. Actually, it was a VW van, parked just around the corner from the phones. He'd been speaking from a mobile phone. As the van hurtled past me, its number-plate muddied out, the rear doors flew open and a body was flung out of the van, for a horrific moment flying straight at me before it splattered half on the pavement and half on the road. I threw myself at it, screaming silently that it should not be Tim.

* * *

'So much for squeezing her to talk, huh,' I said to DCI Gregory, sipping coffee gratefully from his flask as we sat in the front seat of his car. Wally drove up and, uninvited, slipped into the back seat. Gregory didn't object: Wally had the Commissioner's seal of approval. 'Makes the autopsy results from Baltimore pretty irrelevant.' Annette Mallalieu wouldn't be standing trial, not even before the Medical Disciplinary Tribunal.

'To some,' Gregory said: 'Not to others.'

'What about you, Gregory? Where do you stand?'

'Wherever I'm told to,' he said blandly. 'Read the situation for me, Wadd.'

'Sir.' I'd never heard him call anyone 'sir' except sarcastically. 'She went to Switzerland; correction, she fled to Switzerland because of Dave's visit or the surveillance we were putting on her; probably, she went to meet someone there. We know it can't have been Zeke Zeller, Pat Hughes or Debbie Segal.'

'We don't know that,' I interrupted. 'All we know is that they say it can't have been them she met there.'

'There's Neil Somers,' Wadd added.

'It fits. But so would Joe Leahy; hell, so would a range of other names we don't have. Where's Oswald Chambers, Gregory?' I knew he, too, would have been trying to track him down.

'Having a nice day, I imagine,' he said dryly.

'This is fucking rich,' I snapped. 'We're the ones who've got a lost copper and four M.P.s killed. What happened to hands across the ocean, special relationship, all that jazz?'

'Way I hear it...' Which meant MI5 if his other contacts and sources were as dry as he was implying, 'it's not a lot better over there. They're fighting and falling over each other so hard it's impossible to say who, if anyone, has got any answers.'

'Whoever's got Chambers got the answers. One way or the other.'

'Meaning?' Gregory asked.

'Meaning we've all been inclined to believe Chambers is straight, yes? Everyone, but everyone, says so. De Vries, Prof. Christiansen, Julie said it, I felt it, Navy Department thinks it. But he's the one person in it all who could have known and controlled everything that's gone down.'

'What for? What's his motive? What's his game? What's Leahy's game?' Like Farlowe, Gregory had immediately taken the point that Leahy was too far away from any coherent political grouping to gain anything from bringing down the government.

'Brendan said, don't underestimate them,' the Real IRA.

'So?' Gregory asked.

'So maybe things are moving full circle; maybe there's more people prepared to go back to the old ways, who're against talking to the government; maybe Leahy's back in the fold because they haven't got the muscle of their own, seeing as how they aren't in the ascendant policy-wise....'

Gregory glanced at the back seat.

'Does he always talk in this sort of half-gibberish, pseudo-gangster slang, Wadd?'

'As long as I've known him, sir.'

'There's that word again,' I retaliated without adequate cause. 'Sir. You keep calling him sir. I never heard you call Tim sir.'

Wadd frowned to tell me I could get him into serious trouble. I smiled sweetly.

'Hope so.'

Gregory gave up.

'Tell it your own way, Mr Woolf.'

I breathed on my knuckles and rubbed them against my lapel: I'd recovered my 'mister'.

'What I'm saying is, Leahy's a killer, right? He'll kill for anyone the price is right, right? So why shouldn't he kill for the Real IRA?'

'Where would they get money?'

'They can always get money: in some areas, they're the local taxman - local businesses, local crooks too. Who do you think runs illegal gambling in the province - the mafia? Maybe he isn't getting paid; maybe that's where his own agenda comes in; maybe once it's gone down, there's a power shift, Leahy's back in the fold, right at the top maybe.'

'What I'm thinking about, Dave,' Wally scrambled back into my good books by addressing his contribution in my direction instead of Gregory's. 'If Tim - sorry, sir, DCI Dowell - was in that van, then he's a witness to murder.'

'Not necessarily,' Gregory said. 'Not much blood that wouldn't have resulted from the fall anyway. Could have been killed elsewhere. Anyway, what's your point?'

'Just that, well, they can't be meaning to let him go, can they, sir?'

Gregory shrugged.

'No more than before, nor less. We don't know who - if anyone - he's seen. Besides, don't forget these people know how to play with drugs. For all we know, they could be bringing him in and out of consciousness at will, as it suits them.'

We sat in silence for several minutes, all of us thinking the worst in each of our different ways, until a uniformed police office rapped at the window with one hand, the other clutching Carson.

'Claims she belongs to Mr Woolf, sir.'

'Never seen her before in my life,' I muttered, as Wadd leaned over to open the rear door for her. And: 'You took your time.'

'You took the car, remember? What gives?'

She still didn't know.

I told her.

The blood drained from her face:

'Oh, no.'

I knew what she meant. We'd been there together more than once. First, Margot. Then, Brendan. Then, Julie. Now, Mallalieu. How many before it ended? And who? Them, or us?

* * *

Before we parted for the night, I took Gregory aside. Carson stuck to me like superglue.

'You want me to stay on this?' I asked the Special Branch man.

'Would it make any difference whether I did or didn't?'

'Do you or don't you?' I insisted on an answer.

'The Prime Minister, the Commissioner and Mrs Dowell all seem to want you to; so I suppose for once I'd have to say yes.' Such enthusiasm.

'I want a gun.'

'You. Want. A. Gun?'

'Me too,' said Carson, though it hadn't been discussed between us. I felt an objection rising but swallowed it back like bile, just in time: I didn't want Carson to have a gun; I didn't want Carson to need a gun; I didn't want Carson anywhere near danger, or death; on the other hand, I didn't want to risk her reaction to me being over-protective.

'You heard me,' I said irritably: it was almost dawn. 'They're all words of one syllable.'

'You really know how to charm people, don't you Dave?'

It was the first time he had called me by my first name; we would get our guns.

* * *

Dannie rang.

'Are you all right, dear?'

'Yeah, sure. Why?'

'Someone asked me to give you a message but he didn't want me to say who it was from. He said you'd know, but it was very mysterious.'

It had to be De Vries; anyone else, Dannie would have told to get lost, but a policeman, and one I had mentioned, could persuade her. I'd mentioned Dannie and Lucy to him, during general chatter, talking about previous visits. I couldn't remember if I told him their names, but I had probably described where they lived, opposite the Redwood Library, next to the studios that got burned down, as a part of establishing common ground, inviting him to treat me as less of a stranger than he might otherwise. It was a small town; it wouldn't be hard to work out.

De Vries was scared. He wasn't going to call me from the station; he wasn't going to call me from his home; he wasn't going to call me on any line that might be bugged at my end, on which his voice might be recorded. Dannie, on the other hand, could always be denied before the disciplinary tribunal that tried to take his badge, gun, pack of bridge cards and pension.

'What was the message?'

'He said to tell you the man you want is in hiding. He said in hiding from everyone. He said you'd understand.'

'Yup. I do.'

De Vries was not the only one scared; so was Oswald Chambers. He had reason to be: scared of his own government; scared of Joe Leahy or whatever Leahy represented; scared of who knew what or who else.

'And that was it?' Carson asked as I repeated the conversation to her.

'That was it.'

'Hm.'

'Gee, that's helpful.'

We were lying in bed but not yet asleep when the call came. So much for independent space, we hadn't spent a night apart since. I snuggled up to her:

'Hey, how you wanna do it?'

She nibbled my ear and whispered back.

'Over easy.'

I was discovering a new side to Carson. Soft and sensuous, funny and fragile, super indulgent. Arrayed on the table her side of the bed was a stash of Body Shop products. Massage creams and oil: oh, yeah, really, who do they think they're kidding - massage? I stretched out to hook one of the plastic jars between my fingers. It was slippery and slightly tacky.

'Just how old is this, anyway?' I asked.

She giggled.

'Long past its fuck-by date.'

We fell asleep in sheets greasy with overspill, stuck to each other and happy at it.

* * *

Grease-top Farlowe, on behalf of Boller he said, called a full council of war, which he decided to locate in the Commissioner's office, where it would attract less attention than Number Ten. Boller himself was, of course, not present. Millward was, below Dunlop, still technically the ranking officer in the search for Tim; Gooch came next in seniority but was increasingly irrelevant now that no one believed dope had anything to do with the case; Gregory was the rising star, in charge of the investigation into the four MP deaths and thence into the murder of Annette Mallalieu. Even Wadd was allowed in to watch, though not to speak in such elevated company.

Gregory drew the threads together.

'We start with a request by the American government - Navy - to Chambers to play around with the development of a new drug, one they suspect has killer qualities and - we now know, though don't know if this was known to them - that leaves no apparent traces anyone would be looking out for'. Not for the first time, I was struck by how everyone had come to take the idea as being next to normal.

'It's unclear why they did so, or what they were looking for. One can imagine enough uses for it not to find their interest surprising. Chambers allocates the work to Hilton, who pretends there's nothing in it, and convinces Chambers of it, but in fact has it worked out. I think we have to - and can - presume that Neil Somers finds out about it, presumably from Hilton as his sometime roomie. We have a network that runs from Neil Somers to Joe Leahy; we don't know what their purpose is. Potentially embroiled in this network are the remaining elements of the Gant's Gully group, meaning all of them - Julie Somers, Helen Thornton, Patricia Hughes - Neil Somers' clown partner, Debbie Segal, with her own, more intimate, link to Leahy; then there's the mentor himself, Chambers, and the unknown wild-card Zeke Zeller; also there's Mallalieu. Hilton, Julie Somers, Thornton and Mallalieu are now dead. If we presume that means they were never the leaders of the plot, we can focus on Neil Somers, Patricia Hughes, Zeke Zeller and Joe Leahy.'

'Why not Segal?'

'Maybe, but she strikes me as unlikely. She's married to the Navy and your pal de Vries doesn't think that's phoney; she gave up Leahy's name; she's sitting at home raising a baby. I like her for the initial link between Leahy and the others, but probably nothing more.'

Carson was unimpressed, by either the thought or the forum.

'For all we know she may be the mistress brain.'

Ignoring her sarcastic political correctness, Dunlop intervened.

'One has to work on probabilities, Miss, uh...'

'Carson,' I said quickly before she ripped off his goolies. 'Just Carson.'

'Miss Carson,' he compounded his error. 'What about this man Chambers? Why omit him from the frame?'

I had not told them about the call from Dannie; he appeared not to know about it. That told me that if my phone was being bugged by Gregory, it was unofficial. I had not told them mostly for de Vries' protection, even if he'd buried his name; also, because I still hadn't made up my mind what it meant. My initial reaction - that Chambers was hiding because he was scared - had been supplanted by one less charitable: that the only thing he was scared of was getting caught and for hiding we could read on the run.

Gregory struggled.

'I'd assumed that the Americans have him - probably under wraps, probably finishing the drug for use.'

The Commissioner shook his head.

'If that was true, they wouldn't be working as hard as they are at their end.'

'Exactly what are they doing, Sir Randolph?' Farlowe asked him.

'They're trying to establish if Leahy has been in the States, or if he's there now; they're using their IRS to investigate all the participants' financial records and accounts.' As I had suggested to de Vries. 'It seems there are strong financial links between Zeller and Hughes,' he added, also as I had suggested.

'What about the Irish?' Farlowe meant the Eireann officials. 'How co-operative are they being?'

'They've put more people onto looking for Leahy and I'm hoping for an account of activities in and around the Galway area before the end of the week.'

'The Prime Minister is grateful for the personal interest you're showing, Sir Randolph,' Farlowe sounded as if it was a message he had suddenly remembered and did not want to forget. Carson snorted. 'What about Commander Millward's men?'

It was time for some light relief. We all enjoyed the sight of Millward blustering about his efforts, trying to conceal the full extent of his failure to turn up a single real clue to Tim's whereabouts. The West London link had produced nothing and was now believed to be a wild-goose chase. The meeting lasted less than ten more minutes and I found myself, as we started to file out, wondering why it had been worth Farlowe's while. Dunlop signalled for me to remain behind. Carson hovered. He looked at her balefully until I shrugged and nodded for her to wait in the outer office.

'I'll tell her anyway.'

'Yes. But I won't.' No witnesses.

'What?'

'Who do you trust, Mr Woolf?'

'Wadd,' I replied promptly.

He waited.

I said nothing until he got the point.

'When did you meet DCI Dowell, Mr Woolf?'

'During Disraeli Chambers.' I gave him an approximate date.

'Which was soon after he was appointed to special duties?'

'Yes.' I knew that was true.

'And I was appointed when?'

I nodded.

'Got your point.' Dowell was his creation, his notion, his man: someone outside the system, to ride herd on it, mop up after it. 'Doesn't mean I should trust you now. Maybe the man has got something on you.'

He smiled evenly.

'Yes.' He knew that if Dowell had found something out about his own boss, he wouldn't hesitate to deal with it the way it needed. Maybe he also meant it was entirely possible he would have Dowell dealt with. 'But no.'

'Why does it matter to you?' That I should trust him.

'It doesn't. I only rose to it through vanity.' Each time we spoke, I realised how disingenuous was his public and political image as a high-level doofus. It was an additional reason for mistrust. He continued. 'What is important to me is that you should not trust anyone else.'

This was marvellous: the chief of police was telling me not to trust his own men. I admitted:

'I was beginning to trust Gregory.'

'Oh, he wasn't who I had particularly in mind,' he said airily, lighting a fresh cigarette. 'Though I'm sure he has his own aims, apart from recovering DCI Dowell,' he dissembled. 'I wasn't thinking of my own people, really.'

The politicians.

'Small wonder they don't trust you either.'

'It's an odd world, politics,' he said. 'Shifting alliances, shifting ideas. It's not because they're on the left,' he added quickly, 'though I know that's what they think. Don't think the others trust us any the more; they're just a bit more discreet about it. It's a question of what position they want to take in public. And don't think I trust them any the more either.'

'What are you saying, Dunlop?' I was irritated. I wasn't here to listen to mind games.

'I'm trying to explain to you, Mr Woolf, that my mistrust of politicians has nothing to do with their policies but with the nature of the beast. How can I, a policeman, be expected to trust someone whose existence depends on the expendability of erstwhile allies?'

'Isn't it a part of your job to do so?'

'Now there's an interesting philosophical question,' he smiled again. 'Is it my job to trust them, or is it my job to mistrust them?'

'But you didn't ask me to stay back for a philosophical debate, did you?'

'No,' he sighed. 'Of course not. I asked you to stay back to have a chat about the weather, the size of your Southern Comfort account,' he used the illustration to remind me that he knew a lot more about me than I about him. 'And, uh, whether you thought the meeting had really been worth our while - ours, Mr Woolf,' he emphasised. 'As, uh,' though it obviously cost him to include me: 'As detectives.'

* * *

Sheila had accepted the suggestion of coming over to Islington, but insisted on staying with us regardless of the danger.

'Anyway, if he got free, he'd probably call you first,' she told me, managing a moment of humour. Her state of mind had improved since we had confirmed Tim was alive, but not by much.

Her own children were with her sister, Mary. They had still been told no more than that their father was away on work.

Jada and Frankie wandered down the road to join us, eat with us, make a family party out it, let Alton feel a little bit back at home: he was enjoying his own personal diaspora; talk about the wandering Jew.

I couldn't cope. It was too many people, too much distraction. I was surrounded by too many emotions: Sandy's lurking presence, Alton, Carson, there was also an emotional underside to Tim's disappearance - the unavoidable if unspoken fear that he would never return. Carson was right: he was my best friend; I had never had one before. Carson suggested:

'Why don't you go down to the club for a while, Dave? Nat'll be feeling left out, huh?'

* * *

'Hiya, stranger.' Nat was so pleased to see me she even kissed me, but only on the cheek. 'Spot check?'

We hadn't even done an accounting session since Tim took off.

'You wearing polka-dot panties?' I leered. 'Thanks,' I said to Joannie as she brought my bottle and a bowl of ice. 'Suppose you haven't changed your mind yet either?'

'About what?' The waitress replied archly. 'You want a drink, Natalie?'

'Sure, spritzer.' It was early; there was only one other couple in the club. 'You gonna eat, Dave?'

I shook my head.

'The girlies're cooking; I got let out on a leash, but only for an hour. You want to come back eat with us? Sheila's staying; Alton's over; Jade, Frankie.'

She was tempted, but:

'New cook.'

'What happened to the last one?'

'Got fresh.'

'You ever going to settle down, kid? Or you gonna pine away waiting for me?'

'I don't know,' she admitted the subject had been on her mind. 'Sometimes I think, another few years of this and I'll become one of those characters you read about in fiction - you know, middle-aged, single woman, bar-keep, mother-confessor to a parish of equally middle-aged, single boozers; heart of gold.' She paused, then added harshly: 'Dry.'

Our eyes met; we'd been enough to each other for long enough for me not to have to tell her I was there to listen. I asked:

'Anything particular?' I had a fair idea of what the answer would be.

'You going to behave, Dave?' With Carson.

'I'm going to try.'

She gripped my wrist tightly.

'You going to succeed, Dave?'

I pulled it free.

'Do you want me to?'

'It's always scary when someone that close,' like she and Carson were close: 'Gets it together with someone new and you're still alone. It's scarier still when it's two of your closest friends. Scary...and jealous. But only in the abstract,' she finally answered my question.

I took her hand and stroked the back of it.

'Carson said the other night... when was it? On the plane from the States, I think. She said: a relationship's got to be more than the sum total of its individual parts.'

'Sure. So?'

'So you get three friends instead of two: her, me and us.'

'Maybe. Or maybe I get only one.'

She was surprisingly affected and surprisingly bitter.

'I'm sorry, Nat.'

She shook her head violently.

'No, no, I don't mean I mind you've done it. I've been expecting it; I think you're the only one who didn't see it coming. It was only a matter of time.'

'Why didn't you say so, earlier, when...' When she and I had done the deed.

She shrugged again.

'I'm not sure. Maybe it was too early. Maybe we had to get that out of the way. Maybe you had to find out for yourself.'

I frowned: she was holding something back.

She finished her spritzer and poured me another rocky Comfort.

'Yes, alright. Maybe I was frightened for Carson. Don't forget how fragile she is.'

'Oh, I don't.' I tossed her words back and forth, working out what she meant, surfing the waves of my own insecurity. 'You said you were frightened; mean you're not anymore?'

She smiled and patted me on the cheek.

'Let's just say a bit less, okay?'

I laughed and tossed back my drink.

'Gotta run, kid.'

'See you, Dave.' She got up with me and gave me a light hug, wriggling away as I tried to take advantage of it. 'Be careful.'

I was still glowing in the warm embrace of her love and affection, with more awaiting me at home, as I descended the stairs to the Old Brompton Road. It had turned dark during my visit. I had parked right outside the door as usual. Staring out of the rear window of my own car, staring directly at me, her face pressed cruelly flat against the Perspex, was Siobhan Cunningham, her mouth slightly open like she was hyper-ventilating from fear. The front passenger window lowered electronically and a man wearing sunglasses, a sailor's hat pulled low and a turtle-neck sweater pulled up high pointed a pistol through it at me.

'We'd like you to come for a ride, Mr Woolf,' he said in a voice so low it was almost a whisper, but a threatening whisper with a trace of accent barely identifiable, just enough to confirm my worst fears: Joe Leahy's lads was my first and last assumption. 'We'd really like it,' he emphasised as I hesitated.

I guess he thought I was stupid and needed the repetition.

What I was wondering was, would they pay for the petrol they used?

CHAPTER TEN

Now Dave had disappeared as well.

I had rung Natalie and learned what time Dave had left the club - to my surprise, more or less when he was supposed to have done so - but I didn't begin to worry about his failure to return to the house until Jada and Frankie had taken Alton back home with them, Frankie carrying Alton like a prize doll she'd won at her school sports day. Sheila had to restrain the impulse to go with them, to see him settled in properly for the night. Even then, as we did the dishes, we were more narked off about Dave than truly concerned.

'He's so selfish, he lives in a world of his own, he thinks the rest of us only exist to provide a bit of entertainment when he gets bored with his own company. I don't think he was that much different with Sandy.'

'They're all like that,' Sheila replied dryly.

'Funny that; I always assumed Tim was, well, secretly, different - like closet okay.'

She laughed: I think it was the first time I heard her laugh since Tim was taken. I guess she thought the same thing, because the next I knew I had my arms around her, drying-up cloth dangling from one finger, and she was letting the tears go the way I knew she'd been doing in private - knew without being told - but that she'd been too proud to let happen in front of any of us up until now.

It didn't last long.

'You were right. I needed to get away from the house.'

'Come on, let's have a drink. We'll leave the rest for Dave.'

We giggled matronly at the idea of Dave coming in to find a pile of washing up left over from the dinner he'd copped out of and made our way up to the living room with a bottle of Frascati. I'll say this for Dave: just because there's only one thing he drinks doesn't mean he won't keep in supplies for others; he'd even brought home some Fosters, which he thinks I like because I'm Australian but I only drink because it's expected of me.

'Where do you think he is, Carson?' Sheila meant Dave, not Tim.

'Probably found it too much to handle, too many people he cares about all at a time. He's an odd sod. Booze and bluff and bad jokes, but underneath he's pretty sensitive. I think he'd quite like to lead a much quieter life, be a much quieter bloke, but he's frightened to.'

'What of? Do you know?'

That's the thing about Sheila, the reason we became friends. On the surface, she's an ordinary, suburban housewife married to a police officer; underneath, though, she has this reservoir of understanding that puts her a step ahead of others. I figured the right answer was:

'That no one will notice him; no one will ever know he was here. He was never going to be a great lawyer; very few solicitors ever get well-known or noticed outside their own firms and clients...'

'It's the same for policemen,' Sheila intervened, lapsing back into silence without elaborating.

'Right. Maybe. But Tim stuck with it and made himself stand out. Stand out in a crowd. That's hard. Dave did a dive instead.' Sheila knew about Dave's time in the coke trough.

She said gently:

'He doesn't do badly, Carson. Dave, I mean. That's why deep down I do believe Tim'll be back.'

'I think it's easier for him to do something he feels is important as a private eye than as a solicitor. That's what I mean.'

'You're so hard on him. Why?'

'Habit, I suppose.'

I was having difficulty adjusting to our new relationship, my new role in his life and his in mine. I'd always been rough with him until now and didn't really know how to stop. No, that's not right. I knew how. I didn't know if he wanted me to. Or if I did. I still wasn't sure, but his thing with Julie had convinced me I couldn't keep putting off a decision or the next time I might lose the chance forever.

'Is it him you're punishing, or yourself?'

'You should've been a shrink, Sheila.'

'Oh, I know. I did one year of psychology at university.'

'I didn't know you had a degree.' I felt ashamed. I'd always talked far more about myself, assuming maybe she didn't have that much to say. 'I'm sorry. I take you too much for granted, don't I?'

'No, it's alright, Carson, honestly.'

I flushed, realising how much I wanted her approval, forgiveness. When I first started getting friendly with her - against all the apparent odds - I'd wondered to myself if I was using her as a substitute mother; I must have buried the thought without ever admitting it, because now I felt like a little girl again, basking in my mother's favour.

That's another thing about Sheila: she leaves you time to think. She said:

'I don't have a degree. I didn't finish. That's why I don't talk about it. You see, well,' she smiled wanly, back on the edge of tears, 'that's where we met. At university. I dropped out.' She shut her eyes for a minute, then decided to tell me. 'We were careless; I became pregnant; I was pregnant when we were married.' She watched me struggle with dates, then saved me the trouble. 'She died, Carson, when she was five months old. Cot death. Jane. Her name was Jane.'

'I didn't know. Any of it.'

'No. We don't talk about it.'

'Does Dave...'

'No. Not unless Tim's told him without telling me. No,' she repeated. 'No, he wouldn't do that.' Personal confidences were not a hallmark of the relationship between our two men. 'And I'd rather...'

I nodded emphatically: I wouldn't tell him. I asked:

'Didn't you think of going back to college?'

'I was too depressed.' She reddened. She couldn't even equivocate, let alone lie. 'I had a breakdown. I was in a hospital, for six months. Tim was...' She took a deep breath to prevent the tears taking over. 'Tim was wonderful. He was in his last year, law finals. You knew that?'

I nodded again; Tim's law degree was one of the first things Dave had told me about him, forewarning me not to assume he had the average copper's below-average IQ.

'He came to the hospital every single day. I mean every single day for six months, without exception. He sat with me and held my hand and talked to me for more than an hour every day, often when I wouldn't talk to him. I blamed him, you see; for no reason at all, I blamed him for having Jane, for dropping out of college, for Jane's death. And every day he'd tell me it was alright to blame him, if that was what I really wanted, but it wasn't going to help me get better. And remember, Carson, we're talking about a university student; he was, oh, what, twenty-two at the time, and doing his finals, and this is what he did. We don't...'

She hesitated again. I sensed why. One last confidence. I said:

'Don't tell me if you don't want to, Sheila. Keep it for yourselves.' I only just avoided saying 'yourself', in the singular.

'No, I want you to know. I want to explain why we don't talk about it. It's not because we're ashamed of it. It's because it's that most private time, when we finally knew we were going to build a life together forever and worked at it in a way I suppose very few people ever do. It was like all my preconceptions of life and marriage had broken down - my personal infrastructure, if you like - and I was rebuilding it, and I had to make a decision whether to do so with him or without him. And he knew our whole lives were on the line and he waited and helped, and even though he hadn't been as hit by Jane's death as I was, and even though he had to get through his finals, he broke down his own defences to share the time with me, so we were taking an equal risk, both of us building from scratch. So now you see, don't you?'

'Oh, I see.' I saw why they were happy together, why they worked, why each of them meant so much to the other, and yet had something left over for others; the way they'd taken Alton into their lives and home, and had, by association, done the same for Dave and, I suppose, me. 'Why did you want to tell me, Sheila? I mean, now? Because of Tim?'

'No, not because of Tim. Because of Dave.'

Here come those famous last words.

'It isn't Dave who's missing.'

'I don't mean because he's late tonight. I meant because of what you two are doing together.'

I had to puzzle it out; she made me get there on my own. I said:

'Because of Sandy? Because everyone's got their own private story of how they came together?'

'Yes. And sometimes that story's sad; anyway, not a tale of romance and nights of tender love.'

'I don't know,' I said. 'There's enough romance in what you told me, and tender love. Enough to last a lifetime, I'd say.'

'Well, maybe that's what I mean. That's how it seems to me, to us, now. Looking back, we can see it that way. Just not at the time.'

Then I started to cry and I realised how much I'd been suppressing the sad underbelly of the happiness I'd been feeling since Dave and I got it together. I had looked up to Sandy; she had been a mother substitute, too. She had been my boss and, above all, she had been my friend.

'It's part of it, too; the sadness, I mean?'

She smiled, now entirely without tears. She got up to pour us both another glass of wine. I said:

'Shall I tell you something back, Sheila?'

'If you want to. If you're sure you want to.' She didn't want any information in exchange that I might later regret revealing.

I grinned.

'It's only a little secret. When Dave started going with Julie, I was pissed off. I thought I'd know when he was ready to start something new. I was waiting, you see. And I swore that if it didn't work out with her - well, I never thought it would though, sure, I wouldn't have wanted it to happen the way it did - so I swore that when they were finished, I wasn't going to take any more chances and I'd make my move so fast he wouldn't see me coming.' I blushed and used a Dave expression. 'As it were.'

She laughed.

'If you think that's a secret, you don't think much of the rest of us.'

'Was I that obvious?'

'Let's say,' she said with a twinkle in her eye: 'If you hadn't done it, I'd have given you a talking to.'

'You're pleased, aren't you, Sheila? You think it's alright, don't you?' There I went again, begging for her approval.

She smiled all the answers I need and said:

'Let's decide what we're going to do to the idiot when he gets back.'

* * *

'It's my fault,' I moaned at Natalie.

I was pissed as a newt. It was ten o'clock the next night, and I was at the club. I hadn't had a wink of sleep the night before. Around one in the morning, I'd made Sheila go to bed, swearing I wasn't at all worried, before I settled down with the telephone directory to call all the people who he might have gone to see, the office, and every police station and hospital between Islington and the club. I called a lot further than that, too; if he was more pissed than Natalie realised when he'd left, who knew in what direction he might have driven.

Funnily enough - or stupidly enough - it didn't occur to me during the night that he, too, might have been snatched by the people who had Tim. That didn't begin to dawn until Sheila got up in the morning and came downstairs to find me semi-comatose but still conscious on the sofa, an empty bottle of Frascati on the floor beside me and not the one we'd polished off before she went to bed. It was the look of sheer horror on her face when she realised Dave still hadn't come home that made the point I should have made for myself hours before. Damnit; I was supposed to be his fellow detective.

Once the thought had occurred, we had no doubt of it at all; thoughtless, selfish, pig-headed and drunk though he might be, there was no way he'd fail to make contact if he was at liberty to do so.

Sheila rang Millward, ostensibly to sound him out for news of his hunt for her husband, secondarily to tell him where he could reach her, casually to ask if he knew where Dave was at the moment. She left a message for Wadd to call. For myself, I went straight to the top and - not without some heavy duty Aussie aggro - managed to get put through to Dunlop, to whom, not without hesitation, I admitted what we feared. Unless he was a better actor than he was a policeman, the notion that someone somewhere might now have both our aces was news to him: he promised to pull in Gregory and to call back if the SB man had any info.

I also called Ted Farlowe at Number Ten, who voiced due concern, which seemed to me to reflect a great deal of indifference.

The media now had enough of the tale to allow the government to run both outstanding by-election campaigns on the basis of unfair intervention, probably by the Irish, despite a flat denial from Sinn Fein, the Provos and the Real IRA. Because it had gone public, there appeared to be little risk to the lives of the remaining marginal MPs, although, for appearance, a number had been afforded full-time, high profile police protection.

Wally did not ring but showed up halfway through the day. He did not draw the same conclusion that we had, of capture by Tim's snatchers.

'Why? What would they have to gain?'

'What do you mean?'

'We've worked on the assumption they originally took Tim to prevent him getting any closer to their operation, right?'

Sheila and I nodded in unison.

'But by last night, it had already been in the news how much was known. So what would they gain by snatching Dave, too?'

'He's not been mentioned,' I reminded him. 'They know he's involved - from their calls - so maybe they want to know just how much has been uncovered. I mean,' I knew I wasn't very coherent, 'whether the news have got it all. Which,' I reminded him, 'they haven't.'

All they knew was that it was now believed the dead MPs had been poisoned, and police were working on both the nature of the poison and the identity of the poisoner, within a general description that caught anyone with an Irish great-grandparent, any sympathy for the Irish cause or a set of Waterford crystal. They didn't have Leahy by name, nor anything about Gant's Gully and the American naval establishment, nor the death of Julie Somers in Baltimore or that of Annette Mallalieu here, nor the simultaneous disappearance of Oswald Chambers.

'It's possible,' he admitted. 'But if the game's over, why would they care? Their interest now'll be to get away with it.'

'Which you think is what they want with Tim? Protection? Bargaining chip?'

'Something like that. With Annette Mallalieu dead, Julie Somers dead, Helen Thornton dead, Steve Hilton dead, there can't be that many more loose ends to tie up. Until they are, though, Tim's bound to be valuable.'

'You wouldn't have thought it,' Sheila muttered. 'Not the way it's being handled.'

Wally said gently:

'They are doing their best, Sheila. If there isn't a lead, no amount of manpower can dig one up. There aren't enough policemen in the whole world to dig London up by its foundations, let alone anywhere else.'

'What do you think, then, Wally?' I didn't like the idea it was someone different; it was hard enough to think of finding one set of kidnappers, let alone two.

He shook his head slowly, like he had an idea but it wasn't yet fully formed.

'I don't know, Carson, I really don't. Listen,' he said, getting up. 'I need to get back to the Yard; I need to think.'

He meant he needed to think uncluttered by the combined emotions of two women. Any other time, I'd probably have made something of it, like teased him gently or torn off his goolies; right now, we were running out of allies.

* * *

By evening, I couldn't sit still. Sheila shooed me out of the house much as I had sent Dave on his way the night before, and

I used her car to go to the same place of first resort: Natalie at the club.

'It's my fault,' I said for the nineteenth time.

'It's not your fault,' Natalie said. 'Just because you suggested he come here...'

'No, that's not it, Nat.' I was crying openly and relieved she had insisted we talk - and I drink - in one of the corner booths reserved for lovers who did not want to be seen. She had been my best friend for the last five or more years, and it was not the first time I'd wept in her arms like a baby. 'It's because of what we've been doing, it's because I love him,' I hiccoughed.

'Ah, Cars, don't do this, you don't have to do this. It's not true, Carson, you know it's not,' she hushed.

'I don't, Nat, I don't know that. It's everyone, isn't it? Everyone I love dies.' I hiccoughed again and enumerated: 'My mother; my father; my uncle...'

It slipped out without my meaning to say it, and Natalie didn't miss it.

'Your uncle? Your uncle who...'

I covered my ears. I didn't want her to remind me; my uncle who I killed when, as the court heard, he went drunk-crazy and attacked my father, who couldn't defend himself; oh, yeah, that uncle. It was my deepest secret, and the one thing no one would understand; I had loved him; I had loved him more than anyone, more than my father.

She didn't press me; like I said, best friend. She put her arm around my neck and kissed me on the face, kissed away my tears.

'He's not dead, Carson; Dave's not dead.'

'I swear, Natalie, if I get him back alive, I'm going to break it off with him before it goes any further. You've got to understand, I loved Sandy, too.'

'You love me, Cars,' Nat whispered into my ear. 'And I'll take the risk. Dave loves you; don't say it, don't think it; it's not the choice he'd make.'

'But it's my choice,' I insisted. 'Isn't it? I mean, it's my choice that counts, isn't it?'

* * *

I got two calls at the club. One was from Wally, at around eleven o'clock, telling me he was coming to get me and to wait for him. He hung up before I could tell him about the other call, which had been from Sheila about an hour beforehand.

'You just had a call,' she said. 'Or perhaps we did, I'm not sure.' She was uncharacteristically obscure.

'Who from?' I asked, my drunken depression set immediately to one side.

'That man Farlowe.' The PM's PA.

'What did he want?'

'He wanted me to pass on a message to you from the Prime Minister - to tell you that Dave is no longer retained by them.'

'He told you that?' Leaving aside the spectacularly insensitive timing, it was an irregular way to convey such a singular piece of news. 'Did he know who you were?'

'I told him once I realised who he was. Was that wrong? He didn't seem surprised. I think he already knew I was staying here.' It wasn't impossible, or surprising; it was no secret from the police; they had to be told - just in case they accidentally stumbled across Tim.

'What did he say about Tim?'

'Quote, the Prime Minister has decided the matters of my husband and your employer are best handled by the proper authorities.'

'Not even would we like to pop in for a glass of sherry and will we be voting for them in the next General Election?'

'Not a cup of tea.'

'How did he sound?' I Dave said Farlowe had been keen to keep us on the case, even though the Prime Minister was not.

'Formal, business-like.' She picked up my meaning. 'I'd say he wasn't too happy with his boss' decision. He did hesitate at the end, as if he had something else to say.'

'And?'

'He said if we wanted to keep in touch with him, if we needed his help; well, he'd do what he could.'

'Great.' Maybe Farlowe was still with us, but what was Boller doing thinking for himself? I wished I had a number for Horace Black; I'd get one first thing tomorrow. 'What's this going to do to our relations with Dunlop?'

'I don't know. I imagine Millward will be pleased. Gregory's the one that counts. I've tried to reach Wally. He's not at the Yard; he's not at home.'

'I dunno,' I said listlessly, not specifically about where Wally might be, but about everything.

'Carson? Are you alright?'

'I'm alright, Sheila, I'm fine; I'm talking to Natalie. I'll be home soon.'

More famous last words; I was full of them.

Natalie had ordered food for me while I was on the phone to Sheila; also, she insisted I stick to spritzers, suspecting that my night's work was not over yet. Once Wally had rung, I was grateful. To kill time, I helped out behind the bar while she did a relief stint in the kitchen. The temporary cook hired from an agency was good, but stuck to the split-second of his rights. Mid-steak? The order might have been for rare, but if it wasn't ready by the time his break started he would have served it up afterwards, burned to a cinder and tougher than charcoal.

'What've you got?' I demanded as soon as Wally arrived.

'A parched throat,' he admitted.

I ignored a customer, filched a lager and led him and it back to my table. I even offered food but he said there wasn't time.

'Where're we going?'

'They've found Dave's car,' he said slowly, like it was the beginning not the end of the news-flash.

'Where?'

He looked sheepish.

'Almost outside Tim's house. It was there all day. No one noticed.'

So much for the police guard on the house.

I lowered my head into my hands. I wasn't sure if I wanted to cry or scream. I was going to break someone's head and do time for it.

'It's still there,' he said. 'I thought we should go and have a look before it's taken away. Maybe be there while SOCO is.'

'SOCO?'

'Scene of Crime Officers - CSI to you. Come on, I'll drive,' he offered, which was good news as I was well over the limit and didn't want to smash up Sheila's car.

'I'll be back for it, later, Nat,' I said confidently.

Like I said, full of 'em.

* * *

At that time of the night, in a cop car, it took less than twenty minutes to get to Tim's house. Wally hardly spoke. When I asked him if he'd found anything else out, he prevaricated.

'I'm not sure.'

However hard I pushed, he wouldn't elaborate. It was the same as that afternoon; it still wasn't sufficiently worked out. To tell me would be like exposing a negative too soon. For the time being, I let it go, but there was no way I was going to let him go that night without showing me a full set of prints, whatever they might reveal.

Because of the location, the media were there, notified I presumed for the usual reason, a tenner slipped into someone's sticky fingers. If any of them had the smarts to take down the number of the car about to be studied under portable spotlights, it wouldn't take them long to track down Dave's name. It depressed me. Dave never got into the papers; it was his trade-mark. If he did now, it was like he had to be dead. I think Wally sensed what I was thinking, because he took my hand and squeezed it tightly. I pulled it away fiercely.

'You're a married man,' I told him. 'And a sexist shit.'

He grinned, pleased to hear me near normal.

'What I want you to do is see if you can spot anything different that wouldn't be noticed by someone unfamiliar with the inside of the car. Okay?'

'I think I can just about manage that,' I snapped. 'I might even have thought of doing it without being told.'

Wally sought and obtained permission for me to search the car before it was pulled apart by the police, subject to the usual warning to be careful not to smudge any prints there might be. My own prints were already all over it. I climbed in and, without permission, shut the door. Wally looked surprised and reached down as if to climb in beside me. I used my elbow to push down the knob which activated central locking on all the doors. He shrugged and said something I couldn't hear to the forensic officer in charge. I could guess: 'Aussie witch' or something that rhymed.

It was only a day and a bit since Dave and I had been in the car together, coming back from the office. After I parked outside the house, he'd reached across me to stop me getting out. Then he'd kissed me, on the lips, open-mouthed, necking like a pair of teenagers. I couldn't get fully into it at the time; I felt too exposed, like everybody on the street was watching. Now I felt bad because I understood what he'd been saying: go back to the beginning, do it all the way it's supposed to be, like I'd told him to. Silly sod, how dare he let himself be taken away. If I wasn't so aware of Wally waiting outside the car, watching me, I could have cried. Instead, I slammed my fists against the steering wheel hard enough to snap it. The wheel shuddered but didn't break; nothing worked.

I went through the motions of examining the car for clues but knew I wasn't going to find any. Warily, while Wally was distracted and not watching, I reached round and beneath the driver's seat, where he kept the radio/cassette player when not in use, and extracted it. I didn't want to listen to music; it was what I might find behind it that concerned me. I breathed a sigh of relief: it wasn't there and there was where I didn't want it to be.

We were already turning Wally's car around to leave when something that had been troubling me unconsciously popped to the surface. I put my hand on his arm.

'Pull in.'

I slid out of the car and, Wally following, strode up the driveway to the Dowells' front door. I snorted and pointed it out to Wally.

'What were those policemen doing last night? Giving each other blow jobs?'

He groaned and shoved the door with his foot; it had been open just the barest crack, as if carelessly closed and - and it was this which made it certain that entry and exit had been unlawful - not double-locked. Unless, of course, he, she or it was still inside. I admit I was glad I had company. We exchanged a glance, then a grin; there were a dozen police outside. I said:

'Come on, cowboy, let's do it.'

There was no one still inside, but the house had been thoroughly searched and whoever it was hadn't bothered to cover their tracks. Unless they brought along their own upholsterer, they would have had a hard time putting it all back together, the damage they'd done to carpets, curtains and covered furniture. It was spooky, like the ghost of whoever it was had remained behind to haunt the house and make sure we couldn't forget the visitation.

We sat gloomily in the kitchen, sipping lager from bottles, not talking for a while, pondering breaking the news to Sheila, wondering just how much more was going to go wrong before... wondering when - and above all if - it was going to start going right. I said:

'Now you've got to tell me, Wally.'

He sighed.

'Yes, I suppose I have.' He paused to put his thoughts in order. 'There are some very strange things going on at the Yard. People in and out of the Commissioner's office. Dunlop summoned me, then left me waiting in the ante-room for hours while he paraded just about everyone else in the case in front of me. Leaving the door half-open so I could half-hear. A lot of talk about Americans, bloody Americans; some references to the

Prime Minister, not a lot more flattering; Millward gloating; Gooch ordered to let it go, let it go right away; Gregory looking pained when he arrived, white with anger when he left; raised voices, then sudden quiet.'

He paused again as if he wasn't quite sure he believed everything he was telling me he had heard.

'When Gregory was in there, he was shouting at the Commissioner, but Dunlop didn't get angry. Why did he want me to listen? I'm a DS, Carson, there's only one rung lower than me; I don't get to listen to rows between senior officers; hell, even Gregory doesn't get to see the Commissioner every day, every month or all things being equal every year. You could do your career as a Superintendent in Special Branch and never meet the Commissioner. He's God, and God wanted me to know something, without having told me.'

'What did he want to tell you?' I was irritated by his self-centred soul-searching. 'Come on, Wal, this matters.'

'I think,' he hesitated one last time. 'I think he wanted to give me an address.'

'An address of what?' I was no longer irritated, I was excited.

'I think... I think it's where Dave is.'

My jaw dropped off my face and landed on my feet.

'Do you know what you're saying?'

'I do,' he answered solemnly, like the preacher had just asked if he'd take me as his lawful wedded.

I spelled it out, more for myself than for him.

'You're telling me Dunlop knows where Dave is. But he isn't supposed to tell anyone?'

'Maybe not knows, but has a good idea, if I've got it right. I've been thinking about it ever since. It's the only thing that makes sense.'

Sense was the one thing it didn't make.

'He started talking about what he described as known locations. As I said, I couldn't hear all of it. Suddenly, he's spelling out an exact address, quite loudly, loud enough for me to hear. Then Gregory asks why they didn't just take it, and then a reference to possible immunity, which I took to mean diplomatic immunity. Then Gregory's voice was raised, almost shouting; the word resignation came up but it wasn't clear whether he was offering his or suggesting Dunlop's. I don't know. What you have to try and bear in mind is that when this all started, I didn't know it was a set-up. Oh lord, Carson, I still can't be certain.'

'Be certain,' I ordered. There was nothing else to go on.

'Alright. At the beginning, it isn't just that I couldn't hear and didn't know I was supposed to hear, but I was positively trying not to listen. You know, I'm a DS waiting to see the Commissioner, there are senior officers having a row, I'm not supposed to overhear or eavesdrop, it was automatic to try and not listen. You won't understand that, but...'

'I do, and it doesn't matter. When Tim gets back he can kick your teeth in. Just get on with it, Wally, before I do. What did the Commissioner tell you when he saw you?'

'Well, that's it,' he admitted, as sheepish as when he'd been forced to tell me the police guard on the Dowell's house had failed to notice Dave's car for a whole day. 'He didn't. The buzzer went and his secretary's yes sirring and no sirring and telling me the Commissioner's awfully sorry to have wasted my time - which is also suspicious because Commissioners live in order to waste people's time and never apologise for it - and he'll see me tomorrow, she'll ring and tell me what time.'

'Which means you got what out of it?'

'That the Commissioner's angry, that Gregory's angry, that Millward's happy...'

'And an address?'

'Yes. A known location,' he repeated.

'What does that mean?'

'I'm not positive. But they weren't talking about Hole in the Wall.' Where American wild-west bandits used to go hide and hang out.

'Not positive, no. But you're going to tell me what you think.' I confirmed my prophecy by gripping his wrist across the table and twisting it.

He told me.

'And I don't suppose you managed to remember where it was, by any chance? You know, just in case it happened to matter?'

He nodded sombrely.

'Oh, yes, I do. Would you, uh, happen to like to see it for yourself?'

'I was thinking, you know, if you don't think it's too awfully late to go visiting.'

'Trouble is, Carson, I'm not tooled. All I've got is this,' he said, and pulled back his jacket to reveal a blackjack, the plain-clothes man's traditional, if unsanctioned, substitute for the truncheon lawfully carried on the beat.

'Well, that's alright, then,' I said, about five million times more confidently than I felt. "Cos I am.'

* * *

The house was in Barnes, which is technically also in West London but a damn sight nicer than Ealing, way out of the centre of town, almost country. Wally's speculation - informed speculation - was that it was a safe-house belonging to the Americans, though he couldn't say whether CIA or some other agency. The conversations in the Commissioner's office he had been invited to overhear coincided with Wally's earlier belief that the Irish - or Leahy himself, or whoever had Tim - was not who held Dave.

Gooch was off the case. That didn't mean much; everyone knew by now that snort, smoke or shooting up weren't the game. Gregory was probably being told to cool off so far as Dave was concerned. Theoretically, he could have been told to cool off Tim, too, but I doubted either that Dunlop would give that order or that Gregory would accept it. A private eye's one thing; a colleague is another.

Millward was happy, which certainly matched his attitude to my bloke and boss. Also, we'd been sacked by the Prime Minister. It added up to a high-level conspiracy in which co-operation with the American authorities provided an obvious - probably the only - answer. Dave had been yielded up to them.

Wally's observation about not being armed told me that he didn't expect them to hand over Dave without some argument, even if only for form's sake. Neither of us expected to have to use the gun Gregory had provided me with, as he had also provided one for Dave which, as of when the man drove down to the club, lay behind the radio/cassette beneath the driver's seat of his car, but that wasn't there when I felt for it. I also found it significant that Wally did not try and relieve me of my weapon, if only to use it himself. He had have been a better marksman, and would have known it; I had no training at all; as a matter of fact, I had no relevant experience, though I'd hunted with my cousins as a kid and knew how to handle a rifle. I'd held a gun on someone during an earlier case, but it was Dave who had pulled the trigger.

We parked a couple of streets away and examined the road-map. There was a railway at the end of a row of parallel streets. Wally had Googled the address and confirmed that the house was at that end. We clambered up the embankment and over the other side, stumbling and cursing silently in the dark until, gingerly, we poked our heads back up it to find we were within sight of our target. It was two-thirty; whoever was in that house didn't go to bed early. There were lights on the first floor and in the solitary attic window. Though the temperature was not low, I was cold. Through chattering teeth, I asked him in a low whisper:

'How're we going to do it?'

He was as cold as I - or as nervous.

'Abscond, elope and forget we ever knew them?'

'On your pension? Forget it.'

There were really only three options. We could call for reinforcements, but it was already implicit that these would not be forthcoming, even if Wally could convince the night-watch at the local nick that he wasn't drunk and hadn't escaped from the funny farm. We could do a full frontal assault, with Wally in the forefront waving his warrant card. Or we could try and get clever.

They weren't expecting an invasion. They considered themselves secure and on friendly, protected terrain, with carte blanche to do their worst; we could bank on something less than an army on full alert. Accordingly, I was stationed at the back of the house, hand wrapped in my jacket to break a tiny pane of glass in the kitchen door as Wally banged on the front door, loud enough to wake the dead and - hopefully - to conceal the noise I would make. I waited until I could hear his voice raised at the front of the house, joined in argument with whoever had come to answer him, before I did it. Just beforehand, I saw the first floor lights go off. There were now no lights in the back of the house at all.

The kitchen door was bolted top and toe, but not otherwise secured. I pushed it almost shut behind me; we might be grateful for an easy exit. I could hear Wally at the front, still trying to argue his way inside. From where the kitchen opened onto the hallway, I could see no one in the corridor, while no one on or at the top of the stairs would be able to see me.

I tiptoed into Wally's line of vision until he could see me pointing the gun at the back of the man he was talking to. Wally's voice dropped to a low growl, and I could only just make him out ordering the man to turn around and lead him into the kitchen, explaining why it was in his interests to comply. I studied the man closely as he approached me, watching his eyes to see if they flickered in the direction of the stairs. Wally followed him equally carefully, stepping tentatively into sight of the stairs until he too was satisfied no one had him covered. They were too cocky by half, which confirmed Wally's theory. He shut the front door behind him, almost ran to catch up and, without another word of warning, hit our host with his cosh.

'Come on,' he hissed. 'He won't wake for a while.'

'I hope you're right,' I hissed back, less convinced than him but too scared to argue; all I wanted was to get this over with and get out as fast as we could.

Simultaneously, we heard a door shutting at the top of the house. Whatever the other or others had needed to do while the door was answered had been accomplished; a retreat from first floor to attic was my guess, as the first floor light came on again.

The risk was all Wally's. He strode purposefully into the corridor, holding his warrant card out in front of him like a cross to ward off evil, shouting:

'This is the police. Come down.'

I held my breath. If Wally was right about who had Dave, they were unlikely to open fire; if he was wrong, I was on my own with nothing but funerals in my future, one of them my own.

The silence was so loud I would have been able to hear his heart beating at three metres but for the noise of my own.

'What's the problem, officer?' an American asked, strolling down the stairs as if he had not a care in the world. 'Where's Bob?'

'Your friend is in the kitchen, sir. He said you would be able to produce documentation proving diplomatic immunity. Is that right, sir?'

'Sure.'

I could see his back now.

Wally lowered his hand and slipped the warrant card back into his jacket pocket.

'What's this about, officer? Why do we need to prove anything to you?'

'There've been complaints, sir.'

'Yes?'

Interestingly, at a distance, I'm not sure I would have been able to tell, without forewarning, whether he had an American accent or Irish; at the least, it had to be an American of Irish descent.

'Shouting, sir; and some screaming.'

'Not from here, officer. Besides,' he had to show off: 'Hardly the sort of matter that would interest a detective, is it? Boring beat-bobby business.'

Now I knew Dave was here; the guy was alliterating like someone who'd been listening to him for a lifetime.

I said:

'Put your hands above your head. I'm pointing a gun at you. I mean it.'

I was so convincing I could see Wally's hands twitch as if it was he who was the subject of my command. He said:

'I'd do as she says, sir. She's an amateur, and I'm sure you know what happens when nervous amateurs are holding guns. Oh, and, uh, yes, she has taken off the safety. I watched her do it myself.' His emphasis was intended to convey that he appreciated the victim's professional status.

Slowly, the man raised his arms. Wally cuffed and frisked him quickly and, I hoped, efficiently, as he emerged from the exercise without a gun of his own.

'Have you begun to wonder how you'll be able to talk your way out of this, Sergeant?'

'Well, I could always say she held the gun on me,' he proffered. 'But I'm thinking, sir, I'm not going to have to; I think there isn't going to be a complaint. Now, sir, I'm going to ask you to lead the way upstairs. It's the attic I'm interested in. If I'm right about who I think you are, and you can see who I am, there's no real reason for all of this to turn at all unpleasant, is there, sir?'

The man's failure to reply unnerved me. I think it unnerved Wally, too, because he reached back inside his jacket for the cosh and twirled it unpleasantly.

'Lead on, sir. Don't look around. One step at a time. One slow step at a time.'

As he turned, I stepped into position so that Wally was not left like a bulletproof buffer between us. The man took me in without a glimmer of expression.

As we approached the steps to the attic on the first floor landing, I noticed that the doors to most of the rooms were open. Not wide open, but carelessly ajar. I retreated to the top of the stairs which we had just mounted, switched off the landing light and hissed at our guest to move back towards me until I could grab the chain between the cuffs and jerk his hands roughly back behind his head. I heard him grunt but he made no effort to cry out. With my head, I signalled for Wally to check out the three open rooms. He shook his head as he emerged from the last of them, nodding in turn towards the one door that was shut. I held my breath as he turned the handle and swung inside, unable to fling the door back without risking too much noise, so dropping to his knees as he did so instead. He knelt there so long I was beginning to think someone must have a gun trained on him, but then he rose and stepped fully back into my view, his face grey and grim.

I pushed the man along the landing until we were outside the now open door. Wally grabbed him by the neck and flung him onto the floor inside, following him into the room and kicking him in the head before I could see why. He must have known more about what he was doing than I had appreciated, because the man made no sound at all other than that of his body as it fell; he was out as cold as the one in the kitchen. While I studied what had turned Wally's blood, Wally made sure of the job by an apparently casual, but well-placed, additional blow with the blackjack to the man's head.

'Any ideas?' he whispered.

I was too numb to speak. Remembering where we were, I turned around so as to watch the door behind us, and the landing outside, though I had not heard any sound emerging from above. I gritted my teeth as I told him, as noiselessly as I could manage.

'It's Siobhan. Siobhan Cunningham.' It had been Siobhan. Her face was bloody and bruised. It was unclear how she had died. There was no visible bullet wound. Nor any sign of any perversions.

He drew in his breath sharply.

'Bastards.'

I knew what he meant. These people believed they could kill anyone and get away with it. They were right. Everything that had happened that day said so. I hissed:

'I'm going first, Wal.'

He shook his head.

'Not now, Carson. I don't care anymore.' Meaning he didn't care if he was caught carrying an unauthorised firearm, in a house without a warrant, with a companion whose status was as dubious as it was difficult to justify.

I taunted him:

'Take it from me.'

He didn't try. I walked around him, keeping him at a distance, the gun pointing at him. With the blackjack dangling loosely from one finger, he held up his hands, but with a wry grin on his face that said he understood.

'Be careful, Carson.'

'They better be,' I muttered as I slid back onto the landing, slipped out of my shoes, and began the slow climb up the attic steps, treading only at the edges so the boards didn't creak, ninety percent of my sight on the door at the top, ten percent making sure Wally didn't try and come after me too soon.

From outside, I couldn't hear a sound.

I took a deep breath.

It did nothing to slow down the rate of my heart-beat.

I placed a hand on the knob.

As I did so, the door flung open, almost taking me with it.

There were two more men inside. Both of them had guns on me.

'Put that down, girlie,' said the one nearest to me.

If for no other reason, he was dead meat for the 'girlie'.

Dave lay on the floor of a room lined with computer, televisual and radio equipment, his face more bloody and bruised than Siobhan's. His half-open, vacant eyes met mine. Unseen by his captors, whose attention was focused on yours truly, he reached behind his back, down into his trousers, and emerged holding the gun Gregory had given him. He croaked:

'You put it down.'

The other man swung his gun on Dave as I screamed:

'Don't do it.'

Dave screamed:

'Don't do it.'

From the stairs, Wally screamed:

'Don't do it,' distracting them as much as me.

Then it was nothing but noise.

CHAPTER ELEVEN

Then it was nothing but noise.

It wasn't noise to begin with: more like chilled silence as the car drove away from the club, me on the floor wishing I kept the car cleaner and that Siobhan wasn't wearing high heels, one of which was sticking in my calf. Whose side was she on?

These weren't my only worries; it took me a while to feel easy about the steel sticking into my neck.

From the changed quality of light outside the car, I could tell when we left the centre of town. The front-seat Mick said, still sotto voce:

'Search him.'

Back-seat Paddy sneered:

'They don't carry.'

'Search him,' repeated the driver.

'Here we go,' my guard muttered. 'Enjoy.'

Everyone was a joker.

'I'd prefer it if she did it,' I whispered back.

He ran his hands over and under me quickly and at the last whopped my backside almost affectionately.

'He's clean.'

After that, he didn't bother replacing the gun barrel at my neck. I was grateful for small mercies.

The car came off the motorway and hit a roundabout: it didn't slow down. It took the roundabout somewhere in the fifties, and several times over; it was worse than being at the fairground. During the third or fourth time they played this trick - to confuse me as to where we were headed - I managed to get my hand behind the radio/CD player beneath the driver's seat, where I stored both music and muscle while away from the car.

Now all I had to do was find a place to stash it and hope they didn't decide to search me anew. Recalling Paddy's closing bit of slap and tickle, waiting until his attention had wandered, I slid it awkwardly through the front of my pants and around until it was all but buggering me. I prayed I hadn't knocked the safety off. I thanked God that what Gregory had liberated for me from the unofficial armoury to which all experienced senior detectives have unrecorded access was small: a Smith & Wesson Combat Masterpiece with a four-inch barrel. Imagine if he'd given me the model with an 8.38 inch barrel.

* * *

They threw blankets over our heads to take us inside. They were dirty blankets and stank, so I only caught a quick whiff of the river in time to recognise the recycled sewage, untreated waste and illegal dumping that is the Thames' special contribution to nasal history. I heard one thud, a curse, another thud and then a new voice say:

'Pick her up; carry her in.'

During the early exchanges in the car, I had reviewed my assumption about the Irish extraction of my captors: use of the word 'enjoy' seemed more American than Eireann, though I knew that many IRA activists either came from, or had spent time hiding out in, the States; the truth is, I've always had a hard time distinguishing between some Irish and American accents. The new voice was even less clearly accented than that of the driver, or of my bum-buddy from the back seat.

I was led and, I guessed, Siobhan was carried, up to the first floor. I heard yet another thud as they tossed her into one room and shoved me hard into another. My gun nearly got its rocks off. I lay on the floor unmoving as someone whipped away the blanket. The first thing I noticed was that the room was completely unfurnished save for a single upright chair, but that the walls were lined with egg-shell sound-proofing and the windows were double-glazed.

I stared up at a new friend. He did not trouble to hide his face. He looked nothing like the description I had been given of Joe Leahy. He said softly:

'You're very welcome, Mr Woolf.'

'Call me Dave,' I suggested, not entirely for humour's sake. I didn't like the canned respect comprised in the use of my surname. Cans get tossed out. Sometimes, they get crushed first. I was, as all the How To Be A Good Hostage books say to do, trying to strike up a relationship.

He smiled and kicked me in the balls.

I screamed: it hurt. It hurt a lot more than he realised because the tip of his boot caught the edge of the gun handle. For a few moments, I lost the power to breathe. I remembered what Tim had done when I had similarly assaulted the parts that, as the

Heineken advertisements would put it, other beers cannot reach. I drew breath fast and shallow and tried like hell to remember the mantra Karen and I had chanted for her son Abey, until the pain had passed.

I remembered something else it is sensible to do in such situations: I didn't laugh or make any more wisecracks. Instead, I asked:

'What happened to her?'

He tossed his head in the direction of the door, to ask if I meant Siobhan. I nodded. He shrugged.

'She passed out in the car. Fell when they were bringing her in.'

'And one of your thugs kicked her when she was down? Nice.'

He knelt down beside me and whispered in my ear.

'Not as nice as what will happen to her if you don't start talking.'

'You haven't told me what you want to know,' I protested, suppressing the desire to add, childlike, 'no fair'.

He sighed and got back to his feet. It wouldn't have troubled me so much if he hadn't at the same time taken a firm grip on my ear and hauled me up with him by it. I was getting fed up with being treated like a sack of potatoes. I swung out with one arm. I don't know what kind of martial art he used, but the next I knew I was lying face down on the ground, my arm beneath his knees, chewing carpet. Yet when he arose the next time, he lifted me gently and guided me across the corridor to take a look at Siobhan.

They hadn't tied her up. There was no need. She was barely conscious and in less of a mood for a fight than I. This room was also hardly furnished and equally well sound-proofed, though there were three chairs instead of the one in mine. Two men were guarding her. One of them was from the car, but the other was a new face. They were making no further efforts to conceal themselves. I knew it augured ill. As Wally had said of Tim: if they let you see their faces, they aren't doing it so you can pick them out in a line-up.

My handler - the boss - said:

'Wake her up.'

Siobhan was shaken roughly. There was a look of resignation on her face, like she knew what to expect and, maybe, no longer cared. Our eyes met mutely. I wanted to remind her about Declan, her son, their son; that she should fight on for his sake. I couldn't find the words. She watched indifferently as my man took a single step across the room to where she lay on the floor, leaned down, pulled her into an upright sitting position by her hair with one hand and drove the other straight into her mouth. She didn't even scream or cry out, just fell back, blessedly unconscious once again.

I said, dryly:

'I think I have your point. If you'd tell me what you want to know, I could answer your questions and then perhaps the lady and I could call for a cab.'

My man smiled.

'I heard that about you, Mr Woolf. It's very British: humour in adversity.'

I corrected him.

'It's your tradition; read Marlowe; read Spenser.'

He ignored my verbal trap.

'But you don't consider yourself British, do you, Mr Woolf. Jewish, and vain about it.'

'I gotta be vain about something,' I mumbled. 'I could hardly brag about my good looks.'

Especially not when they were about to be re-arranged.

Suddenly, he snapped:

'Where's Chambers?'

I made one, final, half-assed effort.

'You want a dictionary already?' Another way of confirming what I knew about his nationality: only an American or someone of superior education would make the connection, and I didn't think he was the latter.

One of the others hit me from behind. I collapsed onto the floor, trying not to land in a way that would send the barrel of the gun up my backside.

Then they decided to get really funny. They danced around me, kicking me in turn as I curled into a foetal position to protect my face and my favourites. I did a lousy job on each.

'I asked, where's Chambers?'

'How the hell should I know?'

Foot in eye.

'Where's Chambers?'

'I don't know,' I screamed.

Foot in face.

'Where's Chambers?'

'I don't know, I don't know,' I sobbed.

Foot in mouth.

'Where's Chambers?'

'I don't know.' I blacked out.

* * *

That is what I remember from what was left of the first night.

What I remember from when I awoke was that Siobhan lay unmoving against the opposite wall, and that I was seated upright, handcuffed to a metal chair that was bolted to the floor. It seemed they were more afraid of me than of her, though I couldn't imagine why.

Siobhan was watching me.

I said:

'Are you alright?'

She nodded almost imperceptibly.

I asked:

'Where did they get you?'

She mouthed 'Belfast'.

'Do you know who they are?' I whispered, taking my lead from her.

She shook her head. Then she added:

'Not Irish.'

'No,' I said, almost sadly. I had worked it out for myself and twice confirmed it. I hadn't yet worked out, though, why they had gone to such effort to make me think they might be. For the second time, I thought how much had changed: just as I was no longer surprised by poison as a weapon, nor was I surprised at the notion of Western governments - US, UK or otherwise - engaging in torture, cruelty, outright contempt for any of what used to be the basic rules of a civilised society, with a complete disregard for human life. That was what had changed: along with greed is good in the City, winning was all in government.

The door opened and two of them - my chauffeur and the second member of the home guard - entered. I suppressed a groan at the thought of what they might be about to do with me but, to my relief, they had no more immediate intent than to unshackle me. I was lifted - not especially violently - to my feet and led back across the corridor to the room in which I had first been placed, where the boss-man again sat, straddling the solitary chair. I was tossed through the door and needed no help to collapse at his feet. He rolled me away from him like a dry cow-pat. He asked:

'Where's Chambers?'

I shook my head, bemused: if they couldn't find him, how the hell did they expect me to do so?

I heard a thwack from the other room. This time, Siobhan did cry out. I said:

'She has a weak heart, you know.'

'I didn't, but it doesn't matter.' He wasn't trying to maintain the Irish cover by now. Possibly he had heard the exchange before they came to fetch me; probably, he no longer cared if I knew.

'Do you really, really think you can do this - here - and just walk away from it?' I was genuinely curious: at the time, I did not know either of my dismissal by the Prime Minister or that Dunlop had been ordered to let them do whatever they wanted with me.

He shrugged philosophically.

'Don't know; don't care.'

'Why the violence, then? For God's sake, you people can be more sophisticated than this.'

'As I say, I don't know. I could guess, but I don't know.'

I waited for him to tell me, though I was halfway there on my own.

He said:

'I think it might be something to do with the state they want the bodies found in.'

'Hers too?'

He confirmed:

'Hers too.'

Our bodies found together and beaten bloody beforehand would be all the evidence the court of press attention would need to convict the IRA and support the Prime Minister's by-election sympathy strategy.

'I don't know where Chambers is,' I assured him. 'I really don't.'

He sighed.

'Maybe. Maybe not. It's not up to me. The way it's been read to me, you were close to the Somers girl, she was close to Chambers…'

'But you had Chambers in Baltimore,' I probed. 'Why'd you let him get away?'

'No one thought he'd walk.'

'Why'd he do it, then?'

'That's what we call the sixty thousand…' He paused, then beamed ahead of his own witticism. 'The sixty thousand euro question.'

'How long are you going to keep this up?'

He asked:

'Where's Chambers?'

This time, there was no cry from next door. Instead came a high-pitched, long drawn-out whimper which ended with a second blow and silence.

* * *

By nightfall, I didn't think for a moment they cared whether or not I knew where Chambers was. I hardly thought at all. It felt like I had no bones left: it didn't hurt when they hit me anymore; it didn't even hurt me when they hit her. All I knew was that they wanted me dead come what may: they could afford no loose ends.

Siobhan died just before ten o'clock. One of them came in and gave my interrogator a look that said it all. I know the time because shortly after was when they went down to watch the news on television. I'm not sure how much impact it made on me. I know I tried to remember the words to the kaddish and couldn't; instead, I said the only Hebrew prayer I knew, which is the one said before dinner on a Friday night before sipping the excessively sweet Passover wine - Palwin - that came from Israel. I wasn't making sense anymore.

Sometime during the late afternoon, the questions changed direction. They started asking how I knew how the drug worked. I should have kept my mouth shut in Baltimore instead of bragging how I'd worked out about the alcohol and the effect on hair. Since none of their side had spotted it, they wouldn't believe I could have done so without knowing something extra, something undisclosed.

I repeated how well I had known Margot, how much of a deductive advantage that gave me. By the time I finished, it was like it was her I had lived with rather than Sandy. By the time they finished, I couldn't remember what Sandy looked like, or Carson. And who the hell was this Tim Dowell they kept referring to?

* * *

Then there was banging at the door. They tried to conceal their panic. The leader went across the corridor and returned to say:

'Just one man. Bob, go see.'

'What am I supposed to do with him, Dick?'

For a moment, I thought I had a name for my tormentor. I wondered how many Dicks there were employed by his outfit, and then remembered they were all called Dick, except the ones called Bob. They weren't using real names. Dick said:

'Get rid of him. No fuss, no argument.'

'But...'

'Bob,' he said patiently. 'There's no problem here. We're covered.'

Bob didn't look convinced but complied with his instructions. Dick told the other two to carry me upstairs, out of the way. I hadn't known there was any more to the house. The light in the attic was already on. The room was where they kept their communications equipment. This was the command centre.

What followed for me was the long silence. I could hear nothing of what was going on downstairs. I presumed the attic was also sound-proofed, perhaps more so than the rooms below, because the door itself was more solid. They must have been used to it, because at a certain point they exchanged a knowing glance and one of them stood by the door with a gun in one hand and the other on the knob, while his partner kept him covered from across the room. The next I knew, Carson was half-falling into the room, barely keeping her balance.

Idiotically, my first thought was that she wasn't wearing any shoes, and only secondarily that she was armed.

'Put that down, girlie,' said the one nearest to her.

I could imagine Carson's reaction to 'girlie': I almost felt sorry for him.

While their attention was focused on Carson, I reached behind my back, into my trousers, and emerged holding Gregory's now less than fragrant Combat Masterpiece. I croaked:

'You put it down.'

The other man swung his gun on me as Carson screamed:

'Don't do it.'

I screamed:

'Don't do it.'

From the stairs, a voice - Wally - screamed:

'Don't do it,' distracting them as much as us.

Then it was nothing but noise.

* * *

'Jesus,' Wally said as he studied the room. 'Take it easy, take it easy, both of you.'

Both men were dead. I had half-risen. I don't think either Carson or I knew what we were doing any more. We had swung our guns on each other, automatically, only slowly registering who we were pointing them at, unable to stop ourselves. Our eyes held, our guns held, we were frozen in a moment so intense there was no way to think either of us could survive it.

Wally stepped carefully forward, reaching out gently for her gun first, then mine, pocketing them as she and I came down off the identity-warp. She let out a sob and grabbed me and kissed me all over my face so hard it hurt like hell, crying:

'Hurt you, hurt you, hate you, hate you, love you, damn you, damn you, damn you, love you.'

I hugged her as hard as I could, which wasn't very. Wally waited to make sure we were alright before he picked up the men's weapons and went back downstairs where, though I didn't yet know it, the remaining pair of deuces lay face down and unplayed. We held each other for a while longer. She said:

'Siobhan... She's...'

'I know. I told them: she had a weak heart.'

'What the fuck were they playing at?'

'We'll have to find that out. But I wasn't supposed to walk away from it, nor Siobhan, and the IRA were going to carry the can.'

She sniffled.

'Carry the can? They'd probably give them a medal.'

'You would, huh?'

'Right.' She grinned. 'Wrong. Hey.' She hugged me again and whispered in my ear that she loved me even if she hated me which was fine by me.

We followed Wally down. Both the other men were in what I had come to view as 'my' room, the one I'd spent the day and evening in, into which I'd first been tossed, rather than the one in which I'd spent a less than romantic night with Siobhan. They were both still in a stage of recovering consciousness. Wally was covering them, grinning like an idiot. I asked him what was so funny. Once he was sure they could understand him, he explained.

'You know all those rules about how we have to handle a villain? Like five minutes interrogation and five hours television, hot food and drinks to order, would they like a visit from the girlfriend?'

I had the idea.

'You're a lawyer, Dave, you tell me why those rules apply?'

I frowned: I was entitled to be a little crazy; not he.

He answered his own question.

'See, it's because a confession extracted by duress, well, a court can't rely on it, can they?'

'Right, Wally,' I said reassuringly. Like I said, he still had our guns.

'So,' he said proudly, as if he'd just worked out the solution to a serious problem. 'There isn't going to be a court, is there? Not this time. So…'

He offered us each our own weapons back, which we took from him eagerly, regretting that he hung onto those he had taken from upstairs. Then he got down to business. I don't have to admit it, but I'm going to: I relished every bloody, bone-breaking moment of it.

* * *

I stopped him before he killed them or put them out again for the count. I wanted to talk with them first. I acted like it was an effort to restrain him, but the whole time I could see into his eyes and I knew there wasn't a second he was out of control. He knew what he was doing, which is why they were still conscious at all. I said:

'Go downstairs, Wally. Take Carson with you.'

Carson shook her head.

'Just Wally.'

I shrugged: I'd had a rough thirty hours; I was ready to handle these two, but I wasn't up to an argument with Carson. Without argument, Wally went.

I pointed to Dick.

'He's number one, Cars. He did this to me.' I pointed with the barrel of my gun at my face, parts of it turning black, most of it swollen so bad I doubted if we found Tim he'd want to kiss me.

She stood over the cowering American and smiled pleasantly.

'You think I'm going to hit you, don't you?'

He nodded almost imperceptibly.

She said sweetly:

'I'm not. I'm going to kill you. Him,' she tossed her head in my direction, 'he's going to hit you. He's going to hit you until you ask me to kill you. Do you get it?'

His eyes wandered loose and unfocused from her to me, looking for confirmation. I shrugged.

'I dunno, Dick. That's an I dunno about the kill bit, you know.' I kicked him in the balls the way he'd kicked me to get acquainted. 'She's right about the hit, though,' I added conversationally.

He didn't appear to be listening.

I knelt down beside him and - once he had finished writhing - whispered in his ear, the way he'd done in mine.

'We've got some unfinished business, Dick. Let's start with where we are.' I held up a hand. 'I don't mean the address; Carson got here, she's probably got some idea. Who owns this house?'

Between gritted teeth, he answered without any delay.

'CIA.'

'You're CIA.' It's what I had assumed.

'No. Borrowed. ONI.' He saw the blank look on my face and elaborated. 'Office of Naval Intelligence.'

It was probably true; if he was walking at all, it'd be bow-legged for a while.

'Why'd you use it?'

'Untouchable,' he mumbled. 'Agreement.'

'Alsatia,' I nodded understandingly.

Everyone looked bemused.

'Means Wal was right.' I said cheerfully.

Since that didn't seem sufficient elucidation, I elaborated.

'Where the King's writ runs not. There used to be these areas of sanctuary, for criminals, until the end of the 17th century. Alsatia was Whitefriars, between Fleet Street and the Thames, fittingly enough next to where the Inns of Court are now. Well, Inner and Middle Temple. 'Course,' I added informatively, 'most of it belongs to KPMG now.' The accountants and management consultants.

'Dave,' Carson said gently, meaning she feared for my sanity and ability to concentrate on the job in hand.

'All I'm saying is, there's no law here. Like Wally said. Like you said.' I referred to her threat to Dick.

All the time, Bob was watching. He thought we'd forgotten him. I could see him out of the corner of an eye, surveilling the terrain, preparing his move. I pointed the gun at him and said:

'Bang bang. I mean it.'

'Look,' Dick said urgently. 'We know less than you.'

'Doubt that,' Carson quipped. 'He's ignorant as a pig.'

Mistaking the nature of our banter, Bob half-rose. I shot him in the arm. He screamed once and blacked out. The blood drained out of Dick's face as fast as it was running from Bob's arm. He said:

'You're crazy. You'll never get away with this.'

'Now where've I heard that before? Start talking, Dick.'

'What do you want to know?'

Total reversal.

To give him credit, he got the point and summoned a wry smile.

'Then maybe Bob and I can catch a cab to the nearest hospital?'

'Your brief changed during the day. You started off thinking I knew where Chambers was. Who told you I knew?'

'Washington.'

'Name?'

'I don't have a name. Chinese walls.' The operation was being run from discrete boxes: somewhere up the line, someone would be able to identify who or what was piling them in the right order to get a result, but not a lowly prick like Dick.

'Why did your instructions change?'

'I don't know. They didn't tell me.'

'When did you know you were going to kill me?'

He didn't equivocate.

'From the beginning.'

Bob groaned behind me. I didn't know if it meant he had been awake for a while and despaired at Dick's answer, or if it was just because he had awoken to find his arm in agony. I didn't care: anything Dick didn't know, Bob wouldn't.

Carson asked:

'Why'd you search the Dowell house?'

Though it was the first I'd heard of this, it came as no surprise. I saved Dick the trouble of answering.

'To see how much he'd found out before he was taken.'

She said:

'It's going to get light soon, Dave.'

'Right.'

Dick looked confused. I explained.

'We wouldn't want to be seen leaving.'

His eyes met mine.

'You're serious, aren't you?'

'Gotta be, don't I? Like you said, we'll never get away with it otherwise. Same as it was for you, really. Same story, no?'

The mad-dog Irish were to be presumed to have killed me and Siobhan, why not them instead?

'Dowell. Do you know where he is?'

He shook his head.

I tried to recall his exact questions from the day before. It was difficult. Just snatches. I said:

'You've got an idea?'

He mumbled:

'Maybe.'

'Where?'

His eyes met mine again, as if to confirm his earlier instinct about my intentions. I repeated my question. He said:

'North East. We were told - that's what happened during the day - we were supposed to go to the North East next.'

'Why?'

'Meet up.'

'Where?' I pressed my point and my gun at his forehead.

'Cramlington New Town.' It sounded like Cramla-Motown. 'Newcastle, North of Newcastle,' he gave up any show of resistance.

I shook my head in amazement. How the hell did Newcastle get into it? Where the hell was Newcastle? Why was Newcastle? Whoever went to Newcastle?

'He wouldn't've lived, would he?'

This time, when his eyes met mine, it was to make the candid admission that Tim Dowell was no more intended to come out of this alive than I was.

* * *

I sent Carson to wait on the stairs. Two shots later, we joined Wally in the kitchen. He was drinking tea. He offered us some. I asked:

'Is there nothing better?'

He said:

'In the car.'

We waited for him to ask. He didn't.

I said:

'They were going to kill Tim, Wally. They were going North - Newcastle, some place outside Newcastle called Cramlington New Town - to find him and kill him. They know where he is.'

I looked to Carson for support. She was uncharacteristically silent, so I continued.

'Remember, we already killed two of them.'

He said dully:

'I didn't ask.'

'Didn't you, Wal?' I snarled: 'Didn't you?'

He said something to me that he'd said before:

'I'm a policeman, Dave. Just a policeman.'

Carson awoke from her reverie.

'Yeah, right, really. The Americans - the American government - know where Tim is and are going in there to kill him, and what are the British police doing about it? Nothing. Sweet Fanny Adams. The Prime Minister - that arsehole - has made a deal. Why? What?'

I said:

'When he has to call a General Election, the Americans will help him out.' It couldn't be overt, by convention, but they could nonetheless make damn sure everyone knew where they stood.

They both goggled in amazement: the American President was well known to favour a return to the former administration. The current gaggle had kicked more than half his nuclear arsenal off British soil. Far worse, the financial regulations they had introduced effectively limited American ownership of our heritage to marginally less than the whole of its national worth.

'It's the only thing that makes any sense.'

Wally asked:

'The drug itself? No one wants it found?'

'Wrong. Everyone wants it. But they all want to be the only one; it's only if they're the only ones that it's got any value. No, I'd say that was the best trade Boller could get. Finding the drug first, for the British, wouldn't do anything for his electoral chances. He could hardly go public as a major coup for the administration. But the Americans want it badly enough to help Boller stay in a while longer.'

'Why kill Tim?' Carson asked.

'Why kill me?' I countered. 'They want everyone out of the way who knows about it or might know about it. Tim was too close for anyone ever to be sure how much he would have picked up; I was too close to Julie Somers, who clearly did know enough; Chambers, of course, is the vital target. And that's just the roll-call of the innocent.'

'Where's Chambers at?'

'My guess?' I reminded them I didn't know any of it for sure. But I didn't wait for them to nod before I went on. 'I think he's straight. I think once he realised what Steve Hilton had done, he felt guilty about it; he'd created a monster. I don't think he'd figure on being able to destroy it - though maybe that was what he was trying at the time he persuaded the Americans not to make a deal with Hilton, so as to leave him in jail. I'd say he got what he wanted from Julie's autopsy and did a runner to give himself time to work out a way of dealing with the problem, before he handed in the results.'

'There'd be plenty of time afterwards, wouldn't there?' Carson said.

For once, Wally was ahead of her.

'No. That's the point. He knew there wouldn't be.'

They'd kill him too.

* * *

Wally drove us home without another word about the bodies we'd left behind. But he wouldn't come in with us and wouldn't tell us what he planned to do.

I held out my hand, palm upwards:

'For Tim,' once we found him.

He hesitated, then yielded up one of the captured guns.

I thought he was going to give me some kind of lecture about it, but all he said before driving off was:

'Talk to you later.'

Within a short while, I was pretty glad he planned to talk to me later: at least someone would be talking to me; Carson wasn't.

From the moment we stepped into the house, the atmosphere was frigid. It wasn't quite true she wouldn't speak to me: she told me she was going down the road - where Sheila had left a note to say we could find her - and that she would sleep there, but she wouldn't tell me why. I reached out to hug her but she jerked away before I could touch her. I protested:

'You're acting like I raped you, Carson.'

Her eyes looked like she wanted to answer 'Didn't you?' But she just shrugged and left the house without another word. I was still puzzling over what had happened to change her between my recovery and our return when I climbed out of the bath and slid under the duvet to grab a few minutes' shut eye. I was still puzzling over it when I awoke six hours later.

I hit the phone before I finished swallowing paracetamol and downing my coffee. I was no longer concerned who might be tapping my line. It made no difference. The hell with Tim having disappeared; it seemed like everyone else had done so too. Wally was 'out of the office' and Dunlop 'out of town'. Gregory was 'on leave'. Millward didn't have time to speak to me. On the political front, Boller was no longer 'available' to me; Carson had told me

I was fired. Farlowe was the only one willing to talk to me and interested in what I knew, but he didn't even commit himself to passing it on to Boller, though he admitted he would be seeing him soon. So far as the Americans were concerned, Newport PD might as well never have heard of de Vries, nor Baltimore of an officer called Carmen Lovell.

By the time I finished trying, Carson returned. She said Sheila would be over in a while but wouldn't discuss the reasons for her earlier abandonment of me, nor talk about anything other than the case.

'Here's what I've found out. Cramlington is a New Town, north of Newcastle; not far north, maybe ten miles; it's in Northumberland. There's a lot of Irish in that part of the world. Also, most of Northumberland is owned by the Ridley family.'

It took me a moment to register who she meant: a cabinet minister a government or ten back.

'So?'

'So, when he was in government, a lot of his pals used to go up to see him, shoot a few peasants or pheasants or whatever it is they shoot up there...'

'And?' She could take the devil's time to get to the point.

'And they used to stay in a place called Seaton Burn - not even a village, a collection of farms – in a hotel called Horton Grange.' I yawned: I was tired as well as bored. 'And the way all these politicians pal up together, it seems it became quite a popular haunt for politicians of all colours.'

'Including members of the present administration?'

'Exactly. It's convenient; well-known to the security people; they're comfortable with it. It's handy not to have to work out all the systems over again each time a politician wants a weekend away, the staff are all well-cleared, everyone knows everyone else. Supposed to be pretty good, too, 'specially the food.'

'Where'd you get all this from?'

'Friend on a paper.'

'What else?'

'It's a convenient place to stay during a campaign in the North East.'

'Where Margot McAllister had her constituency?'

'Right. And where the hardest fought by-election campaign of this Parliament is coincidentally about to take place. To be precise, tomorrow.'

She had already made the plane reservations for us.

CHAPTER TWELVE

'You see, it really started before your election, Boller. In fact, it had very little to do with you at all.'

It was the most hurtful thing that could be said of and to any politician. Then I said the second.

'It was all about money. All and only. Isn't it always?'

* * *

'You took your time,' Tim grumbled once I had loosened his gag sufficiently.

'And you're going to pay for every hour of it I can remember, and a few I can't,' I hissed.

'Ouch,' he bit his lower lip.

It was not the prospective payment that pained him. He had been tied so tight his wrists were raw and scabbed from previous occasions when knots had been reworked. The nylon rope had to be torn from his skin. He was frighteningly thin. There were no more smartass wisecracks before I helped him - hauled him - to his feet.

He smiled weakly.

'I don't suppose you...'

I extracted a hip flask from my jacket.

'Easy now, Tim, easy.'

It was usually the other way round; I could think of at least twice when he had brought me around the same way and given me the same caution, which naturally I had ignored. Tim wasn't me: he took only a tiny sip. I finished the flask.

We were in the garage of Joe Leahy's house in Cramlington. It was a modern suburban close, where the houses and the front lawns were laid out with military precision, speed-humps kept cars in first gear, children could play in the roads in safety and there wasn't a public sector housing development in sight.

It was hard to think of a more suitable hideout for an Irish terrorist: Joe Leahy had style. It confirmed Wally's rumour that Leahy also did contract hits: the house represented a lot of money to leave lying around for occasional use. I wondered what story his neighbours had been given: travelling salesman; area manager for some large enterprise - perhaps some civil service-style organisation too big for anyone ever to check up on; maybe he stashed a wife - even children - here.

'What's out there?' Tim nodded vaguely in the direction of the door, the street, the world.

'The gauntlet, at an educated guess,' I replied grimly.

He squeezed his eyes shut as if it was difficult to concentrate, then sighed heavily.

'Them or us?'

'Them and them and us and us and Uncle Tom Cobley too for all I know.'

He gripped my arm for support.

'Did you...'

From the other pocket of my jacket I extracted the gun Wally had given me for him, a Ruger Bisley Single Action, standard .32 mag. As he hefted it in his hand, I showed him my own. He said:

'Both American guns, huh? Appropriate?'

'Right, that's one of the us-es.'

'They responsible for re-arranging your face?'

'Yup.'

'Who's the other us?'

'Some of our own spooks.'

'Fits. Figures. Them being Leahy and his allies,' which he knew because that was who had detained him. 'And?'

'How much do you know?'

'Some. They have loose mouths. And, uh, I don't really think they planned on sending me home gift-wrapped for my birthday.' He gripped my arm again. 'They're alright?'

'They're all fine. The kids are with Mary. Alton's at Jada's. Sheila's sort of there and at the house.'

'Carson?'

'With me,' I said, meaning a lot of different things, not all of which I was sure about.

'Listen, you know I'll never say it again, not when there's anyone to hear, anyway, but thanks, okay?'

I shrugged.

'I'd do it for a pig.'

He snorted.

* * *

By the time Carson and I arrived, we were too late to contact Boller. We rented a car at the airport and checked into the Holiday Inn, same as Julie Somers. Single rooms. Straight to bed. I was still catching up from the previous twenty-four hours, not just physically, but emotionally. I slept deeply but badly, reliving too much of it.

I told her to go, to get out. She hesitated. She wanted to be with me, but she didn't want to be what that entailed. I hissed:

'Do it, Carson, go on, wait outside.'

She rose slowly, awkwardly, still keeping her eye and gun on the bleeding Bob. Neither of them sought again to use the momentary division between us. They were too far gone. She backed out of the door, pulling it shut behind her. I couldn't hear any more movement in the hall. She was doing as I'd told her, waiting before going down to Wally.

'I ought to hate you,' I said conversationally. 'I can't figure out why I don't. You were going to kill me; you were going to kill Tim; you killed Siobhan. Did you kill Brendan, too?'

Dick's eyes told me 'no', but he still couldn't find his voice.

I sighed out loud.

That was when I shot them.

* * *

As ever, Carson had been up before me, hard at work making calls. The Prime Minister's participation in the by-election was a hot story: there was, apparently, a convention that sitting PMs never did so, because by-elections are so commonly lost by the ruling party. In their present circumstances, however, there was little choice: not only were they desperate but they were running out of people to campaign.

Posing as a national reporter who had just arrived, Carson had extracted Boller's schedule from the local party office. Mid-morning, he was due to visit the shopping mall that doubled as town centre for the sprawling mass that constituted the New Town. I wondered what Ebenezer Howard, designer of the Garden City concept, would think about this particular bastard offspring. I was still wondering about it as Boller and buffer-zone strode purposefully into the precinct, glad-handing supporters and glowering at protestors in equal proportions. I was not surprised to see Ted Farlowe in his crowd. More so to see Horace Black, though I shouldn't've been: it was his late wife's constituency. Naturally, the party would have wanted to cash in on the grief.

In the middle of the mall was a mini-stage where a couple of amateur clowns were entertaining the waiting crowd. They appeared to be unscheduled, because there were no signs to announce their presence and the mall staff and police looked confused about how to get them out of the way. They could hardly arrest them in front of the watching children. Coco the Clown crushed by copper's cosh?

The Prime Minister himself took the initiative and signalled to allow them a few more moments, applauding enthusiastically at a final display of juggling, which ended with the clowns tumbling backwards off the set and into the crowd, running and whooping and laughing and looking around over their shoulders as if being chased until they disappeared through a door, which I presumed led to where they had changed.

I don't suppose I would have paid them as much mind - though with hindsight, I ought to have made the connection - if I hadn't noticed Farlowe detach himself from the political entourage and follow them. I told Carson to keep an eye on Boller while I followed Farlowe. For a while, I hovered inside a book-shop, browsing with an eye through the window towards the door, praying there wasn't a back way out. I was beginning to despair when Farlowe and the two former clowns, one male and one female, emerged. The man's face was familiar: even though I knew he was younger by some years, Neil Somers and his sister could have been twins. It gave me the name of the woman: Pat Hughes. A right pair of clowns.

It produced a dilemma: did I go back and warn Boller about Farlowe, or follow Neil Somers and his companions to where I expected to find Tim? It wasn't a dilemma that vexed me for a moment. I went after them, spotting them entering their own car and pulling out of the car park in time to see the route they took.

* * *

I followed them to the estate. They weren't pros. They weren't expecting to be followed. They weren't a difficult target to keep in sight. Finally, they drew up at a house and went inside quickly. I parked in the driveway of a house nearby and strolled to the door, knocking hard, hoping no one would be home. At first, I was annoyed that there was, but was relieved to see that it was only a child, who I instructed firmly to tell her parents that Roger had called in to speak to them. I hoped they knew someone called Roger. I didn't.

All the time, out of a corner of my eye, I was watching the front door of the house Farlowe, Somers and Hughes had entered. I was climbing back into my own car when Hughes emerged and looked around, shrugged and went back inside. Though she had shut the front door behind her, it wasn't locked. Next to the house was a garage: its most noticeable feature was the way the glass frames within its own front doors were all covered up.

I drove away before Farlowe came out for a similar look around. Emerging from the close, looking for somewhere to put the car out of sight while I worked on my next move, now completely incapable of finding the shopping mall even if I wanted to return, I saw another car, loaded with grim-looking men, Dick'n'Bobs one and all, driving slowly past. They had known where to look but not, from their expressions and navigation, an exact address. I flicked my indicator light from left to right and went in the opposite direction. If they - or their colleagues - had been around to the house in Barnes, I wouldn't be popular. The encounter enhanced my resolve to get Tim out of there before anyone else arrived.

I was puzzled. Why had Hughes come out like that to look around? Why was the door unlocked? It had to be Leahy they had come to meet, but it was inconsistent for him to give out an address and wait like a trapped rat, even for an avowed ally to arrive. I snapped my fingers at my own stupidity: of course he would not be there himself, nor indeed would be any others involved. Hughes' brief excursion was the act of a person arriving at an empty house, checking she and her companions were truly alone.

Next to the house was a pea field. It was too shallow to try to crawl through unobserved. I crossed it openly, hardly glancing at the house even as I drew near, hoping I was too far away to be identified should Farlowe glance out: neither of the others knew me by sight.

From the path across the field, I could see an alleyway between a couple of nearby houses. I took it. It brought me out at an angle which permitted me to approach the house next door to theirs without a full frontal. At the last moment, out of the line of window vision, almost at the front wall line of both houses, I swung left and slid past the garage to the front door through which they had disappeared. I stood there, grateful for the absence of security spy-hole, protected from view by the porch, my ear pressed against the door.

They were not on the other side of it. They were inside, at a guess off to the right once I entered. They were arguing. All of them were arguing. I drew a deep breath and gambled on my hunch that they were the only current occupiers. If I was wrong, I was dead. I gripped the door handle so tightly I almost couldn't turn it for sweat. I entered the hall, silently I hoped, gun drawn, and pushed it shut behind me so that no sudden draft would alert them. I couldn't see them at once and the noise they were making masked any noise of my own. There was a doorway ahead of me. I could see that it was to the kitchen. That was where they were, shouting at one another.

I watched for a while, unnoticed as they argued. As I listened, I grew more confident: they were at a complete loss; they already knew the game was up; all they wanted to do was to survive it. Only when Hughes pulled a gun awkwardly from her bag and pointed it at Farlowe did I announce my presence.

'Drop it,' I ordered.

They all swung on me from their different directions, giving Farlowe enough room for manoeuvre to grab Hughes' gun hand. Instinctively, I ducked, but the safety must've been on - or we all got lucky - and the weapon didn't discharge by the time Farlowe had a hold of it.

'It's okay, Dave,' he said.

'Drop it, Farlowe; I'm not that stupid.'

He hesitated, but he didn't have a choice: he had probably never held a gun before, and I wasn't convinced Hughes or Neil Somers were that experienced either. They were a band of rank amateurs who had wrought successful havoc with national - arguably international - repercussions, predominantly because they were operating outside all recognisable parameters or for an identified purpose.

Without Leahy, Hughes' gun notwithstanding, they weren't capable of physical confrontation: that was why they needed Leahy. Their collective intellect - years of training and practice in different, demanding disciplines - was of no value: they were pathetic prisoners of war. Farlowe bent down to place the gun on the ground and, without instructions, kicked it towards me. When he stood up again, I could see that he was crying.

I knelt carefully to take the gun.

'I want to make this very clear before we go any further. There's four American navy officers with bullets in them in London. I have used a gun before, to kill, and I can and I will do it again if there's any trouble. We're outside all the rules now and I'm not going to catch any flak for it if I do. To be honest with you, I'm tempted to do it anyway, but we'll have a chat first and then I'll decide. You want to talk, don't you? I mean, it's all you've got left, isn't it?'

They had failed and knew that they had failed; they would never enjoy whatever rewards they had been aiming for; the only thing they could do now was to try and convince themselves - through the only mirror available, me - that the game had been worth the gamble. It's why most people talk when they're finally caught and know there are no escape routes left, legal process included.

All the fight had gone out of them. Or, perhaps, they were relieved it was me rather than Leahy: in the back of each of their minds must have been the knowledge that they were as expendable as anyone else.

I glanced around and saw what I could use. I ordered them to pick up kitchen chairs and carry them in single file into the hallway, where I seated them in a semi-circle facing the front door, tying their hands to the chairs behind them with a roll of kitchen wire, the stuff used to tie garbage and other bags shut: thin, jagged wire protected only by thin, easily torn paper. I tied their ankles, too, not to the legs of the chairs but up underneath the seats and thence back to their wrists. I wasn't careful about it. The carpet would need a bit of a clean; they all bled as I worked, but none of them complained.

It was eerily quiet outside: country quiet. Every external noise was five times as loud as it would be in the city. Each sound put me on edge. A car drawing up at a neighbouring house. Its door banging shut. A stereo turned on momentarily at too high a volume. A dog barking. Children playing on the estate.

I had a choice. I could go for Tim at once, in which case by the time we got back it might be too late and I would never find out all the answers, or I could use whatever time was left to ask the questions, before anyone, everyone and the Band of the Royal Marines arrived to claim whichever prize most took their fancy. I said to Hughes:

'Start talking.'

* * *

'It all began a long time ago. Soon after most of us had moved to Newport and were working for Oswald at Gant's Gully; all of us at that time - Debbie, Helen, Julie, Steve, me - all of us except Zeke Zeller.'

'Who was doing what?'

'He started in a brokerage house on Wall Street. He played his own money well, branched out on his own - all within that first year.' She could not conceal her pride in him. Her voice was gathering strength as she spoke; her natural arrogance had begun to reassert itself.

'He's your boyfriend?'

'Sometimes,' her eyes flashed the message that she and Zeller were beyond the norm, could pick up and leave off at will.

'That was when Hilton discovered the drug?'

'Yes,' she said flatly, as if my question had brought her suddenly back to the uncomfortable present reality. 'That was how it all began.'

At the time, Hilton was still working at Gant's Gully. Chambers offered him the opportunity to work on the Navy's brief, as a last chance to redeem his declining reputation, damaged by the amount of drugs he was doing, including the one he had developed himself and for which he would yet do time.

Hilton was unappreciative. He believed he would be thrown out of the institute, come what may. He decided to retain the research. It was not his intention to use it the way the others later came to use it, but to conceal the information until he was placed professionally elsewhere, to make a mark of his own with it then. Like much other research, it would be impossible to prove where and when the effective, central techniques had been developed. So what if he had failed to find them while he was at Gant's Gully? He had pondered and probed and eventually come out with the process that worked.

Hilton moved from Gant's Gully to Cambridge, Massachusetts, to stay with Julie's younger brother, Neil, who was engaged in postgraduate work at MIT following his undergraduate degree at Johns Hopkins - the university, not the medical school. Hilton's first mistake was to confide in Somers; his worse mistake was to do so within hearing of Somers' other roomie, an unprepossessing, flabby limey taking a sabbatical from work in and around English politics while his party was out of office to study American democracy at Harvard: Farlowe.

When Hilton was busted, Somers and Farlowe went through his belongings, including his personal papers, not yet knowing what they intended to do with the material, sure only that it could be turned to advantage. Unable to translate Hilton's notes into a saleable commodity, they took the formula to Somers' former comic colleague in Newport: enter Hughes. The weekend they did so was also a weekend when Zeke Zeller was visiting his sometime girlfriend. That was when the team was formed and the initial idea hatched.

'Whose idea was it?'

Hughes said:

'Ted's.'

Somers said:

'Hers.'

Farlowe said:

'Zeller's.'

I said:

'All of you. Did you already realise the next administration - whatever it was - was bound to be by a small minority, Farlowe?'

'It was the common wisdom for years before the election,' he reminded me, flushing.

'Why, Farlowe? Why?'

He almost shrugged but the way I had tied, it would have hurt too much. He said, despair in his voice:

'Look at me. Where was I going to end up? A political assistant for life; no constituency would ever want me.'

'And it was Zeller who worked out the financial implications?' I didn't disagree: charm and charisma were not terms that came to mind.

My question didn't need an answer. Like all brilliant ideas, it was only too obvious - and simple - with hindsight. If one could predict, with near certainty, exactly when a government would change, if one could manipulate the timing with a degree of exactitude, the fortune available was unlimited. Zeller already had money: he had helped Hughes buy her house; he had established his own business; he was, I had been told in Baltimore and elsewhere, a financial alchemist.

'You couldn't be certain your party would win, though?'

'No. No.' He paused, drew breath to suppress further tears, then added, 'I didn't think we would, you see. That was the worst of it. I really didn't think we would.'

'Then how...' I bit off my question. His position was largely irrelevant; it had brought tactical advantages, but it wasn't a necessary element. 'Mallalieu. Annette Mallalieu. You knew about her position. You knew about her being gay?' I asked.

He nodded.

I said:

'It wasn't enough. On its own.' By then, the rapid change in attitudes meant that it would not even have threatened her job; given political correctness, it was more likely to have bolstered it. 'She could have just quit. If she had a decent bone in her body, she would just have quit.'

Somers grinned, the clown to the end.

'It wasn't just her job she would have lost.' I frowned. I didn't get it. He giggled. 'Pat said she was only Zeller' girlfriend sometimes.'

I had the background; now I wanted the remainder of the tale. I asked:

'How did Joe Leahy get into it? Through Debbie Segal? Is she a part of it?'

Hughes said quickly:

'No. Really, no. It was Ted's idea. It was later, when things started to go wrong.'

'When Helen Thornton, under Chambers' direction, began putting it together?'

'That, and Ted knew your Prime Minister had arranged for the police to be talked to.'

I glanced disgustedly at Farlowe: he had the most direct responsibility for Tim's disappearance.

'What about Hilton? When he got out of jail, I mean?'

They looked at one another shiftily. Hilton was the one who could have put a spanner in their works. Hilton's final mistake was to return to stay with Neil Somers before going home to Oxford, not so far from Baltimore - to which Somers had by then returned with his additional qualifications - that Somers could not easily visit for a day or two. Once Somers realised Hilton planned to pick the drug up where he'd left off, there were only two choices: take him in or take him out. Somers said:

'He was too unreliable, far too unreliable.'

'Shit.' I shook my head in disbelief: Julie didn't have it far wrong about greed and the good life. I didn't ask how they'd managed to get rid of Hilton: he'd died of a drugs overdose and, but for Julie's suicide note, we still wouldn't know it hadn't been self-inflicted. Thornton was an altogether more difficult target. 'You suggested Leahy, Farlowe? Didn't he scare you?'

'Not at the time. I knew him, long ago, in the very earliest days.' What had Dunlop said? Something about former allies? 'I didn't really mean it, originally. I knew what he'd become; I really meant we needed someone like him, to take care of Thornton, not him in particular. That was when I found out we had a line to him.'

'How?' I asked Hughes.

'He'd stayed in touch with Debbie. On and off. One way traffic. You see, well,' she bit her lower lip, 'he did love her, in his way.' And she had loved him: hence, the dangerous abortion in Dublin instead of a safe scrape in London. As she realised, as the years passed, just who her former lover had been or had become, how could she fail to share the knowledge with one or more of her long-standing close friends - including Pat Hughes?

'And you asked her what? To invite him over for a quick kill of your mutual friend Helen?'

'No, of course not,' Hughes scorned my question. 'I told her Ted was trying to get in touch with him, that Ted was an old friend of Leahy's and wanted to make contact. That it could help Leahy. Given Ted's position, we could bank on Leahy rising to the bait.'

'And it was just luck he got in touch with Segal in time? What would you have done otherwise? No, don't bother: it doesn't matter. How was he paid? No, forget it: Zeller again. Right, Switzerland.'

'Zeke has a house outside Lucerne,' Farlowe said.

'Where you and Mallalieu used to meet for your trysts?' Hughes said:

'There and elsewhere.'

'How did he get on to Dowell?'

'Mallalieu told us about his visit; we told Leahy. He said he'd take care of it.'

'For more money?'

Farlowe shrugged.

'We persuaded him not to kill him; we knew what it would mean.' To kill an English copper. 'We said we wouldn't pay him if he did.'

'Was it always just money? Was there nothing more to it?'

'We were all political to begin with, to differing degrees,' Farlowe said. 'We were all disillusioned.'

'This is disillusionment? Jesus wept. You're out of your minds, all of you.'

There wasn't time for my disgust. I knew it; they knew it; it was all out of control; I was probably their best, if not only, chance of staying alive; now they had been uncovered, Leahy could not be relied on to help them.

I needed also to know:

'Julie. What was her role in it?'

I knew the answer I wanted.

Her brother said listlessly:

'She worked it out. Or some of it, anyway. She was around too many of us for too long not to pick up clues and hints. She got one of them from you - the connection between me and Ted.' I winced. He continued: 'She worked enough of it out. Enough to want to track me down in Baltimore.'

'She didn't have your address? Your parents didn't?'

'No.' He looked down at the ground, momentarily ashamed, no clown. 'I didn't want to see any of them, not while it was all going down.'

'What about when she was arrested - in London, I mean?' At the Irish demo.

'She was just a kid; it didn't mean anything. She wasn't a part of it, Woolf, I promise you that.' He paused. 'She cared about you.'

I wished he hadn't said that. Now I knew she'd talked about me to him. Which meant he also knew what I wanted to hear. Which meant I would never, ever know for sure what the truth was about her. I couldn't let it matter; there were other things I needed to know more.

'Now tell me about the drug...'

* * *

I extracted the remaining details swiftly. After the most recent police enquiries in the States following Julie's suicide, Zeller and Hughes had left the country, individually, by different routes, across into Mexico and Bermuda respectively and out - eventually - to join Neil Somers in Switzerland. Only Somers had arrived in Switzerland by the time Annette Mallalieu was enticed there by Hughes: only Somers, that is to say, and Leahy. Hughes insisted she had not known what would happen to Mallalieu once she went home although she clearly hadn't cared enough to make a fuss; even when she told me about their relationship, I got it that Mallalieu was the needy one, an older woman chasing youth. As for Zeller, he was still there. Hughes and Somers had - at his instigation - subsequently crossed into France and thence into England by train from Paris, the softest point of entry. They were being sent to see Leahy. By then, they all wanted an end to it. They were all scared.

By the time they contacted Farlowe, he had himself been contacted by Leahy, to find out how near the police were - or I was. Farlowe, too, wanted a meet with Leahy, also to try and bring it to an end. It was convenient; Leahy's English hideout was in Cramlington, near Newcastle. It was where he had stashed Tim. Farlowe was due up with Boller for the by-election.

Once he realised they wanted the same out of Leahy as he did, Farlowe told the two Americans to meet him there before he saw Leahy, to come with to see him. They agreed to meet him in Newcastle, but wouldn't tell him when or where: by then, no one trusted anyone else. The clown routine was designed to draw out Farlowe in circumstances in which, if he had turned traitor on them, they enjoyed their best opportunity for denial or escape.

As for Leahy, he was playing all middles against the same end. With some people, it was political; with others, cash. He had not killed Tim both because they had asked him not to; her had not killed Tim because he could be a useful asset to trade. He had the contacts to have learned about Brendan's enquiries which allowed him to arrange for Brendan to be killed not for money but - he was able to assert to ever-gullible terrorists - for the cause. He could re-establish political authority by claiming credit for a campaign leading to the deaths of British MPs because he could identify them in advance.

He had given Farlowe this address so as to wrap up the loose ends. He cautioned Farlowe that the house would be empty: he would be contacted there if, and only if, he was satisfied he would himself be safe. The door would not be locked. They should await his call.

The three of them secure enough for the time being, I slipped out the back door.

* * *

'Now what?' Tim asked.

I shrugged.

'Any ideas?'

'Butch and Sundance?' Come out shooting and die noisily.

As if waiting for the right line to enter, both the front garage door and the side door through which I had entered swung open. A man and a woman were at the front, wearing light summer wind-jammers hanging open to conceal from any inquisitive neighbours the guns they were carrying: an older man was at the side door, his face in the clearest sight of anyone passing on the street. This would be Joe Leahy, the notional resident. He was not a large man: in his early fifties, with thinning, fair hair, strong and wiry, with huge wrists and hands. I didn't enjoy the thought of my neck between them.

We stared at one another. His eyes were asking if I knew what I was doing with a gun in my hand, if I knew how to use it, whether I'd ever killed. Like he had. He read it right.

Suddenly, it was a war zone. There wasn't enough time for Tim to make introductions or any of us to shake hands before the shooting began, let alone for them to offer me a drink. I'd been expecting the Americans I'd seen on the main road to have followed Leahy in but, as usual, I was wrong. The Americans wanted the Gant's Gully gang taken alive: they still didn't have their damned formula and they didn't know who had it. It was Leahy's Irish troops who by now needed the Gant's Gully guys dead while, to make sure everyone got an equal chance to cross the great divide, the British - MI5 - always wanted to kill the Irish, whether or not it brought them any other gain.

The woman took a shotgun blast in the back; the other man at the front fell to the ground screaming before he began to choke on the blood flooding from his neck.

Leahy? Joe was nowhere to be seen.

Outside, the car from which the attack had come was itself now a target. I didn't know for whom, and didn't much care. I wasn't about to wait around to find out. I grabbed Tim's arm and we ran out the side after Leahy. I don't mean my first priority was to try to catch up with him: I'd be happy if I never saw him again in my life; but I didn't want to be caught up with by anyone else. Especially not any pals of Dick or Bob.

'Where now, sunshine?'

'Sundance,' Tim corrected.

I pointed to a path across another section of the development, a different close.

'Can we make that?'

'Why?'

'I think the car's on the road opposite.'

'You think? You don't know?'

I looked pained.

'You think I thought that far ahead? Me? Nothing's changed, Tim.'

'Too fucking right,' he muttered as, drawing a deep breath, he flung himself at the path as if it were the enemy. For a man who'd spent the last several weeks mostly trussed up like a Christmas turkey, he'd recovered the use of his legs pretty fast.

'There?' I screamed, realising too late that the noise from the development had died out altogether and that I was therefore alerting everyone who wanted to know exactly where we'd escaped to.

We piled in and screeched around a hundred and eighty degrees on the tarmac as the first car in chase flew out of the close, aimed straight at us. Neither of us had a clue who it was or the time to discuss it. I said:

'Your call, kid. My driving skills or your shooting?'

'Some choice,' he growled as he rolled down the window, leaned out, took aim at the astonished driver in pursuit and, without any hesitation at all, put one into their windscreen.

The car went into a skid; I watched in the rear-view mirror as it ploughed into a chain-link fence at the side of the road, facing the wrong way.

I didn't slow down; I could see more cars coming from behind. Also, the wail of police sirens as - it sounded like - everything on two and four wheels belonging to the Northumbrian Police descended on the area. I didn't have a clue where I was going, either, but I knew when to stop: about three miles and thirty twists and turns from the estate, I espied a pub with a car park stretched around behind it. I didn't care who found us: I was going in.

'Food,' Tim's eyes lit up as we entered. 'It's food.'

It wasn't the food that excited my attention.

When we were served and seated, I said:

'And now, sunshine, we'd better start telling each other what we know.'

* * *

It was fortunate Tim still had his warrant card: there was no other way we would get into Horton Grange. Indeed, the card was not enough on its own: the troubles nearby had fourpled the security. He could not even persuade the officers in the police car which barred the driveway to go inside and seek permission for us to enter. Instead, he managed to get them to radio from the car into Newcastle from where, in turn, he was patched through to the Yard. There was no point aiming any lower. The policemen watched with grudging but growing respect as he demanded to speak to the Commissioner.

'Dowell?' Because he was on the car radio, I could hear both sides of the conversation.

'Sir...' I nearly fainted. It had never occurred to me that he'd call even the Commissioner 'sir'. But it was only the first part of his name: '...Randolph. I'm at Horton Grange in Northumbria. The Prime Minister is staying here. We want to get in to see him.'

Dunlop didn't ask why, from which I gauged that he understood Tim was not going to return to work without telling the Prime Minister to his face how much damage he had done, at considerable risk to Tim's life and terminal effect to others.

'What about Woolf?'

'He's here. I suppose he'd better come in with me.'

'Tim, was that you in a car-shoot earlier?'

"Fraid so, Commissioner. Not a lot of choice. Trouble?'

'Nothing I can't handle, but I wouldn't make myself available to anyone else for the time being. Nor Woolf. I think the PM's company is about the best you could do for now.'

I prodded Dowell. He nodded that he understood what I wanted to know and asked the question.

'Who?' In the car he'd shot at.

'One of ours.'

'Sorry, Commissioner,' Tim said despite himself.

'I wouldn't be,' Sir Randolph said tersely. 'I'm not. They're the ones who threw out all the rules. You'll be protected. They're in the hands of the locals now. There were three dead inside the house, including Farlowe.' Leahy - before he'd come for us. 'More outside.' MI5 wiping out Leahy's crew.

'What's Woolf's position?'

'Ah, well, that's a little bit different. His tally's somewhat higher than yours. But at present I'm trying to persuade the main complainants to, well, take their freedom and hobble, as it were.'

'Hobble?' Tim gawped.

Well, I hadn't told him everything, had I?

'Woolf'll explain. But, uh, is he listening?'

'Yes.'

'Well done, Woolf. I think it made all the difference.'

I took the handset from Tim.

'That wasn't why I did it.'

'Who knows, Woolf? Who will ever know? Tell Dowell I'll get a personal message to his family.' He disconnected.

Tim said:

'It'll be a few minutes, gents. Would you mind if, uh, we had a few private words...'

'Not at all, sir.' They'd listened while we'd chatted with the Metropolitan Police Commissioner on the best of terms; we weren't going to nick their police car.

'What was that about, Dave?'

I flushed.

'Something I'm still working out. I let Wally and Carson think I'd killed the other two yanks. I didn't is what he means.'

He digested this information, descending in indecent haste on the obvious flaw.

'Not shots in the ceiling, though?'

'No,' I grit my teeth.

Then he put the Commissioner's word into the picture.

'Knee-capping?'

I nodded glumly.

'It was a sort of compromise. Besides, it gave us more time. I ripped out the phones before we left, did some damage to their radios. They weren't in a position to call out for someone from the street. Would have had to wait to be found.'

'Why did you want Wally and Carson to think you'd finished them off?'

'That's what I'm still working out, Tim.'

We turned to look at each other. He read me as clearly as anyone else could, clearer than I could, probably as only Sandy could. He said softly:

'It's been a bad year for you, Dave. Don't expect it all to make sense.'

'Hasn't been a good year for you either, really.'

'Oh, I don't know. Having Alton around has been a major plus.'

It was as close as he'd ever come to an admission of the bond between us.

'So? Where does it leave me?'

'You're not the first person who's killed one too many times and is beginning to think he might like it, maybe even wants people to think he likes it. The point is, you didn't kill them.'

'I lied to Wally and Carson, though.'

'Sort of, but yes. It's the lie to Carson worries me.' I had told him that part of it driving over from the pub. 'With her background.'

There was no time to take it further. One of the policemen knocked at the window and held the door open for Tim. I had to open my own. Horace Black had come out to fetch us. He said at once:

'Your woman's here, Woolf.' He thrust a hand out at Tim. 'I'm glad to meet you, well, to see you in one piece.' He took for granted Tim would know who he was.

'Thank you. I'm sorry about your wife. I had a lot of respect for her.'

'The fuck with all this politeness,' I snapped. 'Let's do it.'

I led the way up the drive to Horton Grange. It was a mid-nineteenth century stone converted farmhouse, with an arch-way porch and, beyond, stables. Opposite, another farmhouse. It was beautiful, peaceful, idyllic; exactly what everything else wasn't.

* * *

'I don't suppose anyone is confused about the roles of the different government agencies involved here. The drug was the US Navy's original idea; they were very keen on it. Once it became clear - contrary to what they'd earlier been told - that there was something in it, they wanted it. They wanted it for themselves and no one else; to recover it and have it available for use was the only way to prevent themselves being made to look like fools. They've had the co-operation of their own government agencies, but they didn't seek that of ours, for the traditional - and good - reason that they trust our secret services as far as the next bookshop with a full shelf of insider revelations. Our own people have wanted it for no greater reason than to take it away from the Americans: we haven't really got anyone left we actually want to kill, have we?'

I didn't expect an answer and that's the one I got.

'But this thing only works so long as no one else knows what it is. The moment the formula's out in the open, it can only be a matter of time before a tracing agent is discovered and applied in an autopsy.'

I paused to grace Julie with a moment's memory of her lecture on my patio. Horace mistook my motive as being for dramatic effect and fed me.

'I don't understand what's so special about this drug?'

I exchanged a look with Tim then explained.

'Its simplicity, really, its availability. You see, even if you're a government agency, or a military agency, if something requires a lot of preparation, a lot of people have to be involved, and we all know what that means in terms of secrecy. The beauty of this drug is its accessibility and - once the processing of it had been worked out for the first time, as Hilton did - ease.'

'So how is it done?' he asked disingenuously.

I shook my head.

'I can't tell you that,' I lied. 'Unless Chambers shows up, we'll never know.'

He led me down a corridor and we emerged into what might have been called a laboratory but which was far larger. It was a huge hall, filled with vast, glass vats in each of which swam or grew the most disgusting colours, shapes, textures and growths - fungi, algae, plankton - you could dread being served up as a seafood salad. A slice of sewer seaweed would have been more savoury. I gulped. This was what last night's lobster had been eating while awaiting its - his? hers? I didn't want to think about that either - destiny as my dinner. They had the most perfect killing apparatus in the world: dunk me in one of those vats and I'd die of horror. 'That's a lot of what we do here,' he added, meaning medical research, not death by a thousand upchucks.

'What's that?' I pointed at a particularly repulsive moving mass.

'Jellyfish, Dave, plain old Portuguese Men of War.'

'Oh yuk.' I'd meant to keep it under my breath but it slipped out.

He laughed.

'You can find one at almost any beach around here...'

Of course I didn't know precisely how the jellyfish was processed, what part of it was involved or how it was compounded only to activate with alcohol, nor did I understand why all traces disappeared - save in the hair - on death. But I knew enough, and unless Chambers came through, I knew far too much.

'When it gets unravelled, we'll find that Zeller has been investing in this country and in everything that'll be affected by your departure from the scene since the moment you were elected, with that wafer-thin majority that made you the easiest and best possible target. When the idea came to them, it must have seemed like perfection; they even had access to Mallalieu, once they'd worked it out.'

Boller shook his head.

'And all of this for money? Just for money?'

'Just think about it. Think how much money a person could make if he was the only one in the world to know that there's about to be a change in the government of a free-enterprise, capitalist country, one of the largest economies in the world, a change that business would welcome. The possibilities are endless, and so are the potential profits. Not millions but billions. Especially if, like Zeller, there's a lot of money to invest to begin with.'

Black said:

'We still don't know where Leahy is. Or Chambers.'

'No more we do,' I said softly.

'We'll find out, Horace,' the Prime Minister said reassuringly.

'I don't think I want you to talk to me, Alf, not yet anyway.'

'No,' Boller replied sadly. 'I don't suppose you do.'

He could not be faulted for failing to find out how far from the fold Farlowe had flown, but the way he had played the political pieces had postponed discovery of the plot, and greater candour might have meant Margot would still be among us.

It could also be said that Black was a party to the paranoia from the outset, but Boller was not the kind of man who would attack his grieving friend with this vicious reminder. So I did.

'You went along with it, Horace.'

* * *

Boller and Black went to the local party offices; they couldn't risk being at the count; they couldn't afford not to show support for the members. The three of us were standing in the main lobby when Millward and Gregory arrived, together with Wadd. Both senior officers held out their hands to him. Tim shrugged, refused to take either, and said:

'I'll have to think about it first.'

Gregory cut Millward short as Tim's nominal Commander started to complain.

'Take your time, Tim; I've nothing to be ashamed of.'

'There's news,' Wally announced. 'First, the Swiss have picked up Zeller and - because we're in better standing with them than the Americans - they're going to let us have first bite of his cherry. They'll let us at him tomorrow. Secondly, Chambers has emerged.'

'Alive?' I asked quickly.

'Very much so,' Gregory took up the tale. 'He appeared at a press conference, at Gant's Gully, together with a representative of the Department of the Navy.'

'To say what?'

'To tell the press about some important research in which he'd been engaged.'

'Yes,' I whispered. 'Well done, Oswald. Bloody well done. Bloody nice.' Hoist with their own petard seemed, in the circumstances, the appropriate metaphor.

Carson dug me in the ribs.

'Stop showing off.'

I explained.

'Something about a dangerous, lethal drug - untraceable - that had been discovered by... by whom? Who did he lay it off on?'

'No names. Hints of international terrorist organisations. He announced that he had been commissioned by the Navy to find out what it was and that he had done so, and that it was accordingly no longer a threat.'

'How?' I was only checking.

'Once you can identify the ingredients, it becomes a standard autopsy search.'

'Right. Provided the knowledge is public.' Which it never would have been if the Americans had got their hands on it before Chambers made it available to the world of medicine.

Millward snorted.

'It'll be a bit late for the victims.'

It was true, but it was also true of any other number of killing drugs. The only sanction was always after the event. It wasn't perfect, but it was the only one the world had discovered in the last few thousand years.

'Pity they didn't let their people know - or even our own - a bit quicker. It might've made this afternoon a little less hectic.'

'It was this afternoon - over here,' Gregory said. 'The time difference, I'm afraid. That's all.'

That, and one man from MI5, and Neil Somers and Patricia Hughes and Ted Farlowe and various Irish. Yeah, it wasn't much; nothing to worry about.

* * *

'I have to talk with Dave and Carson,' Tim said. 'And Wadd,' he added.

The owner, whistling tunefully as he swung out of the dining room with a flourish, directed us to the lounge.

'It's empty, gents. Whoops - lady and gents. If you need to talk.'

He was unimpressed and unflustered by the incrementally increasing task force of police, politicians and barely concealed fire-power.

'Any chance of a drink?' I asked.

'Certainly. What did you have in mind?'

I reviewed the bottles in the bar-rack by the side of the dining room door, saddened by the obvious omission. He must have been a mind reader, because he opened a cupboard beneath it, with everything in it and anything else any of us might have wished for. I reached in and extracted the bottle.

'Some ice would be nice and bill the PM's party.'

While we waited, I studied the menu.

'Think we get to eat?'

Carson extracted the menu from my greedy grasp and, in the first kind words she'd spoken since we left the house in Barnes, told me:

'You're fat enough already.'

Once the waitress had withdrawn, Tim called the meeting to order.

'Agenda item one. Dave's got something to tell you both.'

I reddened.

'I didn't kill Dick and Bob. I shot them. In the legs.'

Wally nodded: by then, he knew.

Carson frowned.

'But why did you let...'

Tim said:

'Did either of you know what you were doing that day?'

'Not a bunch,' she admitted.

'Well, then,' he wrote a bottom line on the lie.

She studied me closely for a few minutes more, then accepted his edict.

'I suppose we've still a lot to find out about each other, huh?'

I smiled - but couldn't say - thanks.

'Second item?' I asked.

'How bad is it with Five, Wally?' Tim asked.

'Bad but not terminal. If we've anything to feed them, bring them back into the fold...anything to trade?'

Tim shook his head.

'I can't see it.'

'I can,' I grinned. 'I've got just the thing.'

'Well?' Tim demanded.

'Zeller.'

'Nah. He's not political, not in their terms.'

'But they don't know that, do they? And they're not going to believe it, are they? I mean, when he tells them. And it'll be extra sweet because you can tell them the last thing we want is to get him back for a trial.' Which fed them Zeller for all kinds of experimentation.

'Are either of you going to explain?' Carson sighed, concealing how happy she was watching us play games again the familiar old way.

'Is,' I corrected. 'Is either of you,' I elaborated when she looked at me blankly. 'It would be 'are' if you asked are both of us going to explain. It's a common...'

She kicked me in the knee.

* * *

At the PM's telephoned invitation, we did get to stick around and eat, in the private dining room, no less. Millward and Gregory were in Newcastle, clearing up on the day's mess. It was after midnight when we finished. We had to wait. The PM was flying down to London once the show was over, and we were hitching a ride. We were alternately merry and morose. Certainly, we weren't sober. As Wally and Tim fought for precedence in the repetitious anecdotes stakes, Carson and I took a stroll in the grounds to clear our heads.

'We okay, Cars?'

'I don't know, Dave, but I think so. That do for now?'

I held her in my arms.

'Is it ever going to be any more certain than that?'

'I doubt it,' she hugged me back. 'Will it do for good?'

'It'll have to.'

* * *

The others were laughing when we re-joined them. They were toasting each other with champagne. I grabbed a glass.

'I don't believe it. He won? He won after all?'

'Hell, no,' Tim chuckled. 'The bastard lost anyway.'

* * *

A few days later, just after we put Alton to bed, the telephone rang.

'Mr Woolf? Dave?'

'That's right. Who is this?'

'No, that's right, too. We never did get to speak, did we?' The full sentence gave me the breadth of the Irish accent so that it was almost superfluous when he concluded:

'My name's Joe Leahy.'

And hung up.